Cruel Rider

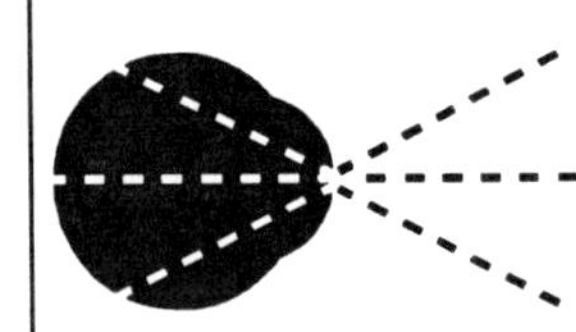

This Large Print Book carries the
Seal of Approval of N.A.V.H.

CRUEL RIDER

CHARLES G. WEST

WHEELER PUBLISHING
A part of Gale, Cengage Learning

GALE
CENGAGE Learning

Detroit • New York • San Francisco • New Haven, Conn • Waterville, Maine • London

GALE
CENGAGE Learning

This is a work of fiction. Names, characters, places, and incidents either are the product of the author's imagination or are used fictitiously, and any resemblance to actual persons, living or dead, business establishments, events, or locales is entirely coincidental.

The publisher does not have any control over and does not assume any responsibility for author or third-party websites or their content.

Wheeler Publishing Large Print Western.

The text of this Large Print edition is unabridged.

Other aspects of the book may vary from the original edition.

Set in 16 pt. Plantin.

LIBRARY OF CONGRESS CATALOGING-IN-PUBLICATION DATA

West, Charles.
Cruel rider / by Charles G. West. — Large print ed.
p. cm. — (Wheeler Publishing large print western)
ISBN-13: 978-1-4104-4551-3 (pbk.)
ISBN-10: 1-4104-4551-8 (pbk.)
1. Outlaws—Fiction. 2. Husband and wife—Fiction. 3. Large type books. I. Title.
PS3623.E84C78 2012
813'.6—dc23 2011043549

Published in 2012 by arrangement with NAL Signet, a member of Penguin Group (USA) Inc.

Printed in the United States of America
2 3 4 5 6 16 15 14 13 12

FD171

For Ronda

Chapter 1

Some folks are born mean. This was not the case with Bill Pike, youngest of three brothers born on a squalid pig farm twelve miles southwest of Omaha. Those who bothered to remember would say that young Bill was a sweet child and, being the youngest, was his mother's favorite. Bill's uncle, Thad Brown, would recall that the boy showed no signs of the downright evil streak so prevalently displayed by his two older brothers. Content to play by himself near the crude shanty that served as the Pike home place, never far from his mother's watchful eye, little Bill remained oblivious to the constant turmoil between his brothers and his father during his toddling years. Jared, the elder brother, was seven when Bill was born, and by the time Bill had reached his seventh year, Jared had already been a guest in the Omaha jail.

John, the middle boy, was two years

behind Jared, but exhibited belligerent tendencies that promised to surpass those of his older brother. One of his favorite amusements was to torment his baby brother whenever his mother was not around to protect her youngest. As a result, Bill suffered a great many twisted ears and numerous knots on his head. He would cry and complain to his mother, and John usually got a licking, which only gave him incentive to take it out on Bill.

Bill wasn't born mean, but thanks to his brothers, he soon picked up the trait. By the time of his ninth birthday, he held a sharp disdain for his entire family, except for his mother, who still tried to watch over him. This contempt for his brothers festered rapidly, and was probably demonstrated best when John, who couldn't swim, slipped on a rotten log and fell into the river. Bill, nearby, searching for blackberries, heard John's screams for help, and ran to the riverbank to see what all the fuss was about.

John was thrashing about in water about fifteen feet deep, trying desperately to keep his head above the surface. Bill could see the panic in his brother's eyes as John cried out for help. A dead limb lay on the ground no more than a few feet away. Bill could have easily reached his stricken brother's flailing arms with it, but decided it more interesting to sit himself down on the riverbank and watch John try to save himself.

John struggled desperately, but his efforts only caused him to tire more quickly, while making no progress toward the bank. The fear was ever more apparent in his eyes as he began to realize that he was helpless — a phenomenon that Bill found fascinating. He sat, watching John's final moments, calmly eating blackberries, until the doomed boy went under for the last time. Still, he sat there, watching until the last bubbles stopped breaking the surface of the dark water. He remained there, waiting to see if John's body would eventually come to the surface again. After a quarter of an hour had passed with no sign of John, Bill became tired of watching. *Don't reckon he'll be twisting my ears anymore,* he thought and got to his feet. *Better go tell Mama that John's dead.*

Later that evening, when Luther Pike pulled the body of his middle son from a snag in the river, some three hundred yards down stream, he passed the lifeless form to his wife. Unable to restrain her grief, she sank down on the grassy bank, sobbing while she rocked her son back and forth in her arms. The scene was particularly disturbing to young Bill to see his mother so obviously stricken. It seemed to him to be an act of betrayal, as if she loved John more than him. This was the initial fissure in the close relationship between Bill and his mother. It would increase in size over the next year, resulting in an impassable chasm when she became pregnant for the fourth time.

The arrival of another baby was not looked upon as a joyous occasion in the Pike household, and Luther seemed to blame his wife for the unwelcome addition. Bill, like his father, felt it was his mother's fault for allowing herself to be impregnated. Two days before Christmas of Bill's tenth year, Grace Pike went into labor with what was to be her final attempt to bring life to another child.

With no one to assist her, Grace steeled herself to deliver her baby alone, for husband and son, Bill, absented themselves from the cabin, neither desirous of witnessing the event. Had he been there, Jared might have helped her, but he was once again a guest of the deputy marshal in Omaha, awaiting trial for stealing a horse.

The birthing didn't go well. Grace knew at once that something was terribly wrong, and she cried out in agonizing pain for help she knew would not come. The baby arrived after hours of torturous labor, but it seemed to be tearing Grace's insides out with it. Finally, the totally exhausted mother struggled to lay the infant on the bed between her legs. She sank back in despair, oblivious to the massive hemorrhaging of her womb. It was not until late in the evening that Luther Pike came home to find his wife dead, lying in the bloody deathbed, the infant between her legs. He barely noticed the small huddled form of his youngest son in the corner of the room.

Luther, the stoic pig farmer, stood staring at the cold dead corpse of his wife for several long minutes. He turned his gaze upon the baby as the infant's tiny hands reached up for him, its fragile cry a pitiful plea for its mother. Without taking even a moment to consider, Luther calmly clamped a huge hand over the helpless child's mouth and nose, and held it there until there was no longer life. The baby was of no value to him without a mother to nurse and care for it. The ten-year-old boy huddled in the corner watched silently, his mind already deadened to the cheap price placed upon a human life. It seemed no different from the culling out of the sick newborn from a litter of pigs.

■ ■ ■ ■

In the years that followed, Bill helped his father on the farm until, sick of the sight of hogs, he found a job in a sawmill near Omaha. He had worked at the mill for a little more than two years when Polly Hatcher entered his life. The owner of the mill took the young girl in when her widowed mother succumbed to pneumonia. There were no relatives to take the child, at least, none living near Omaha. Polly only knew of one relative, an aunt, her mother's sister, and all she knew of her was that she and her uncle Horace had traveled west to settle in Julesburg, Colorado Territory. Polly had never seen her aunt Hattie, but her mother had told her many stories about her high-spirited sister. After her mother's death, Polly worked in the mill owner's house as his wife's maid. She caught Bill's eye almost at once.

Traveling back and forth every day on horseback, between the sawmill and his father's farm, Bill soon began thinking of how much easier his life would be if there was a woman at home to do for him. Although stripped of the compassion he had been born with, Bill could affect a gentle façade when he had to. It was this face that he presented when courting Polly. Romance, and certainly love, never entered the equation from either party. Polly, desperate to escape her role as a servant girl, could see little prospects of meeting the love of her life, and decided she had best take the offer on the table. A marriage of necessity could conceivably grow into one of love, she reasoned. So they were married, and Bill took his bride home to Luther and the pig farm.

Polly's hopes were shattered upon first sight of her father-in-law's farm. There was scant resemblance between the farm described to her and the squalid conditions that met her eye on her wedding day. She saw at once that she had not escaped her life as a servant girl. Her situation was even worse than before. She resolved to make the best of it, however, and resigned herself to cleaning up the filth that Luther and Bill had nested in since the death of Bill's mother.

Her wedding night proved to be a traumatic memory that would forever dwell in the darker regions of her mind — returning as nightmares for months afterward. Steeling herself against the brutal, animallike assaults upon her virgin body, she submitted to Bill's savage lust while aware of his father's prying eyes peering around the doorjamb. The image of the dirty old man's lecherous gaze would return in countless dreams over the next few months, causing her to awaken, shuddering with disgust.

It did not take long before Polly realized that prospects for improvement of her lot in life were slim, if at all attainable. In time, she became calloused to the physical abuse suffered at the hands of her husband, whose regard for her never ventured beyond his carnal lust. In the beginning, she was terrified by Bill's father, and the way he leered at her every move. As far as a threat to her physically, she soon came to know that the old man was harmless. Strong drink and failing health insured that his capabilities were diminished, leaving him with no ability beyond watching. But watch he did, and she soon learned to make certain of her father-in-law's whereabouts before bathing or getting into her gown.

It was inevitable that the old man's lecherous ways proved to be the cause of his doom. One day in early spring he decided to act upon his desire to get a closer look at his daughter-in-law. Pretending to start down to the lower field to feed his pigs, he slipped back to the cabin, knowing that

Polly would take advantage of his absence to bathe. Being careful not to make a sound, he stole up to the back window and peered over the sill. There, he was able to see what he had hoped for. Polly poured hot water into a basin and, stripped to the waist, began cleaning her arms and torso.

So engrossed was he in the despicable intrusion upon his daughter-in-law's private moment, that he failed to hear the soft padding of hooves in the dust behind him. Furious to discover the old man spying upon his wife, Bill set upon his father with a whip, lashing him until the helpless wretch collapsed, unconscious and bleeding. When Polly heard the attack, she quickly pulled up her bodice and ran outside to see what had happened. Bill, standing over his father's fallen body, then turned to give his wife a taste of the whip — punishment for tempting the old man. He stopped short of the beating he had just administered to his father only because he had further use for her.

Standing over her trembling body, he glared down at her with eyes still flashing with anger. Almost in shock, she cowered at his feet, afraid to even whimper lest it should set him off again. She knew then that somehow she must escape this violent monster. In that moment she realized the extent of her husband's disdain for human life.

Distracted by the sound of a feeble groan from his father, Bill turned to fix his gaze on Luther. After a moment's thought, he walked over and knelt down beside him. With no show of emotion, he clamped both hands over the old man's nose and mouth, just as his father had done to extinguish the life of his newborn daughter. Luther struggled weakly, but could not overpower his son. Paralyzed by the horror before her eyes, Polly was unable to move. It was not until Luther's feeble struggles subsided, and he lay motionless on the ground, that she drew herself up to huddle fearfully against the wall of the cabin.

Satisfied that his father was dead, Bill turned his attention to Polly once again. "I'm hungry. Git yourself up from there and fix me some supper."

Still in a state of horrified shock, she nevertheless forced her body to move, afraid for her life if she didn't. It was not quickly enough to please him, and he drew his arm back as if to administer the whip once again. It served to hurry her motions. Then, with complete lack of remorse, he turned to look at his father's lifeless body. "I reckon I'll have to bury him," he said. "I oughta feed him to the damn hogs." The idea seemed to have merit, so he dragged the old man down to the fence and dumped his body over in the hog lot.

With her husband seated at the table, seeming to watch her every move, Polly forced herself to prepare his supper. She could feel his eyes upon her as she stood over the stove, her back to him, afraid if she faced him he would read the terror in her eyes. He would often explode in a fit of rage over some trivial thing that didn't suit him — she was used to that. It usually led to verbal abuse and, if he felt like it, a cuff on the side of her face. But on this night his mood was deep and brooding, unlike any night before. He was in a killing mood, and she feared her life was in jeopardy because she had witnessed the murder of his father. With trembling hands, she placed a plate of food before him and backed away.

"Set down," he commanded. "Ain't you gonna eat?"

"I'm not hungry," she replied, her voice quaking with fear.

"Well, set down, anyway." He watched her intently until she seated herself in a chair across from him. Stuffing food in his mouth, he continued to lock his gaze upon her.

There followed a few minutes of silence, with no sound save that of the grunting and squealing of the hogs as they fought over their grisly supper. She tried not to form a picture of the ghastly banquet in her mind, and strained with all her might to keep from sobbing out loud.

He paused in his eating for a moment. "You seen what I did. Didn't you?"

"No," she lied.

"The hell you didn't," he shot back. "I seen you gawkin' at me, your eyes as big as horse turds." He started chewing again. "He warn't no use around here no more — one less mouth to feed." He paused once more, and pointed at her with his fork. "You'd best keep your mouth shut about it — or you'll get the same medicine."

"I won't tell nobody," she replied softly. She hoped with all her heart that he believed her, for she had made up her mind that she was leaving as soon as he went to work in the morning. In the past, she had resigned herself to a life of abuse at the hands of her husband, but the horrifying events that had taken place that evening were more than she could endure. It would only be a matter of time before he decided that she was of no use to him anymore, and her fate might be the same as that of his father. She had to leave. Her plans were altered, however, with Bill's next comment.

"I ain't goin' to the sawmill in the mornin'." One corner of his mouth turned up in the little half smile that usually signaled trouble for someone. "Fetch me that bottle from the pantry. I think I'll have me a little shooter."

Her nerves turned frigid at the thought, for this was his usual preparation before forcing himself upon her body. He liked to get half drunk before having his way with her. *How could he?* her thoughts screamed out. *How could the heartless murder of his own father stimulate lust?* It was macabre and sickening to her. There was no doubt that he was insane, but there was no question that she had no choice but to submit to his brutal assault. Her mind already made up to leave while he was at work, she was now obliged to change her plan. Because he was not going to go to work in the morning, she would have to leave that night. She got up at once to get the bottle, bolstered by the thought that this would be the last time she would submit to his abuse.

As she expected, he fortified himself with half the bottle of whiskey. Once his eyes took on a glazed film, she knew the time she had come to dread was near. Suddenly, he grabbed her wrist and pulled her down in his lap, pawing her in his crude attempts to fondle. Steeling herself to his animallike exploration of her body, she again promised herself that this was to be the last time. He pulled her roughly to the bed and shoved her down on her back. When it was over, he pushed her away, rolled over, and promptly went to sleep. This was what she had prayed for.

As quickly and quietly as she could, she cleaned herself in a basin of water, constantly looking back at the sleeping man, fearful that he might awaken at any moment. Once, while she pulled on her shoes and stockings, he grunted and mumbled something in his sleep, causing her heart to pound with fright. He turned over on his back then, and started snoring, much to her relief. After tying some extra clothes in a bundle, she tiptoed back to the bedside where Bill's trousers lay in a heap on the floor. She hesitated for just a moment before taking the money from his pocket. All of her actions up to that point might possibly be explained away if he happened to awaken. Emptying his pockets meant there was no turning back, but she quickly decided she would rather die than endure another day of abuse from this monster.

There was another place she could look for money if she only had the time. Bill had a can buried behind the front left cornerstone of the cabin. He didn't think she knew about it, but she had seen him digging it up on many occasions when he thought she was busy in the kitchen. It was too risky to take the time to search for it now, so she took what money he had in his trousers and quietly withdrew. As she walked by the kitchen table, she paused to pick up a butcher knife. It would be useful for any number of things.

As she hurried to the barn, the cool night air splashed across her face, providing a welcome purge of the stuffy cabin air. Bill's horse whinnied softly when she approached, and stood obediently while she saddled it. She tied her bundle of clothes behind the saddle and led the animal out. There was no definite plan for escape. At this point, her only thought was to run, to put as much distance as possible between herself and the farm that had been her hell on earth. She would take time to think about tomorrow after she was safely away.

When she walked out of the barn, it was to find him standing there, squarely in front of the door, his pistol in his hand. Like a belligerent demon, he stood blocking her path, the pistol hanging casually in his hand, pointed toward the ground. She could not contain the sudden involuntary shriek that caught in her throat. In a panic, she scrambled up on the horse, her only thought to try to make a run for it. Prepared for such a move, he stepped aside when the horse bounded toward him. He reached up and, grasping a handful of her skirt, pulled her from the saddle. Determined to fight for her life, she managed to grab the handle of the butcher knife as she was wrenched from the horse.

"Fixin' to run out on me, was you?" He threw her to the ground. "Well, say hello to Pa for me when you git to hell." He raised the pistol to fire. She froze, paralyzed by the realization that in the next second she would face eternity. But instead of the explosion of a gunshot, she heard the clean metallic click of the hammer falling on an empty chamber. The gun had misfired. Upon thinking back to that fateful moment, she would think of it as a miracle, the direct intervention by the hand of God. But in the terrifying instant while crouched in the dark of the barnyard, she acted without thinking — a natural instinct to save her life.

In the darkness, he had failed to notice the knife she still clutched in one hand, so he was not prepared for the attack. In the time it took him to cock the pistol again, she lunged up at him, sinking the butcher knife in his gut. This time the pistol fired, but the shot went wide of the target. He recoiled in stunned horror. Staggering backward, he dropped the pistol, and grasped the handle of the knife with both hands in a desperate effort to extract it. He roared in pain as the blade came free, searing his insides like fire.

Horrified by the sight, Polly scrambled for the pistol as her husband lurched toward her, the bloody knife raised to strike. When it was over, she could not recall actually pulling the trigger. The first shot, fired in haste, barely missed the target and creased his cheek. The report of the .44 handgun startled her when it shattered the chill night air. But she continued to pull the trigger, and two slugs smacked into Bill's chest. A horrified look of disbelief transformed his face into a wide-eyed mask, and he staggered backward a few steps before dropping to his knees. Unable to contain her terror, Polly screamed. He stared at her for several long moments before pitching facedown in the dirt.

Half out of her mind with fear, she sobbed uncontrollably as she forced herself to climb up in the saddle. She had not meant to kill him. Now she *had* to run. Guiding the horse to the gate, she dismounted to open it, looking back as she did to see that Bill was still lying where he had dropped. Even with the confusion of thoughts racing through her brain, she realized that she could now take the time to pack more supplies. So in spite of the desire to run, she led the horse back to the cabin. After making up a pack with utensils and what staples she could carry, she took her husband's gun belt from a peg near the door, and returned the pistol to its holster. Next, she went to the left front corner of the cabin and, with the help of the butcher knife, probed in the loose dirt until she felt the metallic clunk she was searching for. There was not much money in Bill's secret cache — a few silver dollars and a gold tiepin, which he had no doubt found somewhere. But it would help. Ready now to travel, she stole another glance at the body lying near the barn door before climbing in the saddle and striking out for a new life.

With pounding heart and fearing every shadow along the dark road, she urged her horse onward toward Omaha. As the first gray light of dawn transformed individual trees from the solid dark forest curtain, she rode silently past the sawmill where her husband had worked, and the home she had known for a short time after her mother's death. The temptation to turn in and seek comfort from her former mistress was great, but she knew she could not. No matter what the circumstances were that caused it, she was a murderer. No, she had best take leave of the vicinity — to where, she wasn't sure. For lack of any better plan, it struck her that she could make her way to Julesburg and her aunt Hattie. She had heard her mother talk so often about her sister and her free and caring spirit. The more she thought about it, the more feasible it seemed. So it was settled. Now at least she knew where she was going.

Chapter 2

Most folks who had dealings with Tom Meadows would tell you that he drove a hard bargain when it came to trading horseflesh and tack. He was in a benevolent mood, however, when Polly Pike rode up to his stable. Either that, or he had a soft spot that the citizens of Omaha knew little of. Near exhaustion from travel and lack of sleep, the slight young woman must have touched a vulnerable spot in Tom's heart. She wanted to sell her horse and saddle so she could go in search of her only living relative, she told him. She would use the money to buy a train ticket, and Tom believed she spoke in earnest. Before it was done, he had bought horse, tack, and some assorted pots and pans. The horse was sound, the saddle in only fair condition, but he really had no use for the cookware. He didn't figure he had been too great a fool in the trade, but he insisted that she should tell no one how much he had paid her. The next morning, she was on the train to Julesburg.

She didn't know what to expect when she arrived at her destination. When her mother was alive, she would talk about her sister, always in genuine admiration. Hattie was the adventurous one, she would say, with more starch than the rest of the family combined. Polly looked forward to meeting her aunt, but how would Hattie respond to a surprise visit from a niece she had never seen? *I can earn my keep,* Polly thought. *Just give me the opportunity.*

With no earthly idea where to find Horace Moon's farm, she decided to go to the post office. The postmaster was sure to know everybody around. She could not help but feel a tensing of her muscles and a sudden increase in her heart rate when she left the train station and headed toward the telegraph office. The thought had occurred to her that a wire might be bringing a message alerting all stations about a woman murderer on the run. She was greatly relieved when the telegraph operator glanced up at her as she passed, and offered a polite nod. She answered with a shy smile, and hurried toward the post office.

She had been right in assuming the postmaster knew everyone, but she wasn't prepared for the information he passed along. Her uncle had died a few years back. Her aunt Hattie and another widow, Maggie Hogg, had decided to team up and leave Julesburg, supposedly to seek their fortunes farther west. There was some talk, he said, that they had planned to follow the gold strikes in Dakota Territory. The news left Polly in somewhat of a quandary, but she had not come this far to give up.

"My advice would be to go on out to Fort Laramie," he said, "if you're still bent on finding Hattie. If her and Maggie was headin' for the Black Hills, they'd most likely have gone through Fort Laramie. Most ever'body does. You could get back on the train, and ride on down to Cheyenne. Fort Laramie's seventy or eighty miles north of Cheyenne. There ain't no train that goes to the fort, so you'd have to find some transportation."

With the image of Bill Pike's body still vivid in her mind, she knew she wasn't going to go back to Omaha. And Julesburg held no appeal for her without her aunt Hattie. So there was really no decision to be made. She returned to the train station, and sat up all night, waiting for the train to Cheyenne.

■ ■ ■ ■

Arriving in Cheyenne after again sitting up all night, this time in the coach, because of an extended delay in Kimball, Polly went straight to the stationmaster to inquire about transportation to Fort Laramie. "There ain't no public transport to Fort Laramie, ma'am," the stationmaster told her.

When she explained that it was urgent she find her aunt, and she had been told that aunt Hattie had most probably traveled through Fort Laramie, he offered a possible solution to her problem. "There's an army patrol got here last night. They was waiting to meet the train you come in on. Colonel Bradley, he's the post commander at Laramie, his daughter and grandchildren were on the train, and the soldiers came to escort 'em to the post. Might be they'd let you go along with 'em."

The young woman with two little girls, Polly thought, remembering the well-behaved children who sat beside their mother at the opposite end of the coach from her. "Yes," she replied hopefully, "maybe they would." She turned to look back at the handful of passengers detraining, afraid for a moment that the woman and her daughters were already gone.

Reading her concern, the stationmaster walked to the door, and looked across the tracks. "They're still waiting for her luggage," he said. "Come on, and I'll go talk to the officer in charge with you." He immediately stepped off the wooden walkway, and strode toward the group of soldiers gathered on the other side of the tracks. Clutching her bundle of clothes in her arms, Polly was right on his heels. Though the stationmaster seemed oblivious to the wheezing, groaning iron monster, Polly stepped lively when they crossed in front of the locomotive, lest it suddenly decide to lurch forward and devour them. Safely across, she hurried to stay close to the stationmaster's elbow.

"Say, there, Lieutenant," he called out, striding up to the officer standing by while two enlisted men tied some suitcases to the back of an ambulance. When the lieutenant turned to face him, the stationmaster said, "This here young lady is lookin' for transportation to Fort Laramie." When the officer's expression conveyed little concern for civilian travel problems, the stationmaster added, "She's all alone, lookin' for her aunt — got no other way to get there."

The lieutenant's expression softened a bit as he turned his gaze toward Polly. She, in turn, met his gaze, looking up at him hopefully. "Lieutenant DiMarco, ma'am," he said, introducing himself. "My orders are to escort Mrs. Castle and her daughters back to the fort. I really don't have any authority to take along civilian passengers on army vehicles. I'm real sorry, ma'am."

"Oh, come now, Lieutenant. I'm sure the army wouldn't mind if you gave a young lady in distress a ride." They were startled by the voice coming from the ambulance behind them.

DiMarco turned at once to find the colonel's daughter leaning over the sill of the ambulance's open sides. "Begging your pardon, ma'am, but I don't want to get crossways with the colonel on this."

"Well, she can ride with us as part of our party. If you get in trouble for it, I'll fix things with my father." She turned a gracious smile toward Polly. "Come join us, dear. You look like you're about worn out. My name is Mary Castle, and this is Charlotte and Julia," she said, laying a hand on each girl's shoulder as she introduced them.

"I wouldn't want to crowd you," Polly replied, looking at the rather cramped confines of the ambulance. "I could ride a horse if there's a spare one." She looked at the lieutenant, unsure if he was going to permit it.

"Nonsense," Mary Castle retorted. "We'll have plenty of room. Won't we, Lieutenant?"

DiMarco grinned. "If you say so, ma'am." He turned to offer Polly his assistance. She immediately accepted his arm.

"What's your name, dear?" Mary Castle inquired.

"Polly," she replied, then hesitated before adding, "Polly Hatcher," using her maiden name. After she settled herself, she looked back to thank the stationmaster. "My thanks to you, sir."

"You're welcome, miss. I hope you find your aunt."

Mary Castle found herself drawn to the young woman who had struck out on her own in hopes of finding her aunt. She was not sure she would have been so bold had she found herself in Polly's situation. The poor girl's husband had been killed in an accident at the sawmill where he worked, and she had no other family to turn to. Mary supposed that Polly saw herself with little choice but to search for her one living relative. Even faced with similar circumstances, Mary was not sure she would have been brave enough to face such a journey alone.

The two young women took to each other almost immediately. Polly, at first cautious, and feeling somewhat dishonest at having to lie about Bill's death, soon relaxed in the cheerful company of Mary and the children. As a result, the dusty, bumpy ride, as the ambulance rumbled over the prairie, became a pleasant journey with each night's camp almost like a picnic. Lieutenant DiMarco was constantly attentive to their needs, and there was a wonderful sense of security with a patrol of fifteen soldiers to protect them. Before Cheyenne was little more than a day behind, Polly was able to place thoughts of Bill Pike in the recesses of her mind.

During the trip, Polly learned that Mary had not seen her husband, a cavalry lieutenant, for more than two months. She and the girls had been back east to visit her husband's parents. Now she was eagerly looking forward to seeing him again at Fort Laramie. Although her father was the post commander, she had never been there before. So in that respect, it was a new adventure for both women. Winston, her husband, had been transferred to Fort Laramie where he would serve under her father. In letters to his wife, he had written that a campaign against the Sioux was forthcoming. The purpose was to drive the hostile bands back to the reservations once and for all. He had expressed some regrets that he had been transferred from General Crook's command, and would therefore miss the coming action.

"We've been apart longer than I like," Mary said. "And since my father is the post commander at Fort Laramie, I decided to meet Winston there. At least, I'll be able to see him for a little while before he goes marching off somewhere to punish the savages." She turned to grace her daughters with a benevolent gaze. "And grandma and grandpa will get a chance to spoil their babies again." Polly suspected that Lieutenant Castle's transfer was greatly influenced by a doting colonel's acquiescence to his daughter's desires.

The second morning of their journey greeted the travelers with a light frost on the prairie. It was unexpected because the days prior to that had been properly springlike. With full knowledge that it was still early enough in the year for just such a possibility, Lieutenant DiMarco had seen to it that there were extra blankets packed in the ambulance. After a hasty breakfast, due to the sudden chill, the party was off again, the women and children all bundled in army-issue blankets. They sat huddled close together for warmth, chattering cheerfully as the ambulance bumped across a silver prairie that glistened with the arrival of the morning sun. Polly suddenly realized that she had not been so content since she had been a child. She almost wished the journey would never end. She and Mary were very close to the same age, and for Polly it was almost like having a sister. It was only a few hours later when she saw her first Sioux warrior.

It was certainly not the first Indian she had seen, but it was her first glimpse of a *hostile.* He was alone, seated on a white pony at the brow of a low line of hills to the west, approximately four or five hundred yards away. He made no move to run from the column of troopers, seeming instead to be content to watch them. At that distance, Polly could not really tell much about the warrior's appearance, but he did not strike her as much of a threat to their progress. She turned her attention toward the head of the column where DiMarco was conferring with his sergeant. She heard him say, "Just leave him be, we're not out here to chase after any stray Indians."

The warrior remained unmoving, silently watching the small patrol as it continued upon its course. Then, evidently satisfied that the soldiers intended to show him no interest, he raised his rifle and fired several shots in their direction before wheeling his pony and galloping away below the brow of the hill. The shots caused no damage, landing harmlessly in the grass some yards short of the column, but they were sufficient to alarm the passengers in the ambulance.

DiMarco gave a few quick orders to his sergeant, then rode back to the ladies. "Everybody all right back here?" He pulled up alongside. "Just some hostile trying to annoy us," he said. "I've sent a couple of men out to see what he's up to — and make sure he doesn't try to get close enough to hit anything." He wheeled his horse and rode along beside them. "We'll reach Fort Laramie tomorrow. I don't think you have to worry about Indians this close to the fort — just some savage showing off," he assured them.

Polly watched the two troopers ride out from the column toward the point where the warrior had disappeared. They had almost reached the ridge when suddenly a rider appeared from the low hills to intercept them. At first glance, it looked to be another Indian, but the soldiers pulled up and waited for him. After a brief conversation, the three turned and rode back toward the column. DiMarco, as interested in the sudden turn of events as Polly, stood up in his stirrups to get a better look.

When the three were halfway back, DiMarco recognized the stranger. "Who is he?" Mary Castle asked.

"His name's Jordan Gray," DiMarco replied.

Polly watched with interest as the three riders returned to the column. DiMarco rode forward to meet them. The man identified as Jordan Gray ignited a spark of curiosity in her mind. As untamed in appearance as the Sioux warrior she had just seen, he was dressed in animal skins, his face clean shaven like an Indian's and tan from the spring winds. He sat straight in the saddle on the ugliest horse she had ever seen. He rode with a bearing that conveyed a casual confidence in himself — unsmiling, almost stern. Mary asked a trooper riding close by the question Polly had in mind.

"Who is Jordan Gray?" she asked. "Is he one of the scouts at the fort?"

The soldier hesitated, taking a long look at Jordan before answering. "Well, ma'am, he is, and he ain't. He's a scout rightly enough when he's of a mind to be. I don't know too much about him. To tell you the truth, nobody much does. He's kind of a loner, stays up in the mountains a lot, but he seems to show up at times when he's most needed. There are a few folks that know him a little, I guess — Sergeant Grant in M Company, Captain McGarity, and maybe Alton Broom over in the post trader's store. That's about all I can tell you."

"Some people just aren't very friendly, I guess," Mary said.

"I expect that's it, ma'am," the trooper agreed. "On the other hand, I wouldn't say Gray was unfriendly. He just don't go outta his way to be friendly." Warming up to the subject, he offered a bit more information on the buckskin-clad scout. "A year or so back, he was on trial for murderin' some folks in a Fort Smith bank, but they found him not guilty. There's talk that he killed some men up in the Black Hills, but there ain't nobody who knows if that's just rumors or not. He's a strange one, all right."

Polly listened to the soldier's appraisal of the man talking with Lieutenant DiMarco and his sergeant. She could not deny a certain element of fascination for the mysterious scout, while at the same time finding it rather odd that the army would employ a man with such a reputation. On this particular day, she and Mary would have been somewhat apprehensive had they been able to hear the conversation between Jordan Gray and Lieutenant DiMarco.

"What are you doing out this way, Jordan?" DiMarco asked, greeting the scout.

One of the troopers answered for him. "He says there's a bunch of Injuns hiding back of those hills, waiting for us to follow that buck that took a shot at us."

This captured DiMarco's interest immediately, and he stole an unconscious glance back at his responsibility in the ambulance before responding. "Is that a fact? How many is a bunch?"

"A few more than you'd wanna tangle with, seeing how big your escort is," Jordan replied. "I counted at least twenty back in a gulch beyond those hills, and there may be more that I couldn't see." He paused to look at the ambulance, only mildly curious. "They were hopin' to give you a little surprise party. If I was you, I'd head more to the east, close by that rise you see yonder. I don't think they'll come after you out in the open — too risky — but if they do, there's a little stream below that rise that would be a good place to stand 'em off."

"You heard him, Sergeant," DiMarco immediately responded. "Head 'em out." And the column started moving again, veering off to the right of their original path. Jordan rode along beside the lieutenant. Far off to the west, the Sioux warrior on the white pony reappeared at the brow of the hill, and watched the soldiers leave. "I guess he's disappointed we didn't come to the party," DiMarco commented. "Of course, I don't know for sure that he isn't the only Indian out there," he said, obviously joking.

Jordan smiled. "Well, there's one way you can find out for sure," he said.

"It's a good thing you showed up when you did," DiMarco said, taking a more serious vein. "I've got women and children back there — the colonel's daughter, for Chrissakes."

"That so?" Jordan responded. "Well, I think you'll be all right. I don't think they'll take a chance on gettin' some of their warriors picked off chasin' you out in the open."

"How'd you know they were there?" DiMarco asked.

"I just happened on 'em," Jordan replied with a shrug. "I've been up in the mountains back there, on my way back to Fort Laramie, and I saw that Sioux on the white horse come up outta that ravine. He didn't act like he was up to anything good, I guess, so I decided to have a look at where he came from. I saw the little party they were plannin' for you boys, only I didn't know who the party was for at the time. But the way they were set up for ambush, it was easy to see which direction they expected you to be ridin'. So I took a wide swing around 'em to warn you."

"Like I said," DiMarco commented, "I'm glad you showed up when you did." Just as he said it, his horse emitted a sudden squeal and bucked, almost unseating the lieutenant. "Dammit!" DiMarco swore, pulling back hard on the reins until the animal settled down again.

"Sorry 'bout that," Jordan apologized.

"Some day, somebody's liable to shoot that damn horse," DiMarco said, though without malice in his tone. Sweet Pea, Jordan Gray's horse, was notorious for her inability to get along with other horses, and she would not hesitate to take a nip out of one that ventured close enough. DiMarco, like most everyone else on the post, knew that the man who was foolish enough to shoot the homely horse better be prepared to deal with Jordan — and that would be a hard day's work.

They rode on in silence for awhile, keeping an eye on their back trail to make sure the Sioux war party hadn't decided to come after them. DiMarco, satisfied that he had been spared from leading the colonel's daughter into an ambush, considered the man riding beside him — now at a safe interval. Jordan Gray was a puzzle not many people had solved. He was not an unfriendly man, far from it. Yet he really had no close friends. Sergeant Hamilton Grant and maybe the clerk at the post trader's store were the only two people on the post that Jordan talked to. He would disappear for months at a time, only to reappear, usually with news of some movement of hostile camps, or a suspicious assembly of warriors that might bear watching. Then the lieutenant couldn't help thinking, *like today.*

Mary Castle's escort detail continued unmolested into Fort Laramie, delivering Colonel Bradley's daughter and grandchildren safe and sound. The post was bustling with activity. There were troops of cavalry and infantry, newly arrived companies of Crook's command, busily preparing for war against the Sioux. There were scores of wagons, driven by ambitious adventurers eager to reach the gold reported in the Black Hills. To Polly, it was an amazing beehive of more people than she had ever seen in one place. At first frightened by all the activity, she quickly rekindled her resolve.

Lieutenant DiMarco had dispatched one trooper ahead of the column to alert the colonel of their arrival. And he, along with his wife, was waiting when the detail pulled up before the post commander's residence. Within minutes, the party was joined by Lieutenant Winston Castle. Polly stood back beside the ambulance and watched the joyful reunion. She was especially touched by the tender embrace between Mary and her husband, and how it contrasted with the brutal touch of Bill Pike. She immediately tried to shake thoughts of her late husband from her mind. It struck her then that the quiet scout who had appeared to warn them of the Sioux ambush was no longer with them. She had not noticed that he left the column as soon as it approached the outbuildings of the fort, and headed upriver to his camp.

Contrary to Lieutenant DiMarco's belief that Jordan had no friends on the post beyond Alton Broom and Hamilton Grant, the scout often shared his campfire with two of the Crow scouts, Iron Pony and Otter.

He was pulling the saddle off Sweet Pea's back when the two Indians rode up to greet him.

"We thought maybe some Sioux warrior finally tied your scalp to his lance," Iron Pony joked.

"Not hardly," Jordan answered with a laugh. "I just had to do a little huntin' — wanted to have something to eat besides the army's beans and bacon for awhile. I didn't think I'd be anywhere near any Sioux or Cheyenne war parties, but damned if I didn't run into one anyway."

When he told them of the ambush that Lieutenant DiMarco had managed to avoid, they nodded knowingly. "Sioux raiding parties have been striking white homesteads closer to the fort than before," Iron Pony said. "I think it is because they have gotten more brave since they whipped General Crook before."

"You may be right," Jordan agreed. He thought back upon the ill-fated campaign Iron Pony referred to. It had been an attempt to strike the Sioux in their winter camps. Crook had set out from Fort Fetterman on the first of March in bitter-cold weather. In Jordan's mind, it was a stupid endeavor. The soldiers almost froze to death, and when troops under Colonel

Reynolds engaged a Cheyenne village on the banks of the Powder River, the Cheyenne sharpshooters hidden in the bluffs made it so hot for the soldiers that they were forced to retreat back to Crook's command. Reynolds ordered the village burned before withdrawing, thinking the whole time that it had been a Sioux camp they had destroyed. He even reported that it was Crazy Horse's village. Crook decided to abandon the campaign and return to base. The news was quick to reach Fort Laramie as well as the Sioux reservations. General Crook wasn't too pleased with Reynolds. He had a reputation as an Indian fighter and Reynolds had sullied it. In fact, Crook was so aggravated that he court-martialed the colonel. Instead of a telling blow against the hostile bands that refused to report to the reservation, the battle served to encourage more reservation Indians to join their hostile brothers.

It didn't take a great deal of intelligence to know that the summer was going to bring a serious clash between the army and the still-free bands of Sitting Bull and Crazy Horse. In the early spring, Jordan had seen numerous trails left by whole villages across the prairie, all heading in the direction of the Powder River Valley. He didn't know if he would take part in what promised to be a war. It was just as well as far as he was concerned, for he felt no personal animosity toward the Sioux. For a man born with an untamed spirit, he could not really find fault in any man, red or white, who refused to be penned up on a reservation. He would continue to scout for the army, however, at least when it pleased him to do so. He had no other source of income.

After a few minutes of small talk, Iron Pony and Otter left him to return to the Crow camp close by the fort. A short time later, Jordan had another visitor. Jim Eagle was half Sioux, not particularly well liked by the Sioux scouts, and despised by the Crows. Although currently accepting the army's pay as a scout, Jim's allegiance to the Great White Father was somewhat suspect among the other scouts. Iron Pony was convinced that the belligerent breed would deliver a patrol into Sitting Bull's hands if given the chance. Jordan stood up when the half-breed left the trail and headed toward his campfire.

Walking his horse slowly, Jim Eagle looked around him as he approached, evaluating the campsite. He spoke not a word of greeting, sitting sullenly in the saddle, his manner contemptuous. Jordan couldn't help but be curious. The breed had never spoken to him before. He wondered what the occasion was for the dubious honor on this day. As it turned out, the visit was solely to satisfy the stoic scout's curiosity.

"Jordan Gray," Jim pronounced with no emotion. He remained in the saddle while he glanced at Sweet Pea, Jordan's gear on the ground, then back at Jordan. "You like to camp alone. A man can get his throat cut campin' alone."

"I expect you'd know about that," Jordan returned, finding it interesting that the half-breed's thoughts ran along that vein.

"That's one damn ugly horse," Jim said gesturing toward Sweet Pea.

"It ain't her job to be pretty," Jordan replied calmly. It was a remark he had heard a hundred times since he and Sweet Pea had formed their partnership. "Now that you've insulted my horse, why don't you get the hell outta my camp?" He had no idea why the detested half-breed had chosen to visit him, but he had no time to waste on Jim Eagle.

The breed's face remained stoic for a few moments before giving way to an evil grin. "A man camping alone out here is askin' to get his throat cut." He turned his horse, and walked it slowly back toward the trail.

Jordan watched the departing belligerent

until he was out of sight around the bend of the river. Still puzzled over the reason for the visit, because the two had never had any use for each other, he returned to the business of preparing his supper. He glanced over his shoulder at his horse. "Surely, he didn't stop just to tell you something you already know," he said.

Polly Hatcher was pleased to spend the night as a guest of Colonel Bradley and his wife, although she was obliged to sleep on the settee in the parlor. Mrs. Bradley promised to find her suitable arrangements on the following day. She knew of several possibilities. Sergeant Major Rankin and his wife had an extra bed, and Captain Beard, the post surgeon, had a spare room since his daughter had recently married.

Colonel Bradley remembered seeing Polly's aunt Hattie when she was at Fort Laramie. "She came through, all right, driving her own wagon — came with a woman named Maggie Hogg, if I recall correctly. I recall seeing the women, but I didn't talk to them, so I'm afraid I can't tell you where they were heading when they left Fort Laramie. Like everybody else, I suppose, they were probably planning to go to the Black Hills to hunt for gold." He thought for a moment. "You might go talk to Alton Broom at the sutler's store. They most likely bought supplies there before starting out again."

The next day, as soon as she and the colonel's wife had made arrangements for her to stay with Captain Beard for a day or two, Polly went to seek out one, Alton Broom, at the post trader's store. It was never difficult to engage Alton in conversation on any subject, and he was delighted to pass on any information he could provide to help the young lady.

"Yes, ma'am," he said. "I surely do remember your aunt and her friend. As I recollect, them two ladies bought my last barrel of dried apples and a short barrel of flour — figured on bakin' some apple pies, I reckon." He laughed at his attempt at humor.

"Can you tell me where they were heading?" Polly asked.

"Black Hills," Alton replied. "Said they were headin' out to the gold strikes. I give 'em credit for plenty of grit — them two women alone. But if any two women could make it, I'd say it was them." When Polly told him that she intended to follow them, Alton tried to discourage her. "Beggin' your pardon, ma'am, but I don't think you know what you're sayin'. That's Injun territory up there, and since the weather warmed up, there's been all kinds of reports of Sioux and Cheyenne raidin' parties between here and there. No, ma'am, you don't wanna even think about goin' into the Black Hills."

She did not take the warning lightly, hesitating for a long moment while she turned it over in her mind. She thought about Bill's body lying in the mud of the barnyard, and knew she could not go back to Omaha. With no prospects for supporting herself, she could not stay long in Fort Laramie. She saw no option for herself but to find her aunt Hattie. "I guess I'll go to the Black Hills," she said softly, reinforcing her resolve.

Alton guessed as much while watching her worry over the decision. He shook his head slowly in bewilderment. "Ma'am, you're gonna need a guide."

"I know," she replied, then paused a moment more. "A man named Jordan Gray rode in with the column. Do you think he would take me to the Black Hills?"

"Jordan?" Alton said, surprised to hear her mention the name. "I didn't know he was back." He paused to consider her question. "I don't know, ma'am. I don't rightly know. I reckon you'd have to ask him."

"Do you know where I can find him?"

"Yessum, I can tell you where he usually likes to camp." He told her to follow the river upstream for about a mile to the point where a narrow stream emptied into the river. "At least, that's where he's been campin' most of the time when he's back here." He smiled. "Jordan ain't much for crowds."

"Can you tell me where I can buy a horse?" Polly asked.

Jordan glanced up from the fire he was tending, and watched the progress of the single rider slowly plodding along the riverbank. It appeared to be the woman who had come in with Lieutenant DiMarco, but he couldn't be sure. He had not really gotten a close look at the woman riding in the ambulance with the colonel's daughter. *Where,* he wondered, *could she be going?* There was a Shoshoni camp about two miles beyond his own. Beyond that, there was nothing. A few minutes passed before the woman spotted Jordan's horse. She abruptly turned toward his campfire. Jordan rose to his feet to await her.

"Ma'am," he said in greeting when she pulled up before him.

"Mr. Gray," Polly returned.

"Jordan," he corrected.

"Jordan," she acknowledged. "I don't know if you noticed. I was with Mary Castle in the wagon you rode in with yesterday."

"I noticed," he said. "What brings you up this way?"

"I was looking for you. The man in the sutler's store told me I might find you up this way."

He stepped back to watch her dismount. Then, remembering his manners, stepped quickly forward to assist her. When she had both feet on the ground, he released her elbow, took the reins, and led her horse over to a willow a safe distance from Sweet Pea. The belligerent mare was already rolling her eyes in the strange horse's direction. "What can I do for you, miss?"

"Polly's my name, Polly Hatcher," she said, extending her hand. "I would like to hire you to guide me to the Black Hills. I can pay you fifty dollars."

Although there was no sign of emotion in his eyes, he couldn't help but be surprised by the young lady's wish. He studied her face for a moment more before responding. "Did Alton Broom tell you I hired out as a guide?"

"Well, no," she replied. "I asked about you, and he told me where to find you."

When he did not speak, but continued to study her face, she went on to explain. "When you met us back there on the prairie, they said you were a scout. I just thought you might be available to take me to the Black Hills."

"If you don't mind me askin', what's a lady like you lookin' for in the Black Hills?" He couldn't help but be curious. He could only think of one kind of woman that followed the gold camps alone, and she didn't fit the image. He was genuinely surprised when she explained that she was on her way to find her aunt Hattie, and that Alton Broom had told her that her aunt had started out for the Black Hills with another woman. "Hattie Moon?" he asked. "Your aunt's Hattie Moon?"

"Why, yes," she replied, surprised by his response. "Do you know her?"

"Yes, I do," he said, unable to suppress a grin, the first sign of emotion he had displayed. "Hattie Moon and Maggie Hogg, they're runnin' a kitchen in Deadwood Gulch — probably makin' more money than the fellows pannin' for gold." Hattie Moon and Maggie Hogg were two of the few friends he considered close, but he didn't see fit to mention that.

"Good, then you'll lead me there?" Polly

asked eagerly.

"Ah, no, ma'am," he immediately replied. "I don't know what Alton told you, but I don't generally hire out as a guide. I do some scoutin' for the army, and I'm supposed to ride out with a patrol tomorrow." Seeing the disappointment in her face, he added, "I'm sorry I can't help you." He also felt it his duty to advise her to reconsider her plans at this time. "Miss, there's a lot of Sioux raidin' parties between here and the Belle Fourche. It's not a good idea to start out that way unless you're with a column of soldiers."

There was another reason why he was hesitant to travel to Deadwood, one more significant than the danger of Sioux war parties, and one he wasn't prone to mention. Deadwood was not a healthy place for him. A year ago he had had a run-in with a vigilante committee there, the result of which left the town shy of about a half dozen citizens. It wasn't his fault. They had mistaken him for a murdering claim jumper. Without waiting to find out for sure, they came after him, hot for a lynching. He had no choice but to defend himself. It was not something he was proud of. He had been forced to kill several of the vigilantes who attacked him. It was either that or take part in their necktie party as guest of honor. The choice was simple. After the bloody incident, he had resolved to stay away from the untamed town. There were still some there who thought he had been the messenger of death who had stalked the isolated claims. Deadwood was a bad-luck town for Jordan.

Thinking he might be holding out for more money, she attempted another offer. "I don't have much money left after selling my things, but I can raise the fee ten dollars."

"It ain't the money, miss," he replied patiently. "I just can't help you right now. I'm headin' out on patrol with Lieutenant Castle in the mornin'. I'm sorry." The final tone in his voice left her with little doubt that the matter was closed. She sighed and turned to retrieve her horse. "Miss Hatcher," he called out after her, "take my advice and go on back east. There ain't nothin' but sagebrush and Sioux between here and the Belle Fourche — no place for a lady like yourself."

A lady like myself, she thought. *I wonder what kind of lady he would think me if he knew I killed my husband.* She favored him with a tired smile, then turned her horse back toward the fort. Disappointed, but far from discouraged, she vowed to go to Deadwood even if she had to do it with no guide.

Chapter 3

"Looks like you're the only officer catchin' patrol duty, Lieutenant." Jordan pulled up to the head of the formation of soldiers standing by their mounts.

DiMarco gave him a half smile. "This was supposed to be Lieutenant Castle's detail, but I offered to take it for him, since his wife just got here."

Jordan looked around at the assembly of troopers. Half of them were foreigners who knew very little English. All of them were green with little training. He hoped for their sake that the patrol wasn't being sent to quell any hostile activity. "Where are we headin'?" Jordan asked.

"Back down toward Scott's Bluff," DiMarco replied. "Some rancher down that way near the old Red Cloud Agency lost some stock, and he thinks it mighta been Injuns."

"Huh," Jordan grunted. "Whaddaya need

me for? You don't need a scout to lead you to Scott's Bluff."

"No, I s'pose not. Like I said, this was Castle's patrol, and he requested you, since he's new out here." DiMarco grinned. "You might as well ride along, and pick up a few days' pay." He knew that Jordan was not on a regular salary, but was paid only for the days he was actively employed as a scout. It was an arrangement Jordan had insisted upon in order to be free to come and go as he chose.

"I reckon," Jordan said. Still, it seemed like another typically useless army patrol. Scott's Bluff was at least fifty miles from Fort Laramie. By the time they reached the rancher's place, any Sioux raiding party would be long gone. *What the hell?* he thought. *I can use the money.*

The column started east along the Platte, following the old immigrant trail. There wasn't much conversation between the lieutenant and his scout as the horses padded along through a region still scarred with the many tracks of settlers' wagons, their perilous journeys long past. The end of the day's march marked an uneventful trek that found them encamped at Horse Creek, where over a decade earlier the government had met to forge a treaty with the many tribes that occupied the plains. After the horses were cared for, and the cook fires were started, Lieutenant DiMarco and Sergeant Demry settled themselves on the creek bank beside Jordan. The conversation was casual, of little interest to Jordan, until Demry mentioned Polly Hatcher.

"Alton Broom said that lady that come with us from Cheyenne is headin' up to the Black Hills," he commented.

"Is that a fact?" DiMarco replied, his interest provoked. "She's gonna end up in some Sioux buck's lodge — if she ain't scalped. How's she planning to get there?"

"Hell, she's already gone, accordin' to Alton," Demry said. "Hired that half-breed, Jim Eagle, to take her."

"My God," DiMarco uttered in disbelief. "Couldn't somebody have told her better than that? I wouldn't trust that damn loafer Injun to find anything but a bottle of whiskey."

"I guess she's mighty damned desperate to find her aunt," Demry said. "She's takin' a helluva risk, though."

Jordan listened to the conversation without comment, but the news of Polly Hatcher's indiscretion troubled him greatly. It was a foolish decision she had made — if Demry had the story straight. In fact, he considered the woman in grave danger. And try as he might to shrug it off as none of his responsibility, he could not escape the feeling of guilt that descended upon him. She had come to him for help, and he refused her. Hattie Moon and Maggie Hogg were friends of his, and she was Hattie's niece. *Dammit! She ain't my responsibility. She should have had better sense,* he thought, determined to put it out of his mind.

The next morning he found that it was not so easily done. The image of Polly's face returned to haunt him, and he knew he was going to have to do something about it or he would never have peace of mind again. *Damn!* He cursed himself for being softhearted. Then he cursed himself for being foolish because the odds of cutting Jim Eagle's trail from Fort Laramie were stacked pretty tall against him. If Jim Eagle meant the lady harm, as Jordan suspected, there was really no reason to believe he would even head toward the Black Hills. But Jordan had little choice but to assume that was the direction taken.

"Mornin'," Lieutenant DiMarco greeted Jordan as the scout led his horse up to the officer seated on a cottonwood log, nursing a cup of coffee. "You look like you're all rarin' to go."

"I'm leavin' the patrol," Jordan stated matter-of-factly. His statement caught DiMarco by surprise, and before the lieutenant could respond, he continued, "You sure as hell don't need me on this patrol, and I've got somethin' I've gotta do."

Amazed by the scout's announcement, DiMarco found his voice. "What will I tell the paymaster? Don't you wanna get paid?"

Jordan shrugged. "Tell him I quit." Wasting no more time to offer an explanation, he climbed aboard Sweet Pea and promptly loped away, leaving DiMarco shaking his head in exasperation.

"Hard man to figure out," DiMarco commented as he stared after the broad buckskin-clad shoulders moving in rhythm with the surprisingly smooth gait of the ungainly gray mare.

"I reckon," Demry agreed.

Jordan arrived back at Fort Laramie just at dusk. The notes of the bugler's trumpet sounding retreat carried across the parade ground as he headed straight for the post trader's store. Alton Broom would be the first person to consult for information regarding Polly Hatcher's departure. It was Jordan's hope that Alton could shed some light on the trail taken by Jim Eagle and how great a head start he and the woman had on him. As usual, Alton was primed with information.

"I told that lady she'd be better off waitin' for a better time to go traipsin' off across the prairie, especially with the likes of Jim Eagle," Alton said in his own defense. "She said that he was the only one willin' to do it for the little amount of money she had to offer. She was bound and determined to go, said she didn't have the time to hunt for somebody better. I warned her she'd best keep an eye on that buck. She said she would, and had me draw her a map to show her the general direction Jim Eagle oughta be takin' her. I told her she oughta be headin' due north, crossin' the Niobrara and the lower fork of the Cheyenne. She should see the hills by then. If she didn't, they was goin' in the wrong direction."

"When did they leave?" Jordan asked.

"Just a little before Lieutenant DiMarco's detail rode out yesterday mornin'."

Two days to make up, Jordan thought. Now he would have to lose another night because he would need daylight to try to pick up a trail. From what Alton said about making Polly a map, there was a good possibility that they set out on the correct path. Jim Eagle wouldn't want to arouse her suspicions before getting out of sight of the fort. "Where'd she buy that horse she was ridin'?" Jordan asked.

"Ike Lester," Alton answered.

"Much obliged," Jordan replied, and took his leave, determined to make a call on Ike first thing in the morning. He led his horse across the parade ground, heading for the cavalry barracks, and was just passing the post surgeon's house when he heard his name called. Stopping abruptly, he turned to encounter the doctor's daughter.

"Jordan, I thought that was you," she greeted him as she stepped off of the porch to meet him.

"Kathleen," he replied. "Or should I say Mrs. Wallace?"

If there was a hint of bitterness in his tone, she did not perceive it, but came smiling to greet him. "It's been a long time since I've seen you. I hope you haven't been avoiding me." She puckered her lips as if to scold. "Thomas said that you've been riding on some patrols, but not in any he has led."

The mention of her husband served to rankle the nerves in the back of his neck. Lieutenant Thomas Jefferson Wallace — Kathleen had chosen to marry the arrogant officer, a decision that Jordan could never understand. *Why should I care who she mar-*

ries? He had often asked himself that question over the past year, knowing the answer full well, but reluctant to admit it, even to himself. There had been feelings between them, disturbing feelings that had caused him to question his solitary way of life — a life that suited him before she had taken his hand in hers and kissed him lightly on the cheek. *But that was long ago,* he thought. Why did it still bother him? Maybe if she had chosen any other man except Wallace, he would have been better able to accept it. Now she was standing before him, offering her hand, greeting him as an old friend.

"I've been in the mountains a lot of the time," he offered as an excuse. "Haven't been on many patrols lately."

"I should have guessed," she said cheerfully. In her mind, she pictured him, as she often had, in his beloved mountains, as wild as any Sioux warrior. Knowing it could be painful to dwell on thoughts of Jordan Gray, she quickly chased them from her mind. "Come," she said, "I'll walk with you as far as the hospital."

As they walked, Kathleen attempted to fill the silence often left by Jordan. There was not much to talk about except the campaign against the Sioux and the massing of troops that had passed through Fort Laramie. She wanted to ask him how he had been, and if he spent as much time trying not to think about her as she spent trying to rid her mind of thoughts of him. Walking beside him now brought back memories of the days she had spent watching over him when he had been wounded, when her father was the post surgeon at Fort Gibson. Though it seemed like a century ago, it had not been that long. She would have gone with him then if he had asked, and lived in his mountains, in a tent or a cave. But he had not asked. Sometimes she thanked God that he had not, for it would have been a foolish endeavor to try to tame a wild hawk. She had made the sensible choice. Still, there were moments when she looked at her husband, preening before his mirror as he made sure his uniform was perfect, and wondered if Jordan Gray might have been a gamble worth the risk. "I'll never know," she murmured.

"Beg your pardon?"

Realizing that she had uttered the statement aloud, she quickly replied, "Oh, I was just mumbling. I was thinking I'll never know what happens to all the time. I've got so many things to do before Thomas gets back. He's out on patrol, won't be back until tomorrow." *There,* she thought, *I put it out there in spite of myself.*

If the significance of her statement even registered with him, he didn't show it. Instead, he continued walking in silence, trying to ignore the closeness of her, and the faint smell of cinnamon that told him she had been baking. When they reached the hospital, Jordan finally spoke. "I reckon I'd better ride on upriver and make camp. It'll be dark pretty soon." He turned to say good-bye.

"Jordan," she said as he prepared to step up in the saddle and ride out of her life again, "I hope I'll see you more often." She fumbled for words, unable to say what she really wished. "Don't stay away so long," she finally said, taking his hand. "I think you'd really like Thomas if the two of you got to know each other." She realized that she must sound desperate, hanging onto him like a child, but she also realized that she wanted somehow to keep him near her — a feeling she would find difficult to explain to her husband — or herself.

He gazed at her for a long moment, thinking hard on what he was about to say. He was a man of few words and simple truths, but he cared too much for her to hurt her feelings. It would be a cold day in hell before he would come to like Thomas

Jefferson Wallace, and it would be a chilly day there when he came to even tolerate the pompous lieutenant. After a few more moments, he dropped her hand and said, "I'm sure your husband has plenty of friends. I doubt he's lookin' for one from the scout company." With a foot in the stirrup, he uttered a quick good-bye, climbed up, and without another look in her direction, rode off toward the river. In spite of his efforts to avoid them, the chance meeting had stirred up thoughts painful to remember. The worst part of it was the deep suspicion in his mind that she would have accepted his proposal of marriage if he had only asked. *It wouldn't have worked,* he had to admit to himself.

Ike Lester was walking from the barn when Jordan rode in. He kept a wary eye on the stranger, and picked up his pace as he made straight for his sod hut and the rifle leaning against the wall. With rifle now in hand, he turned to meet his visitor.

"Mornin'," Jordan offered.

"Mornin'," Ike responded.

"You sold a lady a horse a couple of days ago," Jordan said. Ike interrupted before he could ask the question.

"That was a dang good horse for what she give fer it," Ike blurted, immediately defensive. "She didn't have a whole lot of money, and she wanted somethin' gentle, and that's what I sold her."

Jordan paused and patiently waited for Ike to finish. He had not paid much attention to the horse when Polly had visited his camp a couple of nights before. From Ike's defense of the sale, however, he could surmise that it had definitely been in his favor. When Ike paused, Jordan said, "I didn't come to complain about the sale." He then went on to explain that he hoped to trail Polly and her guide. "And I was hopin' you could tell me somethin' about the horse that could make my job easier."

"Oh," Ike said. "Hell, not much I can tell you. It was just a horse."

"Shod?"

"Well, shore, it was shod." He hesitated for a moment, not certain he wanted to share a bit of information he had withheld from Polly. Deciding to accept Jordan's claim that he was not concerned about the fairness of the trade, he finally said, "That little mare split her left front hoof somehow, and I had to take a wedge and build the shoe up on that side to keep the hoof from splittin' any worse."

Jordan figured the horse was more than likely getting on in years to boot. But at present, he wasn't concerned that the lady had been properly skunked on the deal. He was more enthusiastic about the news that he might be following a horse that left a signature. Concluding that there was little more information he could get from Ike Lester, he took his leave. " 'Preciate the help," he said in parting, "but that still don't make you much better than a polecat for takin' advantage of that lady."

"No trouble a'tall," Ike responded. And as a final statement in his defense, he said, "It were a sight better-lookin' horse than that thing you're ridin'."

"I reckon," Jordan replied without looking back. *There you go, getting insulted again, Sweet Pea.* The thought brought a smile to his face.

Before the sun was fully peeking over the eastern horizon, Jordan was scouting the trails leading north from Fort Laramie. He knew he was taking on an almost impossible task, but he felt that someone owed the lady as much. Walking most of the morning, crossing back and forth across numerous trails, some new, some weeks old, he covered a wide arc over hills and ravines, all to no avail. There were just too many tracks. He was tempted to start out in the direction he had taken when he last rode to the Black Hills, and rely on blind luck to strike a trail. "That would be a damn fool thing to do," he confessed to Sweet Pea. He had to know he was following the right trail, so he continued to search for a hoofprint with a built-up shoe. It was late in the afternoon when he found it.

Plain as day it was, sharply etched in the wet sand of a small stream where dozens of horses had crossed. He knelt beside it and studied it to make certain it was the print he searched for. The discovery gave him hope that he might not be too late to help Polly Hatcher. If Iron Pony were with him, his Crow friend would say it was a sign from the Great Spirit that Jordan was to find the woman. He got to his feet and led his horse in the direction indicated, only to lose the print again in the jumble of tracks in the trail. He was about to return to the stream to start over when he saw what he had hoped for — the built-up shoe again and the tracks of an unshod pony, the two sets of prints veering off alone. Now the job could begin in earnest.

CHAPTER 4

"You ever use that thing?" Jim Eagle sat on his heels beside the fire, chewing a tough piece of bacon while he watched Polly strap the gun belt around her waist.

Polly looked her stoic guide in the eye when she answered. "Yes, I've used it."

Jim Eagle barely suppressed a derisive grunt. He gazed steadily at her as he licked the grease from his fingers. "Did you hit anything with it?"

She hesitated for a brief moment, recalling the image of Bill Pike reeling backward with the impact of two slugs ripping into his chest. "Yes," she said softly. "I hit what I aimed at."

Jim shook his head slowly before turning his attention to the coffeepot sitting in the coals. For some reason, he did not doubt her. She had a strong determination about her that led him to believe she would fight if cornered. For two days, he had watched her strap the pistol on each morning, and take it off at night, only to hold the weapon in her hand while she slept — if she slept. He could not say for sure if she ever did. Each time he had gotten out of his blanket during the night, he would discover her eyes wide open and following his every move. It annoyed him, but so be it, he told himself. He had time. Eventually, she would become exhausted from lack of sleep. Then he would easily disarm her without risk of taking a bullet in the process.

Polly knew now that she had made a dangerous mistake in accepting Jim Eagle's offer to guide her to Deadwood. The half-breed was obviously not to be trusted. After the first day, he had started to lead her off toward the west, changing directions only after she balked at following him. He tried to excuse himself by saying he had only intended to detour around an area where there might be a Sioux camp. She had unfolded the rough map that Alton Broom had drawn for her, and made a show of studying it before pointing to the north, and announcing, "Deadwood is that way." It was a crude map at best, and not useful for any purpose beyond providing a general direction. But she led Jim Eagle to believe it held detailed directions. Her charade was sufficient to convince him that she could monitor his performance. Consequently, he stuck to a proper course toward the Black Hills.

"If you got a map," he asked, "why do you need a guide?"

"I just believe I'll find Deadwood a lot quicker if you can lead me straight to it," she answered. "How much farther is it?"

"That map don't say?" His tone was laden with suspicion.

"Not exactly," she hedged.

He shrugged. "Two, three days — hard to say." He studied her eyes carefully, certain now that he detected signs of weariness. This was what he had been watching for. Suddenly, a slow grin crept across his cruel mouth, causing her to shiver involuntarily.

"Let's get started then," she said in a tone as abrupt and commanding as she could muster. She could not help but recall the lecherous sneer so common on Bill Pike's face when he took a notion to satisfy his lust.

Jim Eagle showed no signs of responding, taking his time to finish his coffee before moving a muscle. She began to fear that he was going to refuse to go, knowing that she would be totally lost in this prairie. Much to her relief, he finally got to his feet and casually walked to his horse.

He led her on a hard day's ride, pushing on until nearly sunset before reaching the banks of the Cheyenne River. All during the long day, she was aware of his eyes upon her, watching her for signs of exhaustion. By the time they sighted the river, her horse was favoring its left front hoof, causing it to limp noticeably. She realized that she had not bargained for much of a horse. Weary to her bones, she bravely attempted to hide her despair as she helped gather wood for a fire. With a healthy fire going, Jim Eagle drew his knife and began slicing off strips of bacon. As he worked, he studied Polly's face constantly, prompting her to make conversation, if only to break the intensity of his gaze.

"How much farther to Deadwood?"

"What map say?" Jim Eagle responded.

Tired of playing the game, Polly replied, "The map doesn't say."

A slow grin spread across his face. "Two, three days," he said.

"That's what you said this morning," she insisted. "Are you sure you know where Deadwood is?"

"Two, three days," he repeated stoically, and turned his attention to the bacon he was ready to cook over the fire. In fact, he wasn't sure how far Deadwood was from the Cheyenne River. He had been in the

Black Hills many times, but never to the mining town of Deadwood, nor did he intend to visit the town on this occasion. The weariness in the woman's eyes told him that the time was near when he could end this pretense.

Their simple meal finished, Jim Eagle promptly spread his blanket, and announced his intention to sleep. "Maybe get to Deadwood tomorrow," he said. "Time to sleep now."

Polly made no comment questioning the revision of his estimate from two, three days. She was just thankful that he was intent upon going to sleep. She withdrew a few yards from the fire to a sizable tree trunk. Wrapping her blanket around her, she sat with her back to the tree. She decided it a good idea to remain awake on this, possibly the last night of her journey. In a matter of minutes, her eyelids were heavy.

It had seemed like only a few seconds. She blinked her eyes rapidly, attempting to chase the sleep from them, realizing she had dozed. Almost at once, she was aware of a presence, and she opened her eyes wide. He was squatting on his heels, no more than a couple of steps from her, casually spinning the cylinder of her pistol. She instinctively reached for the empty holster. Her sudden movement prompted him to turn to look directly at her. The intensity of his gaze caused her to freeze.

He held her there with his eyes, studying her with the same regard he might have had for a trapped animal. Then he deflected his gaze to the pistol in his hand. "Forty-four," he stated. "Pretty good shape."

"I'll have it back now," she said, in an attempt at bravado, and held out her hand.

He moved so fast, she had no time to protect herself. With the back of his hand, he slapped her hard across the face, knocking her back against the tree trunk. Horrified, she sat stunned for a moment before regaining her senses, and tried to scramble away from him. Moving quickly to block her escape, he stepped in front of her and backhanded her again, knocking her to the ground. He stood over her, waiting for her next move, but she made no attempt to get up, realizing she was helpless before him.

He tucked the pistol in his belt, and drew a length of rawhide he had looped over his knife scabbard. Pulling Polly's wrists together, he bound them tightly. In workmanlike fashion, he dragged the helpless woman over to his horse, pulled a longer coil of rope from his saddle, then dragged her back to a tree, where he tied her. Demonstrating very little emotion, he stepped back and seemed to study his captive. Satisfied that she was tied securely, he then spun on his heel, and went directly to her saddle pack. Discarding items he deemed useless to him, he went through her belongings in search of anything that might please him. Finding little of interest, he left the contents of her pack strewn upon the ground.

Returning to the bound woman, he stood over her for a few moments while she cringed before his leering eyes. "Where's the money?" he demanded.

Terrified to think what might be in store for her, she barely managed to answer, her voice trembling with fear. "I've already paid you all the money I had."

Her reply did not please him, and he responded with a kick in her side. "Don't lie to me, bitch! Where's the rest of your money?"

Crying out in pain, she pleaded, "I swear, I don't have any more!"

Finding that hard to believe, he immediately began to search her, roughly ramming his hands in her pockets, ripping apart the seams in her jacket, all to no avail. In a final attempt to find a hidden fortune, he pulled her boots and trousers off and fumbled through her undergarments. Frustrated, he threw the trousers in her face, and stood staring down at her once more, finally convinced that she was indeed penniless. "God damn," he cursed, disappointed. "Well, maybe I can trade you for somethin' in Crazy Horse's village." He left her tied to the cottonwood, and returned to his blanket to sleep.

She remained that way for the rest of the night, unable to sit or lie down, the rough bark of the tree pressing into her back. Stunned and afraid, she tried to tell herself that she was lucky he had not killed her. But what lay in store for her? He had mentioned a trade, which spread a new wave of despair to torment her. She feared she could not endure life in captivity. It would be better if he had killed her.

As the night passed, her thoughts swirled in her head, ranging from debilitating fear to anger at herself for having to pay the penalty for her faulty decision. Hiring Jim Eagle had been a foolish thing to do, but she had been so desperate to leave her past behind that her judgment had been impaired. Now it was almost certain that the hangman's rope would have been preferable to what might lie ahead. Even though exhausted, sleep was impossible for her, and as the night wore on, she became numb to the pain from the ropes that bound her. In the wee hours before dawn, she finally lapsed into a comalike fit of semiconsciousness. Sunrise found her slumped at the base of the cottonwood, supported only by the ropes.

Jim Eagle stood casually observing his captive while he emptied his bladder. He was reconsidering his initial decision to take the woman to Crazy Horse's camp. What if she somehow managed to escape, and got back to Fort Laramie? It would be the end of his ability to go and come as he pleased. Maybe it would be best to take what pleasure he desired from her, and then kill her. *Too bad,* he thought. *There would be little gained beyond the money she had paid him to guide her.* Even the horse she rode was lame, and worthless as trade. The more he thought about it, the angrier with her he became.

Seeing she was in no condition to run, he untied her bonds. She collapsed helplessly to the ground, her legs unable to support her. Looking around him then, he spied a small pot among the articles he had left strewn on the ground. After filling the pot with water from the river, he returned to empty it upon the motionless woman — splashing most of it in her face. She responded by slowly turning over, seemingly oblivious to the shock of cold water.

He remained standing over her, watching with mild curiosity as the stricken woman gradually began to show signs of life. His gaze wandered from her head down toward her undergarments, and he paused to consider the curve of her hip. His curiosity aroused now, he reached down and tugged at her cotton underpants. When they resisted easy removal, he drew his knife and slit them down the front, leaving her naked from the waist down. She made a feeble attempt to cover herself. He continued to stare at her body with an appraising gaze, devoid of passion, akin to the manner in which he had considered her horse. And, again, not unlike his appraisal of a horse, he decided to take a trial ride.

There was little emotion involved in his decision to violate the woman. He did it simply because he had the power to do so, and in keeping with his approach to all living things, his manner was brutal. Realizing the breed's intent, Polly attempted to struggle from his grasp, only to reap a savage backhand across her face. Had she not been in such a severely weakened state, she might have put up a more determined battle to repel him. She knew, however, that she was powerless to prevent what was about to happen, so she tried to separate her mind from her body, and hoped the ordeal would end soon. It was nothing new to her, for she had endured countless criminal assaults upon her body by her husband. Brutality and pain were the only emotions she had ever associated with the intimate relations between man and woman.

When he had satisfied himself, and was finished with her, he allowed her to crawl to the water's edge. Still too weak to properly clean herself, she let her battered body slip into the cold water until submerged up to her waist. He watched dispassionately while she lay there in the water's cool embrace, trying to make up his mind about what he should do with her. After giving it a few moments thought, he made his decision. He pulled the pistol from his belt and aimed it at the back of Polly's head. Realizing what was about to happen, she steeled herself for her departure from life. She heard the shot and the snap of a bullet over her head, but it was not her pistol she had heard.

The shot came from a rifle, and from the sound of it, probably at a distance of more than one hundred yards. Jim Eagle felt the breeze created by the wake of the bullet as it barely missed his nose. Reacting immediately, he flung himself flat on the ground and rolled over behind a rotten log. The pistol, aimed at Polly's head just moments before, was now seeking a target from the cottonwoods that lined the river. At first, he saw nothing as he frantically searched back and forth from the stand of willows near the water's edge, to the cottonwoods on the bluff. He looked at his horse, some thirty yards away, and wished that he had the rifle still resting in the sling. When he was about to make up his mind whether to risk a desperate run for the rifle, he was startled by a sudden explosion of horse and rider from the thick brush around the willows. He was momentarily stunned by the sight of the charging horse bearing down upon him at full gallop. There wasn't time to identify the rider before Jordan opened up with his rifle, sending Jim Eagle diving for cover behind the log again.

With the reins clamped between his teeth to free both hands, Jordan kept a continuous barrage of fire directed at the log that shielded the half-breed. At a gallop, Sweet Pea provided as steady a firing platform as any horse, and Jordan proceeded to tear the rotten log to splinters. In desperation, Jim Eagle hugged the ground and emptied the pistol in a frantic attempt to hit something while a shower of rotten wood fragments rained upon his head and shoulders. Jordan was almost upon him. Jim Eagle could feel the beat of the horse's hooves through the ground. He pulled the trigger twice more, only to hear the fatal click of the hammer on an empty chamber each time. He knew his time was up.

Emitting a loud Sioux war cry in final defiance, Jim Eagle sprang up from behind the shattered log and made a desperate run for his horse and the rifle in the saddle sling. Jordan grabbed the reins and pulled Sweet Pea to a sliding stop. Once the horse was steady, Jordan dropped the reins and took careful aim at the sprinting half-breed. The shot caught Jim Eagle exactly in the center of his shoulder blades, slamming the breed headfirst into the sand.

Jordan dismounted, and cautiously walked up to the wounded half-breed who was struggling to get up. Watching dispassionately as Jim Eagle pushed up to stand on his feet, Jordan stopped a few steps away. A trickle of blood crept from the corner of Jim Eagle's mouth as he steadied himself. Still, there was a wild maniacal glint in his eyes, a signal that he was not finished yet. In one final show of defiance and rage, he drew his knife. "You have a knife," he growled. "Lay your rifle aside and fight me, man-to-man." He seemed to regain strength as he braced himself for Jordan's response. Jordan hesitated but a second, then raised his rifle and put a bullet between the half-breed's eyes.

Finished with the insolent Jim Eagle, Jordan turned on his heel before the body had crumpled to the ground, and shifted his attention toward the shaken woman lying half submerged in the shallow water. With his eyes on Polly, he paused by his horse long enough to reload the magazine and slip his rifle back into the saddle sling. He had been too late to prevent her violation at the hands of Jim Eagle, but at least he had managed to prevent her execution. Now he wondered in what mental state he would find her. It would not be unusual for a woman to be driven insane after the ordeal he imagined she must have endured. Seeing her sitting there, up to her waist in the river, it was hard to guess if she had lost her mind or not. His rifle put away, he took one quick glance back at Jim Eagle's body, then proceeded to the edge of the water.

"Are you all right, ma'am?" Jordan asked.

Still somewhat confused by the sudden turn of events, Polly stared up at her rescuer. *Jordan Gray* — it registered in her bewildered mind — the puzzling scout who had refused her plea to guide her. Then she remembered a remark that a soldier had uttered — that Jordan Gray was a loner. *But he seems to show up a lot just when you need him.* Still, she did not answer at once. Gradually, her mind began to find its way back from the sanctuary it had sought refuge in, and she realized that she was safe. Without speaking, she nodded in answer to his question.

"Can you get up?" Jordan asked.

"I think so," she replied, and slowly turned to get her knees under her. She accepted his hand, and pulled herself up to stand in the shallow water, dripping wet, her body naked below her waist. Too bewildered to be humiliated, she nevertheless attempted to hide her exposed body with her hands.

Seeing her blanket on the ground, he quickly picked it up and wrapped it around her. "Here," he said. "We need to dry you off, get you in some dry clothes."

She gazed steadily into his eyes, seeing the compassion there, and a tear slowly formed. She finally realized she really was safe. "Thank you," she murmured softly. He nodded with a slight smile.

She continued to gaze into his eyes for a long moment until another tear formed in the corner of her eye, only to be forced down her cheek by another. Once started, the tears began to flow freely as the stark realization struck her that she had been scant moments away from death. At a loss, and feeling totally useless, Jordan didn't know whether to reach out to the shaken girl or not. He was afraid to touch her, to try to comfort her, for fear she might become terrified that she was about to be attacked again. She made the decision for him. Stepping into his arms, she put her arms around him and pressed her face against his chest. Then, like a child, she released the fear that had been choking her. Feeling that it would somehow save her sanity, he held her close until she had cried herself out, and gently withdrew from his embrace.

Relieved that she seemed to be all right, he said, "I'll build up that fire, and we can boil us some coffee. All right?" She smiled and nodded, somewhat embarrassed to have pushed herself upon him. He turned away and left her to pick up some dry clothes among the articles strewn over the ground by the late Jim Eagle. Before tending the fire, Jordan dragged the half-breed's body out of her sight and dumped it into a gully.

■ ■ ■ ■

They remained there for the rest of that day. Jordan left her only briefly while he hunted for game to provide some variety from the salt pork she had brought. It was only a rabbit, but it was at least a change. They did not talk about what had happened to Polly before Jordan arrived, but as the day wore on, she became much more at ease. Jordan hoped she would put the ordeal out of her mind.

"I can take you back to Laramie," he offered.

"I'm not going back," she was quick to inform him. "I'm going on to Deadwood to find my aunt Hattie." When he responded with nothing more than a tight lip, she continued, "If you still won't take me there, I'll find it by myself." She hesitated. "Maybe you can tell me how to get there."

Damn, he thought, *too much to ask that she'd give it up.* To her, he said, "I doubt that I could tell you how to get there." *How,* he wondered, *could anybody tell a person how to find their way through all the canyons and over the mountains between the Cheyenne River and Deadwood Gulch? How could he explain to her how dangerous it was for him to return to Deadwood where he was a wanted man?* Still, burdened with the guilt for her treatment at the hands of Jim Eagle, he gave himself no choice but to relent. "Hell," he blurted out. "I'll take you to Deadwood."

Profound relief immediately shined in her face, and she was about to express her gratitude when he cut her off. "Don't thank me for doin' such a fool thing. I'll take you there because you're Hattie Moon's niece, and because you'll most likely end up lost or dead, or both, if you try to go alone. Deadwood ain't exactly the healthiest place for me, so we're gonna have to be damn careful." He went on to explain then. "About a year ago, there was a claim robber workin' the lonely claims — a few miners were murdered. The vigilante committee got it in their heads that me and my partner were the ones doin' the killin' — mostly because I got to one of the claims right after the owner had been killed. Well, they strung my partner up. Ned Booth was as fine a man as I've ever known, and they killed him. After that, some people got killed, but only those who hung Ned and came after me." He shrugged, not wishing to elaborate further. "Let's just say that it seemed like a good idea for me to leave that hellhole and never go back."

She did not respond for a long moment, unable to decide if she should now fear this man who had saved her — or feel guilty about placing him in danger once more. "I don't know what to say," she at last responded. "I guess it isn't right for me to ask you to guide me."

"Oh, I'm gonna take you to Deadwood." His face broke out a smile. "Hattie Moon would kick my behind if she found out I let her niece ride through those mountains alone."

CHAPTER 5

They started out the next morning, Jordan leading on the scruffy, gray mare, and Polly riding behind on Jim Eagle's horse. After some consideration, Jordan released the horse Polly had purchased in Fort Laramie to fend for itself. Although the horse had a split hoof, he didn't feel it serious enough to permanently cripple the animal. It seemed content to remain by the river, grazing on the spring grass, briefly gazing after the departing riders before returning its attention to the grass.

Jim Eagle had ridden a stout horse, a paint, and like Jordan's, unshod. Polly had half expected Jordan to take the paint for himself, not realizing the cantankerous mare he called Sweet Pea was a match for any horse when it came to strength and determination.

The paint seemed content to follow Sweet Pea's lead, moving at an easy pace as Polly gazed up at the steep mountains on either side of them. The slopes were covered with dark pines and etched by impassive rock ledges. It was a strange land, both beautiful and frightening at the same time. She was thankful that Jordan had agreed to guide her. She would have been afraid if she were alone. When they had stopped for the noon meal and to rest the horses, he had told her of the reverence for the hills by the Sioux. Paha Sapa was the Sioux name for the Black Hills, and to them it was a sacred place. It angered them to see white men despoil it.

Her thoughts returned to the man in the buckskin shirt before her, and she wondered why she felt completely safe with a man she knew so little about. Jordan Gray was a mystery not only to her, but even to many men he had ridden with. According to Lieutenant DiMarco, Jordan Gray was content to let people think what they would — he owed no one an apology for avoiding their companionship. A born loner, DiMarco had said, yet she found Jordan courteous and not at all distant. Her thoughts were interrupted when he held up his hand and pulled his horse to a stop.

Backing up to her, he said, "Wait here for a moment. I'll be right back." She nodded and he rode forward until reaching a low ridge where he dismounted. Leaving his horse behind, he made his way into the trees. As soon as he disappeared into the pines, she immediately felt desperately alone, even though she could see Sweet Pea standing patiently at the foot of the ridge. A long moment later, she felt herself relax when he again appeared, not realizing until then how tense she had become. In no apparent haste, he climbed into the saddle and returned to her, holding Sweet Pea to a slow walk. By his casual approach, she could only guess that he may have simply sought privacy to answer nature's call.

When he came up to her, he smiled and said, "I expect it would be better to ride back a'ways to where the valley was split by this mountain, and take the other side." He offered no further explanation for the change in direction, but urged Sweet Pea forward with his heels. She turned the paint and followed, wondering if he had forgotten the way to Deadwood.

Upon reaching the point he had suggested, he guided his horse up into the pines that started at the base of the mountain. After making their way a couple dozen yards into the thick forest, he stopped and dismounted, motioning for her to do the same. She did as she was told. "You just sit down here and rest a bit," he said. "I'll be right back."

This time, she decided to see what his mysterious actions were all about and, after a few seconds, followed him. She found him kneeling near the edge of the trees. She started to speak, but he motioned for her to remain silent. Then he pointed to the valley below. She drew a sudden breath of surprise. Not more than twenty yards below them, she saw four Lakota warriors, their faces painted for war, riding the same trail she and Jordan had just left. Seized by cold fear, she held her breath until the warriors passed by, and disappeared from view.

"Come," Jordan said softly and took her arm. "They don't know we're here. We'll take the other side of the mountain. It'll be a little bit longer, but there's about thirty more of their friends up ahead on the trail we just left."

It was close to four and a half days before Jordan and Polly made camp in a valley some two or three miles from Deadwood Gulch. It had been necessary to take another trail when they had almost encountered the Sioux war party. The detour had cost them a full day. Now, with several hours of daylight remaining, Polly wondered why Jordan chose to make camp instead of riding on into Deadwood.

"I'll take you in tonight," he explained. "There's a good chance I might get shot on sight if I go prancin' up in broad daylight."

Polly understood his caution then. "I'll make some coffee," she said, and knelt beside the tiny stream that wound around their campsite. She was excited to be so close to her aunt, but could not deny some feelings of reluctance to see her trip at an end. The past few days traveling with Jordan were among the more peaceful days of her life since she was a child. Even the close call with the Sioux war party had given her no cause for real alarm. She felt safe with Jordan. Now there were other things to worry about. Aunt Hattie — what if her mother's sister would not be happy to see a strange niece show up at her doorstep? How could she be sure Aunt Hattie was still in Deadwood? Jordan said she was there, but that was a year ago. Any number of things could have come to pass in a year's time. For this reason, she was reluctant to say good-bye to Jordan. The considerate thing to do would be to leave him now. He had said that it was only a couple of miles to Deadwood. She could go on by herself, and not expose him to the danger of being seen by someone. *I owe him my life. Why endanger his? But what,* she wondered, *would she do if her aunt was no longer there?* She decided to let him make the decision. If he suggested that it might be best for her to go on alone, then she would. *No need to fret over it,* she thought. *I'll deal with whatever I find.*

Under a full moon, the two riders made their way along a low ridge toward the thriving mining town. It would have made little difference had there been no moon, for the sky was lit up for a mile or more over the gulch like the glow of a huge lantern. As they neared the lower end of the gulch, the sounds of the settlement reached them. Drifting upon the gentle spring breeze, a cacophony rose up from the saloons and gambling parlors like the woeful lament of the damned rising out of hell. Jordan could not help but think of the outrage felt by the Sioux when they witnessed this white man's town, lodged like a festering sore in the heart of their sacred land.

Feeling more and more apprehensive, Polly pulled up closer to Jordan as they rode down the main street of Deadwood. Walking his horse slowly, Jordan kept a sharp eye, scanning the board walkways, lest some member of the vigilante committee might suddenly recognize him. With that potential in mind, he rested his rifle across his saddle before him, just in case. His caution was unnecessary, however, for the hour was late, and honest men had retired to their beds. The hard-drinking, gambling rabble was far too concerned with seeking their pleasures to take note of the two silent figures riding along the muddy street.

Jordan pulled Sweet Pea to a stop at the upper end of the street, puzzled for a moment until he read the sign scrawled over the door of the wooden structure. THE TROUGH, it proclaimed. He smiled to himself then. *Hattie and Maggie must be prospering,* he thought. Their dining room had been housed in a tent when he last saw them. Because it was well past the supper hour, the door was closed and the building dark. Jordan led Polly along the side of the building to the back and the detached kitchen and living quarters. They were the same as he remembered. As he stepped down, his mind flashed back to the last time he had come here. It was night then, too, and the eve of a killing time that would last for several days. The thought caused his back muscles to tense. They had hanged Ned Booth the day before. *Poor Ned,* he thought, *he had ridden into town for no other purpose than to make sure the committee knew Jordan had nothing to do with the death of a miner up on Hard Luck Creek.* Jordan's mouth went dry with the bitter taste of that memory, and the rage it had ignited inside him.

He had sought to put that time behind him. It was the reason he had rejected Polly's request when she first asked him to take her to Deadwood. *Well,* he thought. *I am here, anyway.* The trouble between the men of Deadwood and himself was over a year past. He resolved not to let his mind dwell there. He stepped toward Polly's horse in order to help her down. Her feet were barely on the ground when he heard the unmistakable metallic click of a pistol being cocked. He froze, his eyes automatically going to the rifle in Jim Eagle's saddle sling. The voice in the shadows anticipated his thoughts.

"Reach for it, and you're a dead man."

Jordan and Polly turned to face the direction the voice had come from. Although it had been more than a year, it was a voice that Jordan could never forget. "This is a helluva way to welcome visitors," Jordan said.

"This is a helluva time of night for visitors," the voice shot back. "Step out in the moonlight so I can get a look at you." Both Jordan and Polly complied. There was a long moment of hesitation, then, "Jordan Gray, is that you?"

"I reckon," Jordan replied. "I see you're as friendly as ever, Maggie."

"Well, I'll be go to hell," Maggie Hogg blurted out. "I never thought I'd see you around here again." As soon as she said it, she immediately remembered. "Have you gone loco? There's still some here that would shoot you on sight." Not waiting for Jordan to reply, Maggie turned her attention to Polly. "Who's this you got with you? You ain't up and married, have you?"

"Not hardly," Jordan answered. "This is Polly Hatcher. She's come lookin' for her aunt Hattie."

"Her aunt Hat—" Maggie blurted out in surprise. "Hattie!" she called out. "Open the door!"

Hattie Moon was fully as shocked as her partner upon seeing Jordan Gray again, as well as being confronted with a niece she had not known existed. She turned the lantern up, and held the door open wide. When all had entered the small shack that served as living quarters for the two women, she stood appraising her surprise visitor. "So, you're Florence's girl. My Lord in heaven," she marveled. "I swear, I can see you favor your mother." It had been many years since Hattie had seen her sister and, looking at Polly, it was like seeing her now. "How is Florence?" Hattie asked. When Polly told her that Florence had passed away some years back, Hattie sighed sorrowfully, disappointed to hear the news. But after the time she had spent on the frontier, she was hardened to the facts of life and death. "God rest her soul" was all she said.

"How on earth did you wind up out here in Deadwood?" Maggie asked.

Polly hesitated for just a moment, reluctant to say that she had come all this way in hopes her aunt might help her start a new life, far away from her past. Looking at her, Jordan had wondered himself how Hattie would accept the news that Polly had come to live with her. He listened with interest as Polly explained. "Well, everybody's talking about the gold strike in Deadwood, and I had nothing back in Omaha holding me." She sighed. "So, I thought I might as well come see if there was some way I could make a living out here."

It was a simple enough answer, and Jordan turned his attention toward Hattie and Maggie to see if they would respond in the way Polly was hoping for. They did. "Why, you could stay right here with me and Hattie," Maggie immediately suggested. "If you ain't too proud to work in a kitchen, we could use some help. Couldn't we, Hattie?"

"We sure could. We were just talkin' about hirin' somebody to help us out. We're gettin' a bigger and bigger crowd to feed every day," Hattie said, beaming her delight. "How 'bout it, honey? We've got plenty of room to set you up a bed right here — if you don't mind bunkin' with two old turkey buzzards."

Jordan was relieved. Even though he considered his obligation ended with Polly's safe passage to Deadwood, he would not have felt comfortable leaving, knowing that she was trying to make it on her own in an untamed place like this. Polly accepted the invitation at once, and all three women smiled delightedly. Polly's eye caught Jordan's, and he nodded approvingly. The new arrangement settled, everyone's attention turned to Jordan.

As Maggie had exclaimed, Hattie was moved to express her surprise at seeing the broad-shouldered scout. "I swear, I never thought I'd see you again, Jordan. You're riskin' your neck for sure comin' back here."

"I know," Jordan replied. "But I just couldn't stand being away from you and

Hattie any longer." He grinned mischievously.

"Bite your lyin' tongue," Maggie replied, giving him a playful look of disapproval. In the next second, however, she returned to serious thought. "Jokin' aside, there's still some around here that think you're the man who raided the claims and killed them prospectors."

"I'm not aimin' to stay long. I'm leavin' before sunup," he assured her.

Still amazed that he had taken the risk of getting shot in order to escort Polly, Maggie commented to the young lady, "It's a lucky thing for you that you found Jordan to bring you here. There's a lot of men who'd just as soon cut your throat, and leave you back in the mountains somewhere."

Polly then went on to relate the unfortunate circumstances that led to her contract with Jordan, and the frightening experience suffered at the hands of Jim Eagle. Maggie and Hattie listened to her story with obvious concern. Polly stopped short of admitting the rape.

"I reckon that explains the bruises on your face," Hattie commented. "I was gonna ask you about 'em."

"Say," Maggie interrupted, "you folks must be hungry. I'll go to the kitchen and put on some coffee — won't take but a minute to heat up the stove. There might be a cold biscuit or two left from supper."

"I expect I'd better head on back outta town before it gets daylight," Jordan said. "I wouldn't want to cause Ben Thompson to have to call out the vigilance committee." He grinned at Maggie. "I guess he's still the top dog around here."

"Hell," Maggie responded, "he's callin' himself the sheriff now."

"We've even got us a jail now," Hattie added. "Ben spends most of the day settin' around there lookin' important."

"A jail," Jordan commented. "Deadwood's gettin' downright civilized. Keep on, and you'll be the capital of Dakota Territory."

"It ain't *that* civilized," Maggie replied. "You sure you don't want some coffee before you go off in the woods?" She glanced at Polly and grinned. "Jordan Gray wouldn't know how to sleep under a roof, anyway."

Polly smiled and turned to face Jordan. "I guess I owe you some money for guiding me here. I won't ever have enough to pay you for saving my life, though. For that, you have my eternal gratitude." She extended her hand to him.

Jordan took her hand for a brief handshake

before releasing it. "You don't owe me anything. You'd best keep that money. You'll need it to get yourself set up here in Deadwood." He broke out a wide grin. "Besides, after a few days livin' with Hattie and Maggie, you'll probably spend it on a stagecoach outta here."

"Don't pay him no mind, honey," Hattie said. "Besides, there ain't no stagecoach comes to Deadwood."

Jordan laughed. From outside, the sound of Sweet Pea snorting carried through the rough board wall. "See," Jordan said, "even my horse is tellin' me it's time to go." Never comfortable with drawn-out goodbyes, he abruptly turned to leave. With his hand on the doorknob, he looked back and said, "Take care of her, Hattie."

"I will," Hattie replied. "You take care of yourself."

Polly stepped quickly up to him and gave him a hug. "Thank you, Jordan," she whispered and kissed him lightly on the cheek. Slightly embarrassed then, he mumbled, "You're welcome." Then he opened the door, anxious to be out in the open air.

The full moon that had flooded the valley with light was dropping lower in the sky, almost resting on the ridge above the town, and casting long shadows behind the buildings. Jordan looked at Sweet Pea. "What's ailin' you, girl?" The ornery mare was stamping nervously. He realized too late that she was trying to warn him.

"Just hold it right there and don't move a muscle, or I'll shoot you down right where you stand."

The voice came from the shadows at the corner of the kitchen shack. Jordan immediately tensed, but he did as he was ordered. In the next second, two men emerged from positions behind the rear corners of Maggie and Hattie's living quarters. With three rifles on him, he had little choice but to give in. He wasn't even wearing his pistol.

"Well, now, if it ain't Mr. Jordan Gray. I didn't believe it when Whitey came to get me, but here you are. I'll tell you the truth, Jordan, I figured you for better sense than to show your murderin' face around here again."

It had been more than a year, but Jordan easily recognized the voice of Ben Thompson. He turned to face the new sheriff of Deadwood, and immediately heard the sound of three rifles being cocked. "I'm not wearin' a gun," he said.

"Step out more in the moonlight, so I can see for myself," Thompson ordered. When he saw that Jordan was, indeed, unarmed, he lowered his rifle, but kept it trained on his captive. "Get his rifle outta the sling, Whitey," he said to one of the men. "And watch yourself around that horse. That mangy-lookin' coyote'll take a nip outta your hide if you ain't careful."

Jordan stood passive while Whitey confiscated his rifle and lifted his pistol belt from the saddle horn. "So now what, Ben? Another hangin' like you and your boys did with Ned Booth?"

"Jordan ain't no more guilty of murderin' anybody than poor Ned was." It was Maggie Hogg's voice that made the statement.

Ben turned to glance at the three women, who had filed out the door when they heard the commotion in the alley. "Maggie, this ain't no business of yours. Why don't you women go on back inside?"

"Why don't you go to hell?" Maggie retorted angrily. "I'll go where I damn well please."

Ben turned his attention back to his prisoner, ignoring Maggie's remark. "Why, no, we ain't gonna hang you. We're a lot more progressive in Deadwood now. We're gonna give you a trial, and then we're gonna hang you." He motioned with his rifle. "Let's go. I'd like to get to bed sometime tonight."

"You've got it all wrong, Ben," Jordan said. "Just like you did when you and your mob murdered Ned."

"Oh, have I?" Ben retorted. "Well, I guess I'd better just let you go, then. Boys, Mr. Gray here didn't shoot them poor fellers in the posse. I guess our eyes were just playin' tricks on us."

"I only killed those who came to kill me. I had no choice in the matter. It was me or them. Any man would have done the same." He knew he was wasting his breath. The question in his mind at this time was whether he should make an attempt to escape now, with the odds of success probably not even fifty-fifty, or wait for a chance later on. With three rifles still pointed at him, he decided it would be foolish to make a move now.

"Get movin'," Ben ordered with a wave of his rifle. "I got a cell waitin' just for you in our new jail."

"What about the horses?" Whitey asked. "Want me to take 'em to the stable?"

Maggie was quick to jump in. "I'll take care of the horses. I can put 'em in with our mules. They ain't both his, anyway. One of 'em belongs to Polly here." She stepped forward and took Sweet Pea's reins.

Whitey stopped and looked to Ben for directions, not sure what to do. Ben thought about it for a long moment, then shrugged and said, "I don't care. If that's what you wanna do, then you take care of 'em." The three men then walked their prisoner off to the jailhouse.

The women watched until the sheriff and his deputies disappeared from sight. Then Polly turned to her aunt. "This is all my fault. The first time I met him, he told me he didn't want to go to Deadwood."

"Don't blame yourself, honey." Hattie was quick to reassure her. "From what you told me, I believe it was him that come after you. He made up his own mind to bring you here." She glanced at her partner for confirmation as she remarked, "Jordan Gray don't do nothin' he don't wanna do. Right, Maggie?"

"I expect that's so," Maggie replied. "No need to blame yourself, Polly."

Hattie gently patted her niece on the shoulder, then turned back to Maggie. "What are we gonna do, Maggie?"

"I'm thinkin' on it," Maggie replied. "I know one thing for sure. I don't intend to stand by and let that bunch of jackasses string up another innocent man."

CHAPTER 6

"I've been in bigger jails," Jordan commented dryly as Ben Thompson held the cell door open for him.

"I'll bet you have," Ben replied, slamming the door and bolting it as soon as Jordan was inside. Holding a lantern, he watched Jordan through the small opening in the heavy plank door as his prisoner took inventory of his cell. One of only two, the room was barely eight feet by ten feet, with a small window opposite the door. A heavy odor of pine from the still-green lumber filled the space. Jordan went directly to the window to stare out at the dark alley behind the building.

Watching him intently, Ben found it hard to believe that he actually had Jordan Gray in his jail. Jordan Gray, the midnight panther, whose very name had brought terror to the miners around Deadwood a year ago. His thoughts were momentarily interrupted when Whitey spoke. "If you don't think you need us no more, me and Andy are goin' home."

"Yeah," Ben replied. "You and Andy go on. I don't think Mr. Gray, here, is gonna go anywhere." He turned away from the cell door to watch his deputies depart. "Much obliged. You boys done a good job. I'm goin' myself in a few minutes, soon as Pete gets here."

When they had gone, Ben turned his attention back to his prisoner. Picking up Jordan's rifle, he looked it over carefully. "Seventy-three model Winchester," he said. "Is this the same rifle you killed them prospectors up above Hard Luck Creek with?"

Jordan continued to stare out into the darkness, not bothering to turn around. "I told you," he insisted, "I didn't kill any prospectors — on Hard Luck Creek or anywhere else."

"You didn't, huh? Well you damn sure killed Barney Lipscomb, and Bob Wooten, and Tom Bowers. I was with 'em when you done it." His ire rising at the thought, he cocked Jordan's rifle several times for emphasis, pumping the live rounds out on the floor.

Still calm, Jordan turned then to face the

door. "Those men died because you came after me with blood in your eye. You didn't take time for talk then, just started shootin'. You didn't leave me much choice, did you?"

Flustered for a moment, Ben calmed down when he reminded himself. "Well, I reckon we took time to talk this time, didn't we? We're gonna have a trial for the citizens of Deadwood to see we take law and order serious around here. Then we're gonna swing your murderin' ass from a pole right in the middle of town."

Jordan didn't reply, but he thought about the prospect of ending his life at the end of a rope, and he didn't particularly care for the idea. *More likely,* he thought, *you'll end up shooting me.* He was not inclined to go peacefully to the gallows.

Jordan heard the front door open when Pete Blankenship entered the jail. Listening to the conversation that passed between them, he learned that Pete slept on the cot Jordan had seen in the office. Ben filled Pete in on the arrest, and advised him to practice extreme caution when dealing with the prisoner. Before leaving for the night, Ben came back to the cell door.

"I wouldn't want you to get lonesome during the night, so Pete here will be right outside this door. I wouldn't advise you to cause him any trouble. Pete's got a short fuse when people aggravate him. If you behave yourself, I might let Maggie and Hattie send you some breakfast in the mornin'." He waited a moment in case there was a reply. When there was none, he chuckled to himself and told Pete good night.

As soon as Ben left, Pete came to the door. A large man, he had to stoop over to see through the small opening. "You heard what Ben said about behavin' yourself, I reckon. Just so's we have an understandin'. If I hear a peep outta you, I'm liable to come in there and break your back for you." Like Ben before him, he waited to see if there was any response from the prisoner. There was none. Jordan never bothered to waste words.

Jordan lay down on the cot in his cell and tried to sleep, but sleep wouldn't come. His brain was too busy thinking through all that had happened, and trying to come up with an escape plan that had some chance of success. *There aren't many options,* he thought, *and that's a fact.* In less than an hour's time, the deep drone of Pete's snoring rattled through the tiny jail. Jordan closed his eyes and did his best to ignore the sound. Although he thought sleep impossible, he nevertheless drifted off sometime after midnight.

At first, he thought he was dreaming. "Jordan." A voice softly whispered his name. He opened his eyes and stared into the darkness. "Jordan." This time he realized that he was not dreaming. He quickly got up from the cot and went to the window. He was not prepared for what he saw. On the other side of the window, he saw Hattie Moon's face. At first, he thought the bars threw shadows across her features. Then, as the sleep left his eyes, he realized they were not shadows. She had painted dark streaks vertically on her face. "Hattie," he blurted out. "What tha hell — ?" He never finished because it occurred to him then that Hattie would have to be ten feet tall to look through the window.

"Here," she whispered, and passed a heavy rope through the bars. "Tie this good and tight around the bars." She looked down then. "Hand me the other one, Maggie."

Jordan couldn't believe it. "Is Maggie out there?"

Hattie giggled. "I'm standing on her. Here, tie this one on one of the other bars. We're breakin' you outta here."

"Hurry up," Maggie whispered impatiently. "You ain't exactly no feather."

"Are you two crazy?" Jordan demanded. "Anybody see you and you'll be in here with me." He took the two ropes, paused a moment to make sure Pete was still snoring, then tied them securely to the bars. As he worked feverishly with the knots, he glanced back at Hattie's grinning face. "What are those streaks on your face?"

Hattie's expression turned to one of surprise, disappointed that he had to ask. "War paint," she crowed. "Me and Maggie dressed up like Injuns, in case somebody saw us."

"Dammit." Maggie's voice came up from beneath the window. "Hurry up with them knots. I can't hold you much longer."

In the next instant, Hattie began to waver back and forth. Then suddenly, she dropped out of sight, and Jordan could hear the sounds of hushed giggling from the ground behind the jail. "Are you all right?" he asked in a hoarse whisper.

"Yeah, we're all right," came back to him. He couldn't tell if it was Hattie or Maggie who answered. "Did you get those ropes tied?" When he replied that he had, Maggie called out quietly, "All right, Polly, let 'em go."

The ropes went taut as Maggie's team of

mules braced against the load. Jordan stepped back from the window. There was no sign of anything giving for a few seconds. He could plainly hear the women ordering the mules to pull, and he marveled that Pete could sleep through the noise. The only indication that the window was under stress was a steady creaking of the green pine lumber. Outside, Maggie exhorted her mules to work harder. The window resisted for a full five minutes before surrendering to Maggie's determined team. Suddenly, there was a loud crack like that of a bull-whip, followed by the helpless protests of cracking wood. Amid a clamor of snapping, creaking pine, and the reluctant shriek of nails pulled from the planks, the window frame was finally torn free. It was a racket Jordan was certain could be heard halfway up the street. It was certainly enough to arouse Pete Blankenship from his slumber.

Jordan could hear Pete's confused mumbling on the other side of his cell door, and knew there would be brief seconds before the big deputy came to investigate. He went quickly to the gaping hole where the window had been, and urged the women to flee. "I'll catch up," he promised.

"By the crick, back of the house," Maggie whispered hurriedly as the three jail breakers disappeared in the shadows of the alley.

Jordan moved back to flatten himself against the wall beside the door just as Pete lifted the heavy bar that secured it. Even in his confusion, Pete was cautious. He opened the cell door wide, and paused to take a look before rushing in. His eye immediately settled upon the open hole where a window should have been, and he charged into the cell. Jordan stuck his foot out and tripped him, sending the charging brute sprawling headlong onto the plank floor. The rifle he held went sliding across the planks. Jordan was quick to retrieve it. Pete scrambled to get up, but Jordan had the rifle trained on him by the time he was on his feet.

"All right, Pete, you do like I tell you, and you won't get a bullet in your gut."

The huge bully growled in reply, "You won't git away with this, you son of a bitch. Who helped you tear out that window?"

"I don't need any help breakin' outta this chicken coop," Jordan replied with a thin smile. "Now, I'd love to stand around here and discuss it, but I've got to be on my way." He motioned toward the door with the rifle. "Now move. I want you in that other cell."

Pete was not a man to be easily cowed. "To hell with you," he snapped defiantly. "I ain't goin' anywhere." He stood his ground.

"Have it your way," Jordan replied indifferently. "It's easier for me this way." He raised the rifle, taking dead aim at Pete's head.

"All right, dammit!" Pete blurted out, his bluff called. "I'm goin'." It wasn't worth the gamble. Jordan Gray had killed before, and Pete knew it. He turned and walked out the door into the office, then went obediently to the other cell.

Jordan followed cautiously, the rifle held ready. He was not willing to believe Pete was completely subdued. The man was an obvious bully, and was bound to make an attempt before meekly submitting. Just as Jordan had anticipated, Pete was not ready to admit defeat. As he started to pass through the doorway to the cell, he made his move. Suddenly whirling around, he aimed a huge fist at Jordan's head, but the big man was not quick enough. Jordan easily avoided the wild haymaker, and rewarded Pete with a solid thump of the rifle barrel against the side of his head. Stunned, but still on his feet, Pete wobbled drunkenly as Jordan shoved him into the cell and closed the door. While he inserted the timber that served as a bar for the door, he reminded Pete, "I could just as easily have killed you if I was the murderer you people think I am. Remember that."

Taking but a moment to check the street in front of the jail to make sure all was still quiet, he then went about retrieving his possessions. His rifle and pistol were in a corner of the tiny office, the Winchester propped against the wall, the Colt lying on the floor. After loading the weapons, he glanced quickly around to make sure he hadn't forgotten any other article that might have belonged to him. His gaze lit upon a box of .45 cartridges. "Might as well help myself to some ammunition," he murmured. "Little enough pay for the inconvenience."

Before leaving, he took another look at the gaping hole in the back wall, and couldn't help but grin. *A helluva job,* he thought. *But I don't reckon I'll take a chance on spraining an ankle by jumping out the window.* He turned and walked out the front door.

There was no clock in the jail, so he could only guess the time. Judging by the hint of gray in the eastern sky, he figured it could be no more than an hour before daybreak. Turning to pull the front door shut, he was startled by a voice behind him.

"Looks like it might be a warm one."

He turned to find a man walking along

the rutted street, apparently heading toward the stables at the far end. Realizing that he was under no threat, Jordan returned the greeting. "Looks like," he said, wondering even as he said it what possible sign the man could have seen that would tell him it was going to be a warm day. At that moment, Pete chose to yell, "Hey! Let me outta here!" He had apparently heard talking outside the jail.

The stranger paused and looked at Jordan. Jordan grinned, and explained, "Drunk — he'll need more time to sleep it off."

"I reckon," the stranger replied and laughed. He continued on toward the stables. Jordan watched until he was sure the man showed no signs of suspicion; then he hurried to meet the women by the creek.

"Where the hell have you been?" Maggie wanted to know when Jordan finally joined the three women waiting beside the creek. She had apparently expected him to jump out the window immediately.

"I had to take care of a few things," he explained. "And make sure Pete didn't follow us." Seeing an instant look of concern on their faces, he assured them, "He ain't hurt. I just locked him in the other cell." He then paused to take a look at his rescuers. "Where in the world did you get those clothes?"

Hattie grinned. "They belonged to Ned. He wasn't a whole lot bigger'n Maggie and me." The last she added to explain the fit.

Looking more like clowns from a circus than Sioux Indians, the two partners of The Trough stood draped in some of Ned Booth's old buckskins. Jordan shook his head and laughed. In spite of the danger in which they had placed themselves, the whole incident was laughable. He feared, however, that they were blind to the seriousness of their actions. "When Ben Thompson finds his deputy locked up, this is the first place he's gonna come," Jordan said, no longer laughing.

"Probably so," Maggie allowed. "But we'll just say we didn't have nothing to do with it. He can suspicion all he wants. There ain't no way he can prove nothing." She looked at Hattie for support.

"That's a fact," Polly replied for her aunt. "We were here the whole time." She couldn't help fretting about the trouble she had already caused Jordan. "You'd better get goin' before it gets daylight."

He hesitated, still concerned for their welfare, until Hattie reassured him. "Don't worry about us, Jordan. It's our word against Ben's, and the men in this town ain't about to let anything shut our kitchen down. Half of 'em would starve to death if they had to do their own cookin'."

"I guess you're right," Jordan said. He stepped up in the saddle, and turned Sweet Pea's head toward the west. He held the homely mare in check while he took one last look at the three women. "Much obliged for springin' me. You girls take care of yourselves," he said in parting, then gave Sweet Pea her head.

"There's bacon and coffee in your saddle bags," Maggie called after him, just remembering. Then she said to Hattie, "We'd better get busy cookin' breakfast, or we're gonna have a lot of explainin' to do come sunup."

Just as the women expected, Ben Thompson stormed into the dining hall before they turned the sign around from NOPE to YEP. "Why, good mornin', Ben," Maggie said, greeting him cheerfully. "You must be powerful hungry this mornin', but we ain't quite open yet — unless you come to fetch breakfast for your prisoner. If you'll just set down a minute. . . ."

"You know damn well I didn't come for

no damn breakfast," he interrupted. "Where is he?"

"Who?" Maggie asked innocently.

"Jordan Gray! I know he came here. His horse is gone, so quit playin' games with me."

"It is?" Maggie went to the back door and looked out at the corral. "Well, I'll be damned," she exclaimed. "It is gone." Hattie walked in from the kitchen at that moment. Maggie turned to her and said, "Jordan's horse is gone."

"Gone?" Hattie responded, and made a show of going to the door to see for herself. "How'd it get out?"

Ben was beside himself with anger, and it was getting worse by the second. When Polly walked in behind Hattie, and her aunt started to give her the startling news, Ben exploded. "Gawdammit, that's enough! You women ain't foolin' nobody. I've a mind to throw the lot of you in jail." He was about to threaten more when Pete Blankenship came in the door.

"I think we picked up his trail," Pete reported. "Jack found fresh tracks down by the crick. Looks like he crossed over and headed west, up over the ridge."

"All right," Ben replied. "Let's get in the saddle." Turning back to the women, he said, "This time, when we catch him, we ain't gonna bother with no trial." He glared at them for a moment before promising, "I ain't through with you ladies over this yet."

"Oh, get the hell outta here, Ben," Maggie snapped. "We've got a breakfast to get on the table." She stood, hands on hips, glaring after him until he was out the door. Then turning to Hattie, she confided, "I hope Jordan ain't wastin' no time, not with Jack Little Hawk trackin' for 'em." Her tone concerned Polly, and she asked who Jack Little Hawk was. Hattie explained that he was a full-blooded Arapaho who could track a water spider across a pond.

CHAPTER 7

"Nope, can't say as I have," Alton Broom replied, stroking his chin to encourage his memory. "What did you say her name was?"

"Polly Pike," the stranger repeated.

Almost everybody who passed through Fort Laramie visited the post trader's store, so Alton was the one person who would have seen the woman in question. Soldiers, settlers, Indians, prospectors — Alton saw them all. But he had no recollection of a woman named Polly Pike who, according to the man standing before him, had supposedly passed through little more than a month before. "There was a lady name of Polly here at about that time," he said. "But her name weren't Pike. It was Harris or Harrison — somethin' like that."

"Hatcher?" the man suggested.

"Hatcher," Alton echoed. "That's it, Polly Hatcher." He beamed his satisfaction for remembering. "Yeah, she was here, all right.

Nice lady, she was lookin' for somebody to help her find her aunt. Last I heard, she hired Jim Eagle to take her to Deadwood in Dakota Territory." Pleased that he could supply the information, he inquired, "Is she kin of your'n?"

"She's my wife," Bill replied evenly, a thin smile slowly spreading on his unshaven face. "Hatcher's her maiden name."

It was not a friendly smile, and Alton had a sudden sinking feeling that maybe he should not have been so free with his answers. Up until that moment, Alton had not bothered to study the stranger standing at his counter. Now, upon closer inspection of the gaunt face and cruel eyes, he decided Bill Pike was not a man one would seek out as a friend. Alton had never been accused of having an overabundance of brains, but it didn't take a genius to figure out that Polly was obviously running from her husband. Someone running from something back east was not that unusual, but in most cases it was a man running from family obligations — or a criminal past. Without knowing the facts of the matter, he nonetheless wished that he had not supplied the man with information. His natural curiosity would not permit him to drop the issue, however, without asking, "How is it you ain't travelin' with your wife?"

"She run off, and left me for dead — took my money, stole my horse, and run off. Left me layin' in a muddy barnyard with two bullet holes in my chest and a knife wound in my belly. Is that a good enough reason why I ain't travelin' with my wife?"

Alton hardly knew how to answer that. The image he recalled of Polly Hatcher didn't match the deed. She just didn't seem like a woman capable of such violence. "Why, I reckon so," was all he could reply to the question. He stood gaping while Bill Pike continued his story.

"I've still got two hunks of lead in me, 'cause the doctor said it was too damned risky to try to get 'em out. I can feel 'em in there like a toothache." His face grew pinched and dark with the bitterness he felt inside as he talked. "The doctor said I'd be in bed for a month, but I was back on a horse in three weeks. The bitch took every penny I had. I had to sell off my hogs to pay the doctor, and buy me another horse." He glared at Alton for a long moment, waiting for his comments, but Alton had none to offer. He didn't know what to think, or whom to believe. He just wished he had not told this vengeful man where his wife had gone. "Well," Bill concluded, "I reckon I'm on my way to Deadwood."

"It ain't a good time to be travelin' between here and Dakota Territory," Alton offered weakly. "Lotta hostile activity."

"That don't bother me none. I reckon I'm pretty hard to kill," Bill replied. "Can you tell me the best way to get to Deadwood?"

Alton had never actually been to the Black Hills, and he was quick to let Pike know. Already regretful that he had supplied as much information as he had, he was as vague as he could be, saying only that it was north and a little east of Fort Laramie. Bill turned and walked out of the store.

Alton noticed for the first time that the man moved a little unsteadily, a fact he attributed to his wounds. *I swear,* he thought, *that little lady didn't seem the kind to do something like that. Even if she did, she probably had good reason. I hope that fellow doesn't find her.*

Bill Pike was not without guile. He detected a sense of reluctance on Alton Broom's part to be cooperative. *North and a little east,* he thought. *He might as well have said it's outside somewhere.* Alton had evidently been taken in by Polly's deceit. Bill had assumed that any man would sympathize with his quest for justice, but realizing now that there may be some spineless excuses for men in the world, he decided to keep his story to himself in the future. With this in mind, he stopped at the stables where he received much more detailed directions to Deadwood.

Leaving the stables, he started out immediately. With a smug grin in place, he thought, *I'm coming, honey. A few more days, and your loving husband will be with you again.* The thought of the reunion caused the smile on his face to widen, and he almost chuckled in anticipation of the slow revenge he planned to extract.

Approximately one hundred and fifty miles north, as the hawk flies, Polly Hatcher suddenly felt a chill. She attributed it to the recent turn of cooler weather in the mountains after it had appeared to be warming in earnest toward summer. She finished patting the dough she had just formed in the pan. Hattie's hot stove would soon dispel any chill in a matter of seconds.

"Do you think they'll catch him?" Polly asked as she opened the oven and slid the pan of biscuits inside.

Hattie smiled at her niece, and wiped the sweat from her brow with her apron. "No, child, I don't think they're likely to catch Jordan Gray. He's as much at home in the mountains as a panther." She paused while she thought about him. "And that ugly horse he rides will run most any other horse into the ground. No, they won't catch Jordan." Even though confident in her own words, she still formed a bit of a frown when she considered that Ben Thompson had been smart enough to take Jack Little Hawk with him.

Polly was encouraged by Hattie's remarks, for she felt personally responsible for his troubles. There was still some concern for her aunt and Maggie, however. "That man, Ben Thompson," she said. "He said he was not through with us about Jordan's escape."

Hattie quickly brushed her concerns aside. "He just thinks he ain't," she replied confidently. "Me and Maggie's been in Deadwood as long as he has. It's our word against his." She paused and winked at her niece then. "And he ain't doin' the cookin' for half the men in town."

"What is it, Jack?" Ben asked when he caught up to the stoic Arapaho waiting at a point where the narrow game trail took a sharp turn around a huge boulder. Jack Little Hawk did not answer, choosing to point instead. Ben followed the direction indicated with his eyes. "Up there?" Thinking that possibility unlikely, he dismounted to take a look at the tracks himself. The Indian was right. The tracks they had been following all morning left the trail and appeared to head straight up the steep face of the mountain. Ben stood gazing up toward the peak for a few moments while the posse behind him caught up.

"You don't think he went up there, do ya?" Whitey Hickson asked. Pulling up beside him, Rufus Sparks asked the question that had occurred to some of the others. "What the hell is he ridin', a damn mountain goat?"

"I wouldn't be surprised if that ugly-ass nag he rides is part goat," Ben commented. He paused and looked around him as if searching for alternatives. "Looks like he went up there," he said, finally deciding.

Jack Little Hawk continued to study the trail while the other men of the posse debated the sensibility of attempting so steep a climb. "Deer go up there," he announced. "He see deer tracks. He think he go, too."

"Me think he crazy," Lester Pierce said, mocking Jack's broken English. "We'd probably come closer to finding him at the bottom of this damn mountain." He grinned broadly when the others laughed at his remark.

"We might all end up at the bottom if we try to climb up there," J.D. Watts chimed in. "That's a helluva steep climb. I ain't sure Buster here can make it without we both take a somersault down this mountain." He patted his horse's neck.

Ben didn't like the direction the conversation was heading. "Well, boys, we sure as hell ain't gonna quit just because the trail got a little steep. Hell, if he rode up it, then we sure as hell can, too." He wanted Jordan Gray, wanted him badly, and he had no intention of letting him get away this time. The last time he had gone after Jordan, he had come back with fewer men than he had started out with. A couple of those who didn't come back, Barney Lipscomb and Tom Bowers, were close friends of his. Also, it wouldn't hurt his reputation one bit if he were to bring in a killer of Jordan Gray's status.

"I don't know, Ben," Lester said, scratching his beard thoughtfully. "I don't know what kinda horse that son of a bitch is ridin', but I'm kinda like J.D. I ain't sure my horse can tote me up that climb without takin' a tumble." He looked at Jack, directing his question to the Indian. "Can't we just keep following this game trail on around the mountain?"

"Sure we can," Ben answered before Jack could respond. "But the fact of the matter is he'll just pick up another hour on us." He stared at his posse in an authoritative way. "We'll dismount and lead the horses up. Jack, you lead off. Now, come on, we're wastin' time."

Just seventy-five or eighty feet below the peak, Jordan Gray knelt on a solid rock ledge, watching the group of men far below as they began the climb up to him. If he had to make the decision again, he wasn't sure he would have attempted the climb. But Sweet Pea had attacked the slope confidently, so he figured she knew better than he. About halfway up, when they encountered an area of loose shale, he had seriously questioned the wisdom of letting the ornery mare have her head. But, as she most often proved, she was up to the climb.

Admittedly, he had expected to lose the posse long before this, but they had relentlessly dogged his every turn. *That tracker is good,* he thought, watching Jack Little Hawk start up the slope. His was a new face to Jordan. He didn't know the man. He decided to linger a little longer to watch their progress, hoping they might decide it was not worth the risk. He had no desire to kill any one of them, and earnestly hoped it wouldn't be like the last time when he had been given no choice.

They all dismounted and, leading their horses, started up the steep slope behind the Indian. Moving slowly out of necessity, the posse soon became focused upon the rocky earth beneath each footfall, the horses sliding and struggling behind them. Although painfully slow, it appeared that they were going to make it — much to Jordan's disappointment. He decided that he was going to have to impede their progress, so he cocked his rifle, and sighted upon a scrubby pine beside the patch of loose shale he had crossed on his way up. Waiting patiently while Jack Little Hawk carefully made his way across the shale, Jordan held his fire until Ben moved out on the shifting gravel. When Whitey passed the stunted pine, Jordan squeezed the trigger.

The Winchester's sudden roar, and the chunks of splintered pine showered down on Whitey's head, was sufficient to startle the horses. Whitey's, a spirited stallion, kicked its back legs up high in the air and tried to bolt. The loose shale began to shift, denying the horse sound footing and, in a moment, it was flailing front and back hooves in an effort to find solid ground. Ben's horse, frightened as well, began skating on the treacherous gravel, but Ben was able to hold the animal firmly until it scrambled to secure ground. Not so with Whitey's stallion — the terrified horse lost its battle with the slope and tumbled. Down it went on its side. Then in a frantic struggle to right itself, it succeeded only in tumbling over on the other side, legs flailing in the air as it slid down the slope. Had Whitey not been quick to release the reins, he would have surely gone down the mountainside with his horse. In the confusion, every man in the posse was concerned only with trying to keep from following Whitey's horse to the trail below. There was no time to worry about where the shot had come from.

Jordan took a few moments to assess the effects of his shot. Only Ben Thompson and the Indian were safely across the loose shale and in the cover of a ring of pines. The others had fallen back to seek cover in a shallow gully — all except Whitey Hickson. Whitey was on his way back down the slope, hurrying as much as possible without losing his footing and plunging headlong after his horse. Jordan felt confident that a good portion of the determination had drained from the three in the gully, and a little more encouragement on his part might send them home. He chambered another round, and sighted on a spot on the ground close to one of the horses. It had the proper effect. The bullet kicked up dirt and gravel on Lester Pierce's leg. He yelled, thinking he had been hit. When he realized that he had not been shot, he deemed himself lucky, and determined not to test fate any further. "Jesus," he exclaimed. "I'm gettin' outta here, boys, before that son of a bitch's aim gets any better."

Without waiting to discuss it, Lester started down the mountain after Whitey, using his horse to shield him from the rifle above on the ledge. There was no more than a moment passed before the other two saw the wisdom in Lester's decision, and followed suit.

"Hey!" Ben shouted after the retreating men. "Come back here! We've got him treed."

J.D. Watts answered for the disenchanted members of his posse. "We didn't sign on to commit suicide," he yelled over his shoulder as he puffed and panted in his efforts to descend the slope as quickly as his stumpy legs would carry him. "You do what you want. I'm gettin' outta here."

"Hell, you're the sheriff," Lester said, but

not loud enough for Ben to hear. "If you want him so bad, you go get him."

Up above, Jordan watched the four posse members retire from the field of battle. His concern was now reduced to two, and they were concealed in a screen of pine trees. With hope that they, too, might be discouraged at this point, he decided to offer amnesty. "Thompson," he called out. "I won't shoot if you go on back with the others and leave me be."

Ben responded immediately, "You might as well give up, Jordan. I'm gonna hunt you down no matter what."

The man's relentless attitude was frustrating to Jordan. "Dammit, Ben," he yelled back. "You've got no call to hunt me. I've told you I didn't murder those men up on Hard Luck."

"Throw down that rifle and give up, and we'll let a jury decide that," Ben said.

Jordan recognized the lie. He knew that he would be shot down as soon as he exposed himself, or hanged when they got him back to town. He decided further talk was pointless, and edged back from the rim of the ledge to the rocks where Sweet Pea waited. Replacing his rifle in the saddle sling, he stepped up into the saddle and guided the mare toward a hogback where he could cross over and make his way down the other side of the mountain.

Below him, Jack Little Hawk listened. Hearing what he knew was the sound of Jordan's horse, he crawled to the edge of the pines to take a look. He was just in time to see Jordan disappear over the ridge. Hurrying back to Ben, he reported. "He rode over the top, headin' down the other side. We follow these trees around, we might cut him off on other side." He made a circling motion with his hand.

"Let's go, then," Ben immediately replied, fearful that Jordan would escape once again.

Leaning back in the saddle, his back sometimes only inches from Sweet Pea's rump, Jordan descended the eastern slope of the mountain. The reins held loosely in his hands, he made no attempt to guide the ornery mare, relying upon her natural ability to pick the best path down. "Easy, girl," he cautioned when her front hooves slid a little in some loose gravel, but she calmly maintained her balance and continued down toward the ring of pines some fifty feet below them now. Forced to remain patient because of the steepness of the decline, he searched the pine belt constantly in case Thompson and the Indian made their way around to cut him off. He figured if he could reach the cover of the trees he had a good chance of losing them.

At the edge of the pines, Sweet Pea stopped suddenly, her hooves sliding on some loose soil. Not expecting it, Jordan lurched forward, thrown flat against the neck of the horse. At the same instant, he heard the snap of the bullet that passed directly over his head, followed by the report of a rifle. It would occur to him later that the ornery mare had once again saved his bacon, having evidently caught the scent of the other two horses. But at the moment, his mind was occupied with staying alive, and his natural reflexes took over. Instead of trying to regain his balance in the saddle, he kicked his feet out of the stirrups, slid from Sweet Pea's neck, and dropped to the ground. He rolled over against the trunk of a tree and lay still, listening, not sure where his attackers were. He didn't have to wait long.

"You got him!" Jack Little Hawk exclaimed when he saw Jordan fall from the saddle.

Thompson lowered his rifle, and peered through the screen of pines before him. It had been a shot of approximately fifty yards, and he had been forced to take it quickly before his target disappeared in the forest.

As soon as he pulled the trigger, Jordan had lurched forward and dropped to the ground. Still, he remained cautious. "I ain't sure," he said. "We'd best be careful."

Jack had no doubts. "You got him," he said. Anxious to take the scalp before the sheriff might decide to deny him the rite, he kicked his pony hard and hurried to the body. Jordan Gray's scalp would be big medicine — big enough to elevate Jack's status among his people.

His rifle ready, in case Jordan was still alive, Jack slid from the saddle. His eyes fixed upon the body lying still against a tree trunk. He stood where he was for a long moment, watching. But there was no movement, no sign of life. Reassured, he took one quick glance back to see Ben approaching. Concerned that the sheriff might want to display the corpse with his scalp intact, Jack slid his rifle back in the sling and drew his knife. Moving quickly, he rolled Jordan over on his side, and grabbed a handful of his hair. With scalping knife poised to strike, he was suddenly startled when Jordan's eyes opened wide to stare right into his face. In almost the same instant, he was shocked by a searing pain in his stomach. Astonished, he looked down to discover Jordan's knife sunk to the hilt in his gut. Stunned by this sudden turn of events, he tried to fight back. But Jordan moved quickly to lock the wrist of Jack's knife hand, while withdrawing his own knife and plunging it deeply into the Indian's gut again. Jack screamed with the pain, and clawed viciously at Jordan's face with his free hand, fighting helplessly in his agony.

Equally startled by the sudden reversal of fortune, Ben froze, paralyzed for a few moments while the Indian's death screams rang out through the trees. He was struck with the sobering thought that he was now alone against Jordan Gray, man-to-man, and the notion was not one he relished. With his courage rapidly draining, his thoughts stampeded toward saving his hide. In one last desperate attempt, he raised his rifle and took a hasty shot at his adversary before turning to flee. The bullet meant for Jordan struck Jack Little Hawk in the back, ending the Indian's agony.

Jordan rolled the body off of him, and scrambled to his feet where he stood for a moment watching the sheriff galloping recklessly through the pines. *Well,* he thought, *I guess that's the end of that.* Still, he was not satisfied with the final outcome. He hesitated for a long moment, trying to decide. Finally, he made up his mind. Collecting

Sweet Pea and Jack Little Hawk's horse, he started out after Ben. There were still some strings he wanted to tie before he was ready to move on.

It was no trouble to follow Ben Thompson's trail back around to the point where he had started down the mountain. The fearful sheriff had left a wide track that a blind man could have followed. In his apparent haste to leave Jordan behind, Thompson had whipped his horse unmercifully, forcing the already tired animal to gallop when the slope permitted. Jordan followed at a more conservative pace, confident that he would overtake Ben in time while the sheriff had no choice but to rest his exhausted horse.

When he came to the edge of the pine belt, where the rest of Ben's posse had turned back when faced with the patch of loose shale, Jordan stopped to study the tracks more closely. The slope was scarred with the evidence of the posse's earlier struggles to cross the treacherous area. It took him a few minutes of close examination to determine that the man he chased had not risked the shale a second time. All of the tracks led across the shale from the other side. None led back the other way. So Jordan backtracked a few dozen yards to a narrow gully that sliced vertically through the pines. He dismounted and searched the pine needles for sign. In a minute, he found what he was looking for. Thompson had taken the time to try to disguise his trail. He had assumed the gully was a quick way down the mountain to intercept the game trail he and his men had originally followed up the mountain. It was an easy mistake to make. Jordan remembered a time when he and Ned Booth had decided to follow the gully to see where it led, only to end up looking out over the valley from a cliff two hundred foot high. Thinking now that he may have Thompson trapped, he tied the horses to some pine boughs, and proceeded down the gully on foot.

It had been more than a year. But if his memory served him, the gully ran no more than a hundred and fifty yards at the most before it emptied out at the edge of the cliff. It was time to be cautious. With his rifle cocked and ready to fire, he made his way carefully along the narrow defile, his eyes constantly searching the way before him. The sheriff could be hiding in hopes Jordan had not detected the tracks he had attempted to cover with pine straw. Or, he might be on his way back up the gully after discovering there was no way out. Jordan readied himself for either occurrence. As it turned out, however, he was not prepared for what he found.

Ben Thompson was almost paralyzed with terror. He looked down at the tops of the pines some two hundred feet below him. The only thing that prevented him from falling into that frightening space was the puny juniper limb he clutched with both hands. Only moments before, he had ridden his horse down the gully, pushing the tired animal for more speed even though the incline was obviously dangerous. The gully had taken a sharp turn and suddenly he was looking into space. It was too late for the horse. The exhausted animal tried to stop, stumbling as it went down on its side and sliding, throwing Ben from the saddle. Their momentum drove both man and horse over the edge of the cliff — the horse to its death, the man to snag the limbs of a juniper.

Ben was terrified. His bleeding hands went unnoticed as he held onto the branch in desperation. He tried to find purchase with his feet, but the overhang was too much to permit him to reach the cliff wall. He tried to summon the courage to pull himself up, but each time he tried to get a better handhold, the juniper gave way just a little, its roots gradually ripping away from the soil. His arms and shoulders rapidly tiring, he realized that he was helpless, and doomed to fall to his death without divine intervention. The miracle he frantically prayed for came, but in somewhat less than divine form. He almost let go of the branch when he looked up into the eyes of Jordan Gray.

Certain now that he was a dead man, Ben could do nothing but peer into those steel blue eyes, knowing that he was powerless to do anything but choose the way he would die. The thought of falling through the air, his body mangled and crushed in the treetops below, was so abhorrent to him that he pleaded for a quicker death. "Please," he begged, "put a bullet in my brain. I'm afraid to fall."

Jordan didn't answer for a second. He had not come after Ben to kill him. Instead, he wished at that moment that he had led his horse down the gully. It was a long way back to the horses to get a rope from his saddle. He doubted that Thompson could hold on that long. With nothing available to use, he lay down on his belly and reached down with one arm. "Take hold," he ordered.

Ben was confused by the unexpected move. Suspecting a trick, he only stared at the extended hand — afraid to try for it, only to have it snatched away. In the next moment, however, the roots of the juniper began to give way, and his natural instincts to grasp for anything to save himself took over. He grabbed for Jordan's hand just as the roots tore from the ground, and now found himself dangling with only Jordan holding him.

The sheriff was not a small man. Jordan's body slid a few inches toward the edge when he took the full weight of the suspended man. He quickly braced himself with his other arm hooked around the trunk of a pine tree, and steeled his body to take the strain. He felt Ben's other hand clamp around his forearm as he gradually pulled himself away from the edge of the cliff. Inch by painful inch, he labored, Ben's dead weight pulling against him as if to dislocate his shoulder from its socket. After what seemed an eternity, the sheriff's head finally appeared above the rim of the cliff, and he managed to get his arms over the top. With Ben able to help now, Jordan pulled him up over the edge.

Exhausted, Jordan was almost as spent as Thompson. Both men sat gasping for air for a few seconds. Still in a state of confusion at having been saved from falling, Ben suddenly reverted back to the fear that had sent him and his horse plunging over the edge of the cliff. He reached for his pistol, only to find an empty holster. His pistol was two hundred feet below in the trees.

Watching the frantic man's actions, Jordan commented dryly, "You're a grateful son of a bitch, aren't you?" He reached behind him and picked up his rifle.

Finding himself once again at Jordan's mercy, Thompson fidgeted nervously with his empty holster. "I was just trying to do my job as sheriff. I was just gonna take you in to stand trial."

"Is that a fact?" Jordan replied sarcastically. "I suppose you took a shot at me back there just to warn me." When Ben couldn't come up with a reply, Jordan growled, "I should have let you drop, but I reckon I'm too softhearted for my own good." He took a step back and motioned with his rifle. "Get on your feet."

"What are you gonna do?" Ben whined, fearing that he might be about to receive the bullet he had so earnestly begged for moments earlier when he dangled helplessly over the edge of the cliff.

"I'm gonna put a bullet in your head if you don't do like I tell you," Jordan replied. "Now start walkin' back up that gully."

The sheriff did as he was told, stumbling

occasionally as he tried to walk while constantly stealing nervous glances over his shoulder. "Just doing my job," he mumbled weakly.

"Just keep walkin'," Jordan said.

In a few minutes, they reached the mouth of the gully and the two horses tied there. "Sit down," Jordan instructed, gesturing with his rifle toward a pine tree. When Thompson did as instructed, Jordan stepped over to check Jack Little Hawk's horse. Then he turned to directly face his captive. "You and that rabble you call a posse have been dogging my heels for over a year, and I'm gettin' damn sick and tired of it. I've never murdered anyone in cold blood in my life. I tried to tell you that, but you were so hot to string somebody up you wouldn't listen. When you couldn't get your hands on me, you strung up an innocent old man. I oughta shoot you for that, but I reckon you and your posse will have to answer to the devil for that one. True enough, I killed some of your righteous citizens, but only because they were tryin' to kill me. I didn't have much choice. Any man would have done the same. I coulda let you die just now, but I reckon I wanted you to know that I didn't kill those miners on Hard Luck Creek." He paused to judge the effect of his words on the frightened sheriff. "I've got no reason to lie about it," he continued. "If I was the murderer you think I am, I would have just let you drop. But I guess enough men have died to make up for Ned Booth's hangin'."

Ben's mind was still spinning. He was hearing Jordan's words, but he wasn't sure what was up and what was down. Brief moments before, he was certain this was his final day on Earth. Now he was seated upon solid ground, listening to Jordan proclaim his innocence. Could he possibly believe him? If he accepted Jordan's word, it would mean that he had hanged an innocent man — a possibility he was reluctant to admit. On the other hand, maybe this act of mercy was no more than a ploy on Jordan's part to put a stop to being hounded by a posse from Deadwood. Jordan had spared his life. More than that, he had saved his life, but Ben didn't want to be taken for a fool. "I reckon I owe you thanks for pullin' me off of that cliff," Ben finally muttered begrudgingly.

Jordan studied the man's face. He could guess what was going through Ben's mind. "I've got no reason to lie. I don't plan to ever go anywhere near that hellhole you call a town back there. But I never murdered anyone, and I wanted you to hear it from me. Now that you have, I'll be on my way." He walked over and untied his horse, keeping one eye on Ben all the while. "I'll leave you the Indian's horse. I expect you can find most of your plunder at the bottom of that cliff back there." He paused then before adding a solemn warning. "Make no mistake about it, if you or anybody else from Deadwood comes after me again, I won't waste time talkin'."

Certain at last that he was not going to die, Ben got to his feet and walked over to stand beside Jordan's stirrup. "I reckon I can admit I was wrong about you and Ned," he said. "Thanks again for savin' my bacon. I reckon I couldn't have blamed you if you had just let me drop. I'll set things right about you in Deadwood." He stepped back then and turned to untie Jack Little Hawk's horse. The Indian pony sidestepped nervously, uncertain about the strange rider approaching it.

Jordan made no reply to Ben's thanks, merely nodding his acknowledgement. He turned Sweet Pea's head, and gave the mare a gentle nudge with his heels. The Arapaho's pony jerked at the reins, taking a few steps to follow. "Better hold him," Jordan advised. "He looks a little skittish." With that final piece of advice, he rode off through the trees.

Ben scrambled up on the horse and yanked back hard on the reins to hold the nervous pony. The horse responded by rearing on its hind legs, causing Ben to grab for the saddle horn to keep from being thrown. When the horse settled down again, Ben's hand slid off the horn to rest on the butt of Jack's rifle. Desperate thoughts flooded his brain as he gazed at Jordan Gray's broad back, and he suddenly saw a picture of his heroic return to Deadwood with the body of the notorious scout draped across his saddle. He hesitated. Although moving at a leisurely pace, he would soon be swallowed up in the forest of pines. The temptation was too great. It was an opportunity to make a real name for himself.

Thirty yards away, Jordan heard the distinct sound of a rifle being cocked. His reaction was automatic. He rolled out of the saddle, his rifle in hand. Ben never got off the shot. Jordan, in lightning fashion, pumped two .45 caliber slugs into the hapless man's chest before the sheriff could steady his aim and pull the trigger.

Stunned for a moment by the suddenness of Thompson's attempt on his life, Jordan remained kneeling on the ground as the sheriff recoiled from the impact of the shots and fell from the horse. A wave of anger swept over Jordan then — anger for the senseless waste of it all. He rose and walked back to the fallen man, still wary lest the sheriff was still alive. But Thompson was dead, one of Jordan's bullets had found the heart. Jordan stood over the body for a long moment, contemplating the sorry turn of events. "Damn you," he suddenly blurted, and kicked the lifeless form.

It was close to dusk when the lone rider, leading the Indian pony with a body riding across the saddle, stopped on the ridge overlooking Deadwood Gulch. Still nursing an anger that simmered at a low boil inside him, Jordan looped the Indian pony's reins around the saddle horn and gave the horse a slap on the rump. It responded by galloping a few yards before settling back to a walk. Then it stopped and turned to look at Jordan.

"Git!" Jordan commanded, but the horse continued to stand and stare, showing no inclination to proceed or to follow. Jordan wheeled Sweet Pea and rode off down the other side of the ridge, confident that Jack Little Hawk's horse would eventually wander on into Deadwood. He had gone to the trouble to return the sheriff's body because he felt it necessary to issue a warning. With no pencil or paper available, he had lettered a crude message on Ben's shirt, using the dead man's blood for ink. *Leave me be,* it read.

Chapter 8

"Maggie, come take a look at this!" Hattie motioned for her partner before stepping outside on the wooden walkway.

"Empty-handed," Maggie said. "I told you they wouldn't catch him."

Hearing their comments, Polly joined them at the door, still holding the knives and forks she had been in the process of laying out by the plates. She shielded her eyes against the sun and peered at the four riders, led by J.D. Watts, their horses walking slowly down the middle of the street.

"Hell," Maggie commented. "There ain't but four of 'em. Where's Ben Thompson?"

"And the Injun," Hattie added.

The three women walked out into the street to intercept the four members of the posse. They were soon joined by a sizable crowd from the saloons as the word spread that the posse was back. The four riders pulled up to relate the news. J.D. took on the role as spokesman. "We caught up to him, all right, and we went as far as we could go before we had to turn back. The horses couldn't make it up to the mountaintop where he was holed up." He nodded his head toward Whitey. "Whitey's horse damn near broke his neck. Jordan Gray had the high ground. He coulda picked us off one by one, but Ben and Jack was lucky enough to get to cover before he spotted 'em."

Someone in the crowd called out, "Where's Ben?"

"Don't know for sure," J.D. answered. "There wasn't no way we could tell, pinned down like we was."

"Didn't you wait to find out if him and the Injun was all right?" someone else asked.

J.D. shrugged and shook his head. Lester Pierce answered for him. "Hell, we was out in the open gettin' shot at. Him and Jack was in the trees. We had to get outta there. There wasn't no way we could say which way they was headin', so we just come on back. He'll most likely show up pretty soon."

Relieved that the posse had been unsuccessful in capturing Jordan, the three women returned to their chores in the kitchen. The usual crowd came in for supper, Whitey

Hickson among them. He enthralled the diners with an embellished account of that day's incident on the mountain. "Lead was flyin'," he said. "I felt one whistle right by my ear just before my horse went tail over teacup down the side of that mountain." He went on to tell of the hailstorm of bullets that forced the four of them back. His fellow diners were properly impressed, and the question was raised concerning what would be done about the wanton murderer.

Overhearing the question, Hattie remarked, "Jordan Gray ain't no murderer. You boys ain't got enough brains to stack a pile of sheep dung, even if it came with directions."

Whitey laughed. "Hattie, you and Maggie has always been soft on that man. But fact is fact, and there's a lot of poor souls dead around here because of Jordan Gray." Then answering the question just put to him, he said, "I don't know, Charlie. I reckon we'll have to wait to see what Ben says."

As it would happen, Whitey was the one who found Ben's body. After supper, he and some of the others adjourned to the Silver Dollar Saloon where he continued to embellish on the standoff in the mountains. It was well past dark when he made his way to his horse, walking on somewhat shaky legs due to the consumption of a considerable quantity of Sweeney's whiskey — the first round on the house, in reward for his heroism. The horse, although showing the scars of a distressful afternoon, had made this trip countless times before, so it wasn't necessary for Whitey to remain sober enough to guide the animal. Teetering in the saddle, fighting off the overpowering desire to sleep, Whitey was intent only upon reaching his claim before falling off. He would have missed the Indian pony carrying Ben Thompson's body had not his horse stopped of its own accord. Whitey sobered up considerably when his half-pickled brain registered the discovery.

For the second time that night, Hattie, Maggie, and Polly joined a gathering of townsfolk in the middle of the street. "Oh, my Lord," Hattie sighed, sincerely sorry to find that Ben Thompson had been killed. She and Maggie had never really found fault with Ben, aside from his hardheadedness at times. She would not have wished this fate for the self-proclaimed leader of the Deadwood vigilante committee.

"I reckon he finally caught up with Jordan Gray," Rufus Sparks muttered under his breath.

"He should have left him alone," Polly

Hatcher was quick to respond. The Jordan Gray who had come to her rescue and seen her safely to Deadwood would not have killed had he not been forced to. She was certain of that.

Hattie put her arm around her niece's shoulders, and turned her away. "Come on, honey, there's no need to fret about it." Ben Thompson was an important man to most of the folks in Deadwood, and there was no use in riling anybody up anymore than they were bound to be over this latest encounter with Jordan. Glancing at Maggie, she said, "This ain't gonna do much for Jordan's stock around here."

It was not until morning light that the undertaker discovered the message written in blood on Ben's shirt. When the word got out, even Maggie and Hattie wondered if Jordan might be developing a bloodlust. "I hope to hell that ain't the case," Hattie lamented. "He was too nice a young man to turn bad."

Ben Thompson had been a key figure in the daily happenings in Deadwood. He had organized the original vigilance committee, and later took on the job as sheriff. Even so, death was a frequent visitor in the unruly mining town, so the shock of Ben's demise wore off quickly, and the town soon got back to the business of prospecting, drinking, and gambling. Not one of the town's citizens was concerned enough to worry about the whereabouts of Jordan Gray — just as long as he wasn't in Deadwood. There was the question of who might fill the vacancy left in the sheriff's office. And while J.D. Watts voluntarily took on the task of repairing the window in the jail, he adamantly refused the job of sheriff.

For Polly Hatcher, life had at last dealt her a peaceful hand. She was genuinely welcomed by her aunt and her aunt's gruff, pistol-toting partner as a member of their little family. The Trough had gone from the original tent to a pine-frame dining hall with two long tables, end to end, down the center of the room. If Polly had not shown up when she had, Maggie and Hattie would have been pressed to hire someone to help them. The town had progressed slightly from the days when Maggie found it necessary to wear her .44, but she still wore it, feeling undressed without it.

Although apprehensive at first when she felt the open stares of the customers as she helped serve the meals, Polly soon became accustomed to them. She had not gotten to the point of exchanging flirtatious remarks with the men, answering suggestive comments with nothing more than a shy smile. But within a few days' time, she became comfortable with her situation. And the horrifying nights, when she would awaken from dreams of Bill Pike's bleeding body standing over her, were occurring less frequently. The town might be wild and dangerous, but she felt safe under the protection of Maggie and Hattie.

It didn't take long for word to get around the gulch that there was a new young lady at The Trough, and that she was a comely lass at that. Most of the town's male population came by to ogle Hattie's niece, resulting in a sharp increase in business. Polly soon became accustomed to the open-mouthed gapes, and politely declined several offers to hitch up in her first week in town.

One soul that seemed to find a reason to frequent The Trough between the regularly scheduled hours was young Toby Blessings. Though no more than nineteen, Toby had pulled a man's load for more than five years, following gold strikes across Montana Territory before ending up in this homely gulch. When he drifted into Deadwood in the spring of the previous year, he seemed to have naturally gravitated toward Maggie and Hattie. Having no family of his own, the two partners of The Trough came to be like aunts to the lonely young man. With the arrival of Polly Hatcher, Toby suddenly found an object of worship. He was smitten with his first glimpse of the flaxen-haired girl, her perfect face marred only by healing scars and bruises. Already accustomed to the shy young man's frequent visits to The Trough, Hattie found it amusing when Toby began to show up between meals, offering to chop wood or repair the roof shingles — anything for an excuse to be close to Polly.

"That boy follows her around like a puppy," Maggie commented one day as she sat before a large pan of potatoes she was peeling. She had paused to watch Toby carry an armload of wood after Polly.

Hattie looked up from the peas she was shelling to gaze after the two young folks. " 'Pears to me, if he's supposed to be a prospector, he's lookin' for gold in a peculiar place."

"Oh, he's prospectin', all right," Maggie said with a laugh. "Only it ain't for gold."

They both laughed at the thought. It would take an earthquake under Toby's feet before the shy young man would make an aggressive move toward Polly, who seemed oblivious to the obvious emotions worn undisguised on Toby's face.

The two women may have been correct in thinking Toby to be shy, but he was also a determined young man. That was evident by his departure from home at the tender age of fourteen when he set out for the Montana gold fields, determined to be his own man. He had never before been struck so helpless by the mere presence of a woman until he first laid eyes upon Polly Hatcher. From that fateful moment, he could not rid his mind of her face, and he realized that he wanted always to be close to her. As a result of that total infatuation, he found more and more excuses to show up at The Trough to offer his help with the chores, following Polly around — as Maggie had said — like a puppy.

If Polly was aware of the effect she had on the boy, she didn't show it. After a few days of constant visits by Toby, and some good-natured remarks by Maggie and Hattie, she had to acknowledge the young man's devotion. "Why, he's just being friendly," she said, knowing full well that it went deeper than that. "I expect he's been all alone for so long that he just wants to be around someone to talk to."

"You think so, huh?" Maggie snorted. Then she looked at Hattie and winked.

"Honey," Hattie chimed in, "that boy ain't

got his eyes uncrossed since he first set 'em on you." She winked back at Maggie. "I expect you'd better get ready for a marriage proposal."

"Oh, I don't think it's that serious," Polly said, blushing. It was flattering, she had to admit, but she had no desire to lead the boy on. Maybe, she thought, his fascination for her would soon wear out. It seemed harmless enough to her, but she soon became aware of just how serious it was to Toby. The occasion came on a chilly spring afternoon when he came by the kitchen to find Maggie out back chopping wood for the stove.

"Here, ma'am," Toby immediately volunteered, "let me do that for you."

Maggie straightened up, and leaned on her ax. "Why, hello, Toby," she greeted him. "Nice of you to offer, but I've been chopping wood for more years than I can remember."

"Well, then," he responded with a shy smile, "you can let me spell you for a bit." When she failed to accept at once, he insisted. "I don't mind."

She laughed and handed him the ax. "All right, if you really want to." She nodded toward the large pile of wood behind her. "I just need to bust up a couple of armloads of that bigger stuff for the stove."

"Yes ma'am," he replied and set into the chore with determination. After a few minutes, Maggie excused herself to attend to something in the kitchen. She left him to his work attacking the woodpile, noticing he was constantly stealing glances toward the kitchen door.

Hattie turned in surprise when Maggie came in the kitchen. "Who's choppin' wood?" Hattie asked.

"Toby Blessings. Who else?"

Hattie laughed. "You must not have told him Polly ain't here."

"No, I reckon I didn't," Maggie said. "I wasn't gonna tell him till after I got my firewood." They both laughed then. "I reckon I'd better go back out there before he goes through the whole woodpile."

Outside, Maggie exclaimed, "My goodness, boy, that's wood a'plenty for now."

"Oh, I've got plenty of steam left. There ain't many men better at splittin' wood than me," he boasted.

"I can see that, but there ain't no need to chop up any more. That'll do me for two days."

He stopped then, but she could see the reluctance in his face, and realized that he hesitated to give up an excuse to hang around. Although he tried to be discreet about it, his eyes were constantly looking beyond her toward the kitchen. With a twinkle in her eye, she grinned and said, "Polly's down at the creek washing clothes. She might appreciate a hand carryin' the basket back."

He couldn't avoid the blush. "Why, shore nuff," he stammered. "I reckon I could do that." And he was off.

"Supper's on the house," Maggie called out after him, "for cuttin' all that wood."

Polly looked up when she heard someone coming down the path. Recognizing Toby, she greeted him cheerfully. "Howdy, Toby. What are you doin' down here?"

"I come to help you," he said. Then he thought to add, "Miss Maggie said you might need help."

"Is that so?" Polly said with a smile. "Well, I'm just about finished here, but you can carry my basket back if you want to."

It burst out before he could stop it. "I'd carry your basket to Kingdom Come," he blurted. Then realizing in horror that the words had dropped out of his mouth, he started to stammer an apology.

She interrupted his efforts. Smiling sweetly, she said, "I really didn't intend to go that far — just back to the house would do."

He was mortified. Feeling foolish and immature, he attempted to extricate himself from the embarrassing situation. "I didn't mean it to sound like that," he said, then paused to think again. He suddenly decided that the cat was out of the bag. He already had a start on something he had been trying to summon the nerve to say for days. So it was now or never. Determined to state his feelings, he bolstered up his courage and came out with it. "Polly, I wanna marry you."

Literally stunned by a statement so unexpected, Polly could do little more than stare wide-eyed at the young man. With no desire to hurt the boy, she thought for a long moment before responding, "Why, Toby, that's the sweetest offer I've ever had, and I'm really flattered you like me that much."

"Wait!" he interrupted, in a panic to stop her before she could add *but*. "I know you think I'm young, but a lot of folks has told me I'm a lot older than my years. You couldn't find nobody that'd work harder for you than me."

The desperation in his face was enough to bring a tear to her eye as she gazed at the still-boyish features, the scraggly attempt at a mustache, the unruly sandy hair. What, she wondered, could she say to this innocent boy? How could he possibly deal with the pain and torment she had already endured in her life? "Toby," she pleaded softly, "you don't know anything about me — where I'm from, what my life has been before this."

"I know all I need to know," he insisted. "All that other stuff don't matter. I'd make you a good husband. I swear I would."

She gazed at him patiently. "I know you will make some lucky girl a good husband." She saw the hurt and disappointment sweeping over his face. "I'm not the woman for you, Toby. But I'm honored that you asked."

Feeling empty inside, his young hopes dashed against the rocks of what could never be, he still refused to accept defeat. "Don't say no, please, Polly. Just tell me you'll think on it."

Not wishing to give him false hope, she had to say, "I can't tell you I might change my mind, Toby. I just can't."

Not another word was spoken between them as he carried her clothesbasket back up the path. She feared she had crushed his hopes with her rejection, so when he set the basket down by the clothesline, she said softly, "There's no need to tell anybody about what we said."

He looked at her with mournful eyes, grateful that she would not expose his earnest confession of adoration, and that made him more smitten with her than ever before. He was certain now that he loved her with every fiber of his body, and he was even more determined to win her love. She did not think him mature enough to marry. That had to be it. He would go back to his claim, and search for the gold that he knew had to be there. Once he had means, she would look upon him in a different light. "I'll be seein' you" was all he said in departing, and left without waiting for his free supper.

He walked into the rough wooden dining hall, standing in the open doorway for a few minutes while he gazed around the room as if searching for someone. "Well, come on in and close the door," Maggie Hogg barked good-naturedly. "We've got enough flies in here already, and we have to let them get a chance to eat before we let in another bunch." Lester Pierce, seated at the end of the table, laughed in appreciation of Maggie's attempt at humor. "If you're wantin' to eat, you'll have to park that gun you're wearin' on the table by the door. Ain't nobody wears a gun in here but me." She patted the pistol in her holster for emphasis.

The stranger grunted a gruff reply, but ignored her request to deposit his pistol. He closed the door and took a few steps into the room, stopping again to shift his gaze back and forth across a room partially filled with uninterested diners. Maggie paused as she was about to place a plate of biscuits before Lester, and studied the face of the stranger. His eyes had a dark, pinched look about them, giving the impression that his face had never known a smile. A long scar ran horizontally across his left cheek, leaving a white streak through an otherwise heavy beard. Her natural instincts told her that he was a man to be wary of. "If you're wantin' to eat," Maggie repeated, this time in a more serious tone, "get rid of the gun and set yourself down any place that ain't got a behind in it."

Still unmoved by Maggie's persistence, he stood where he was for a few moments longer, his lifeless gaze locked now upon her. Finally, when it appeared that he was about to turn and leave the room, he shrugged, and still without a word, took a step toward the table, only to stop again when Polly came in from the kitchen carrying a huge bowl of baked beans.

"Bill!" Polly shrieked as if she had been shot. The bowl dropped from her hands and shattered on the plank floor. The customers seated around the two long tables started as if a gun had gone off.

An evil smirk spread slowly across Bill Pike's face. Polly's reaction could not have been more satisfying for him. "Hello, Polly darlin'," he slurred. "You look like you're surprised to see me."

There was not a sound in the dining room as all eyes were locked on the heavyset stranger with the dirty black beard and the deep-set eyes. Polly, paralyzed with fright for a moment, recovered enough to back away until stopped by the kitchen door. There she stood, stunned, still not sure she was not seeing an apparition.

"Thought I was dead, didn't'cha?" Bill said, gloating. "Well, it takes a helluva lot to kill Bill Pike." The smirk expanded to form a wicked smile. He eyed his wife up and down, as if appraising the property that had been stolen from him. "I've come a long way to fetch you home." He took a step toward her.

"Stay away from me!" Polly cried.

"Now, that ain't no way to talk to your husband after so long a time," he said, and took another step toward her.

"That's far enough," Maggie commanded, her .44 drawn and leveled at Bill. "Looks plain enough to me that she don't wanna go anywhere with you."

The smile was immediately replaced by a scowl directed at Maggie. "Lady, this ain't none of your affair. This is between me and my wife."

"Right now it's between me and you, ain't it?" Maggie said. She cocked the hammer back, her hand steady as she held the pistol on him. "Around here, we believe in free choice. She don't choose to go nowhere with the likes of you, and I don't choose to have you in my business establishment. Now you can choose which way you wanna leave here, walkin' or carried."

Bill paused. His eyes, dead before, now burned with anger, and for a moment he considered drawing his own pistol. But the calm look of determination on Maggie's face told him that would be tantamount to suicide. Still he wavered, unwilling to back down to a woman, until a movement in the open doorway caught his eye. He shifted his gaze briefly to discover Hattie Moon, shotgun in hand, easing quietly into the room behind Polly. "So that's the way it is," Bill snarled. "A bunch of old women takin' up for a back-shootin' bitch that run off with my money and left me for dead."

"That's the way it is," Maggie said.

"I didn't shoot you in the back." Polly finally found the courage to speak, bolstered by the unwavering support of Maggie and Hattie. "You came at me one too many times, and you got what you deserved. Now, go away from here and leave me alone."

Like a cornered badger, Bill snarled as he shifted his angry gaze back and forth between the three women. He was cool enough to realize that he was the loser in this round, but he was determined there would be other rounds. He had not ridden halfway across the prairie to be defeated by a gaggle of women. There was time, he counseled himself, and slowly the pinched look of hatred receded from his dark eyes. His next words were calm and without passion. "We'll just let it go for now," he said.

"Sorry you have to leave so soon," Maggie responded sarcastically.

The thin smile returned to Bill's face, and he glanced around at the silent customers seated at the tables. "I'm in no hurry," he said. "I ain't et for a spell. Maybe I'll just take a chance on your cookin'."

"Not today, you ain't," Maggie replied.

Bill affected an expression of mock surprise. "Why, hell, you're in the business of feedin' folks, ain't you? And I'm a customer same as these fellers."

Maggie's patience was wearing thin. "You can peck shit with the chickens for all I care. You ain't eatin' here, today or any other day. Now get your sorry ass outta here."

A quick spark of anger instantly returned to Bill's eyes, and his heavy brows lowered to cloud his whiskered face. "I'll get what I came for, you crazy old bitch, and anybody gets in my way is gonna be sorry."

"Mister" — Lester Pierce finally decided things had gone far enough, and it was time for one of the men to say something — "you'd best get yourself on outta here while you're still standin'."

Bill cocked his head sharply to see who had spoken. His gaze lingered for a long second on Lester — as if memorizing his face. Then he turned and walked slowly toward the door, leaving a hushed dining hall behind him.

It was Hattie Moon who finally broke the heavy silence as all eyes seemed to be locked on the shaken girl still standing by the kitchen door. Stepping over to put a reassuring arm around Polly's shoulders, Hattie said, "Don't you worry none, honey, we ain't scared of the likes of that trash."

She then turned toward the gawking boarders at the tables. "Show's over, boys. Don't let the victuals get cold."

In spite of her aunt's confident composure, Polly knew Bill well enough to be certain that the show was not over. Bill possessed an evil determination that drove him to get what he was after — no matter what. If she had noticed the knowing glances exchanged between Maggie and Hattie, she would have surmised that they suspected the same. Now she stood staring down at the broken bowl and the spilled beans on the floor as if suddenly wondering how they got there. Nothing was making sense at the moment. Her husband back from the dead, spilled beans on the floor — what did it all mean?

Hattie realized that Polly was in shock. She turned the confused girl away from the tables and led her out of the room. "Don't worry about spilt beans," she said. "Me and Maggie'll take care of 'em. There's plenty more in the kitchen." This last she said loudly for the benefit of the customers.

Maggie, her pistol holstered now, went back to the kitchen with Hattie and Polly. "Why don't you take her on back to the house," she said. "I'll clean up the beans." When they went out the back door, Maggie got another bowl and a big spoon, then returned to the dining room. "There's more beans in the oven," she reassured her guests as she scooped them up. "I'll fetch some more." Returning to the kitchen, she transferred the contents of the bowl into another of the same size, hurriedly picking occasional shards of broken glass from the beans. Satisfied that she had not missed any pieces of a size sufficient to rip a hole in the gut of one of her regulars, she stirred the beans to blend in any dust from the floor. All done, she returned to set the bowl on the table where it was immediately seized upon by the closest man and promptly emptied as it made the rounds.

Back of the kitchen, in the small room that served as bedroom for the three women, Hattie was in the process of calming her niece. "You just need to rest here a bit, honey. Everything'll be all right."

"He was dead," Polly insisted. "He was laying there in the mud — dead — I know he was. I killed him." She began to sob violently. "I killed him. I had to, Aunt Hattie, I swear."

"I know it, child," Hattie cooed softly. "Ain't nobody blamin' you."

Polly seemed intent upon telling Hattie the whole story, anxious to confess what she considered her secret shame and sin. So Hattie sat on the side of the bed and listened while Polly recreated the fatal evening that caused her to take flight from Omaha. When she had finished, Hattie assured her that any woman worth her salt would have done the same. As for Polly, the confession served as a cathartic for her troubled mind, and she seemed to calm down enough to settle back on the pillow.

"You just rest here a bit," Hattie said. "I'm gonna go help Maggie finish servin'. Then I'll be right back." Confident that she would be all right, Hattie left her and returned to the dining room to help Maggie.

As she entered the back door to the kitchen, Hattie met Maggie coming from the dining room carrying an empty coffeepot. "Is she all right?" Maggie inquired.

"Yeah," Hattie replied. "She was mighty shook up from seein' that son of a bitch land on the doorstep. I don't know as how I blame her. He was a mean-lookin' son of a bitch." She shook her head as she thought about the confrontation. "I had a feelin' Polly had a stronger reason for landin' here in Deadwood than just lookin' for a place to make a livin'."

"I don't think we've seen the last of that man," Maggie said. "I don't mind admittin'

I was gettin' a little nervous myself back there. I swear, I thought for a minute he was gonna go for his gun right there in the dinin' room."

The thought caused a shiver down Hattie's spine, and she shrugged suddenly to shake it off. "I'll help you with them bowls. Then I think I'd better go on back to see if she's all right."

Always a fast eater, Lester Pierce untangled his long legs from the bench and stood up. With a brief good night to all in the room, he took his leave, pausing only to take a toothpick from the little glass in the middle of the table. He paused again at the door to work a piece of bacon from between his front teeth before stepping out into the cool evening. Standing on the small covered stoop, he worked the toothpick around in his mouth while taking in the night air, taking no notice of the dark figure lurking in the shadows. As Lester turned to step off the stoop, the figure was suddenly in front of him. "What tha—" was as far as Lester got before the eight-inch steel blade sank up to the hilt in his belly.

Drawing his breath sharply in terrified agony, Lester staggered backward against the stoop, his assailant stepping with him to stay pressed against him, his face almost touching Lester's. "This'll learn you to mind your own business," Bill Pike hissed, even as Lester began to crumple with the pain. In one quick motion, Bill jerked his knife from Lester's gut, and stepped back to let him fall. He stood there, unconcerned that others might come out of the dining room, and watched the wounded man's efforts to save himself.

Lester struggled to his hands and knees, one hand clamped over his stomach in an effort to contain the bloody flow from his insides. In desperation, he tried to crawl back up the step to the porch, gasping out for help. Bill watched for a second before planting a foot on Lester's behind and shoving the suffering man flat. When he heard someone approaching the door, he stooped down, wiped his knife blade on Lester's trousers, and disappeared around the corner of the building.

Tom Blanton was still strapping on his gun belt when he stepped out on the small porch. After pausing a moment to buckle it, he almost stepped on Lester's hand when he started down from the porch. "God-a-mighty!" he exclaimed, recoiling at once. After a moment to look right and left, he moved closer again to see who it was. It was not an unusual sight to see a drunk passed out in the street in Deadwood, and this was his first assumption. Kneeling down beside the body, he said, "Come on, feller, you was just about to get stepped on." He placed a hand on Lester's shoulder and rolled him over, recoiling for the second time when he recognized Lester Pierce. The faint light from the window of the dining room reflected from the dark pool of blood on the step, and Tom quickly withdrew his hand to keep from touching it. At that moment, Lester emitted a weak groan. "God-a-mighty," Tom gasped again. "Lester, what happened?" Not waiting for an answer, he said, "Just hold on. I'll go for help."

Instead of going for Doc Plummer, Tom ran back inside The Trough for help, thinking that Maggie and Hattie would know what to do. When he blurted out the news, almost everyone inside jumped up and crowded to the door to see for themselves. Only a couple of dedicated diners remained seated, pausing for only a moment before resuming their supper. As Tom had figured, Maggie took command of the situation. After a brief inspection of the ugly wound, she sent one of the men to fetch Doc Plummer. "A couple of you fellers pick him up and bring him inside," she ordered.

Without waiting for instructions, Hattie

cleared one of the two tables of dishes. "Put him down on the table," she said. "I'll get another lamp from the kitchen." She only glanced at the two boarders still seated at the other table when one of them asked if there were any more biscuits.

In the little shack that served as the ladies' living quarters, Polly Hatcher lay resting, unaware of the commotion in the dining room. Outside, a dark figure moved quietly through the shadows, pausing at the kitchen window to observe Hattie while she took a lamp from the table and disappeared through the door to the dining room. With no sense of haste, Bill then turned his attention toward the small building behind the kitchen. Trying the latch, he found the door unbolted and pushed it open. The soft squeak of the hinges was not enough to disturb the woman lying on the bed. He stood in the open doorway for a long moment, gazing at the sleeping woman lying helplessly on the bed. An evil grin of smug satisfaction spread slowly across his grizzled features as he relished the deed he was about to perform.

"Wake up, darlin'," he cooed softly as he shook her shoulder. "I want you to see your lovin' husband one last time."

Polly's eyelids fluttered as she awakened.

Confused at first, she opened her eyes wide when she suddenly realized it was Bill standing over her. She immediately tried to bolt, but he grabbed her and held her down. The terror he saw in her eyes was enough to force a chuckle from his lips. "Did you really think you was gonna get away with shootin' me?" he said, smirking. Confident that she was helpless to prevent it, he prepared to finish what he had come for. Just as he had done with his father, he clamped his hands over Polly's nose and mouth. But Polly was not as feeble as the old man had been. She struggled against him, fighting for her life, and was able to scratch his face to the point where he released his death grip with one hand in an effort to defend himself. When he did, she managed to wrest herself free of his other hand and scramble off the bed. Furious to have lost his advantage, he cursed her fiercely, pulled his pistol, and leveled it at her. The wicked grin returned to his face as he watched her cringe against the wall. Enjoying her terror, he kept the pistol trained on her as she slowly edged toward the door. When she was within a foot of the open door, he shot her. The bullet caught her in the chest and slammed her against the wall.

Knowing he had but moments before the sound of the shot brought someone to investigate, he lingered only briefly, regretting the fact that he didn't have the time to watch her die. He considered the possibility of dragging her out the door with him, but the sound of voices from the front of The Trough changed his mind. There was no time left. Gazing at the mortally wounded girl slumped in a sitting position against the wall, her eyes glazed and unblinking, a grim smile returned to his face. He quickly holstered his pistol and slipped out the door, satisfied that vengeance had been served. No more than a few brief moments had passed when a half-dozen boarders, led by Maggie Hogg, came running. No one noticed the shadowy figure sliding along the side of the building to be swallowed up in the darkness of the alley.

Hattie was beside herself with grief. "I shouldn't have ever left her alone," she admitted tearfully. "I meant to come right back, but then all that with Lester . . . I shoulda known that son of a bitch was just mean enough to do something like this." Her guilt was almost unbearable as she stood to one side while Doc Plummer did what little he could to ease Polly's suffering.

Bursting into the room moments after hearing the gunshot, Hattie and Maggie had been stunned to find Polly still sitting propped up against the wall. She stared at them with eyes wide open but unseeing as her life's blood soaked through the back of her dress and smeared on the wall. They had been forced to wait a few minutes for Doc Plummer to finish with Lester before he was able to attend Polly. During that time, the two women carried Polly to Hattie's bed, and tried to make her comfortable. The young girl was lost too deeply in shock to know one way or the other.

"There ain't much else I can do," Doc told Hattie. "She's hurt pretty damn bad. It's hard to say, but it looks like the bullet mighta struck her heart. I know it went through one lung. You can tell that by the way she's pushing up blood." He sighed apologetically. "I reckon it's up to her and the Good Lord now."

Life had not been kind to Polly Hatcher. It had been her misfortune to cross paths with Bill Pike. If this was God's plan, it was a sorry one, according to Maggie Hogg. Polly could evidently see no reason to prolong a life so filled with misery, so she elected not to fight. Passing what appeared to be a peaceful night, she opened her eyes briefly the next morning when Hattie leaned over her, then slipped into eternal sleep.

Later the same day, they buried Polly on a hillside overlooking a small stream that fed down to the creek. As soon as the service was over, Maggie approached J.D. Watts with a question. "Is anybody gonna go after that son of a bitch? I ain't heard no talk about a posse."

J.D. stalled a moment before answering. "Well, you know we ain't got no sheriff since Ben was killed."

It was obvious that J.D. was not enthusiastic over the prospects of joining a posse. Maggie looked around her at the handful of participants at the grave site. Other than she and Hattie, none were really mourners. They barely knew the unfortunate girl they had come to bury. J.D. Watts and Rufus Sparks were there to show a little support for Hattie. The other two men only came to help dig the grave. She turned back to J.D. "We just gonna let a man come in here, kill an innocent girl, knife Lester Pierce in the belly, and just let him get away with it?"

J.D. was clearly uncomfortable with the issue. Finally he stammered, "It ain't up to me, Maggie. I ain't the damn sheriff." Seeing the condemnation in her eyes, he wavered slightly. "I'll talk to some of the others, and maybe we can round up a posse," he said, hoping to appease her for the moment. Nothing came of it, which was no surprise to Maggie and Hattie. The town was content to just be rid of the likes of Bill Pike, and thankful that none of them had crossed his path. Life went on in Deadwood.

Chapter 9

"I knew it was here! I knew it!" Toby Blessings scrambled up the sides of the narrow crevice, oblivious to the scrapes on his knees from the rocky surface. "I just didn't know where to look." There had been far too much sign in the stream below him for it not to be there. And even though he had found little more than traces, he had been convinced that the real dust was hiding close by. His patience and determination had borne fruit, and his first thought was *Polly will see me in a different light now.*

After his disappointing conversation with Polly by the creek behind The Trough, he had stayed away from Deadwood — in part because of embarrassment, but also because he was determined to unlock the mountain's secret treasure. For the past three days, he had labored from dawn till dark, stopping only to eat a hurried meal of salt pork and occasionally some soup beans. The only time he was even close to having contact with another human being was when he heard a rider on the trail below his camp. It was late in the evening, and Toby paused to listen lest the rider might prove to be a claim robber. It was a suspicious time of night for anyone to be riding that seldom used trail.

Deciding it best to have a look, he doused his lantern, picked up his rifle, and made his way down through the rocks to a point where he had a clear view of the trail. In the darkness, he could tell very little about the rider now coming into view. Squinting in an effort to see more clearly, he could only say that the man was a stranger to him. Dark and heavyset, the stranger rode slumped forward in the saddle. From the way he had continuously prodded his horse, Toby figured he must have been in a hurry. That was all right with Toby. He didn't care to have folks discover his camp — especially strangers. *Not many people travel this trail out of Deadwood,* he thought. *Most people take the main trail.* He had continued to watch the rider until he disappeared from sight before returning to his camp.

Now, two days later, Toby rode his horse down from the mountain ridge to take the same trail into Deadwood. In his saddlebags, he had a four-ounce sack of gold dust. "Now we'll see who's a boy and who's a man," he uttered confidently.

It was midafternoon when Toby tied his horse at the hitching rail in front of The Trough. Already he could feel his heart beating faster in anticipation of confronting Polly with his status as a man of means. There was no one in the dining hall, so he walked by the two long tables, already set for supper, and out the back door to the kitchen. Maggie was at the stove, stirring something in a huge iron pot. Hattie was busy rolling out dough for biscuits. Both women paused abruptly when the boy appeared at the open door.

Toby quickly scanned the room, looking for Polly. He greeted the partners with a brief nod, then asked, "Where's Polly?"

Maggie and Hattie exchanged quick glances, but neither woman was anxious to give the love-stricken boy the awful news. Maggie, always the stronger of the two, took on the chore. "She's gone, Toby."

"Gone?" He didn't understand. "Gone where?"

"Somethin' awful's happened," she replied, then went on to tell him of Polly's death.

He was almost staggered by the impact of

her words. His head reeling, he stepped back against the doorframe for support, feeling an icy cold stab in the pit of his stomach, his young dreams shattered. Hattie moved quickly to help him. Taking his arm, she led him to a chair by the table. "Sit down, son," she said, "I'll get you a cup of coffee — unless you want somethin' a little stronger."

"I don't want nuthin'," he mumbled, still in shock, but he sat down heavily in the chair. Devastated, he shook his head, trying to clear it. His eyes were wide and staring, but he saw nothing beyond a blur. In that one paralyzing moment, his world had been destroyed. The hide pouch he held in his hand seemed no more than worthless sand without Polly to share it. He placed it on the table before him and stared at it. As he stared, a sudden recollection came to him: *the stranger.* The thought served to return him to his senses. "When was Polly killed?" Toby asked in a voice so softly that Hattie had to lean toward him to hear.

"Day before yesterday," she replied. "We buried her yesterday."

Two days ago, he thought. *It was him. I saw him.* He formed the picture in his mind of the dark, blocky man on the trail below his claim. He had been unable to get a clear view of the man's face at the time, but he was certain he would recognize him if he saw him again. At that moment, there was nothing in his life that held any importance beyond tracking down the man who had destroyed his dreams and revenging Polly's death. That the man was actually Polly's husband was completely lost on him. In his mind, Polly was as pure and innocent as any virgin born.

His mind made up, he looked up then to find both women staring at him. "I'll be goin' now," he stated simply, and got up from the table. The look of shocked disbelief had been replaced by one of grim determination.

"Where you goin'?" Maggie asked, concerned by the look on his face. "Why don't you set here a while with Hattie and me? We'll fix you somethin' to eat."

"No, thank you, ma'am. I ain't hungry. I've got things to do."

"You ain't thinkin' about goin' after that man, are you?" Hattie wanted to know.

"I reckon," Toby replied softly.

"Hell, boy," Maggie insisted, "that trail's two days old, and nobody really knows what direction the bastard headed when he left here."

"I know," he replied emphatically, still in a voice barely above a whisper.

Both women followed him to the door, attempting to convince him that what was done was done. He politely ignored their efforts. Maggie finally blurted out, "That man's a born killer. We've already lost Polly. There ain't no sense in you gettin' killed, too. It ain't gonna bring Polly back." Two days before, she had berated the men of Deadwood for making no attempt to go after Bill Pike, but Toby was just a boy.

Reading the thought in her eyes, he stated, "I'm more of a man than you think." Those were his last words to them on the matter.

Jordan Gray knelt by the small fire he had built in the crook of a shallow gully. He had selected this spot to make his camp because it was close by a strong mountain stream, but also because it afforded a long view of the valley. He turned the spit he had fashioned to roast the venison evenly. Then he shifted his gaze back toward the far end of the valley where he had been watching the approach of a lone rider.

Even at a distance of perhaps a quarter mile, Jordan was able to identify the rider. Very few white men traveled this part of the Black Hills alone — especially in recent months with Sioux activity what it was. This particular rider was easy to recognize because he rode a mule, and led a packhorse behind him. Most men did it the other way around. *Jonah Parsons,* he thought. Jordan had met up with Jonah on more than one occasion, even shared a camp with him for a week in the Wind River Mountains just that past winter. He couldn't suppress a smile when he recognized the crusty old trapper. Jonah had lived with Crazy Horse's band for many years until his Sioux wife died. After she succumbed to a fever one spring, he had taken to wandering the mountains, trapping beaver and fox, and trading the pelts for the little he could get for them at the trading post. Because he had lived among them for so long, the Lakota knew him well, and he was free to travel their hunting grounds without fear of harm.

"Hey, old man," Jordan called out when Jonah had approached to within fifty yards. "You still got your topknot?"

Jonah pulled up briefly, surprised, but not startled. "Jordan, is that you?"

"Yeah, it's me. Come on in, Jonah," Jordan replied.

The old man nudged his mule with his heels and proceeded toward the low ridge that concealed Jordan's camp. "I thought it might be you," he said. "Solomon smelled that ugly horse of your'n a'ways back." The mule flicked its ears slightly at the sound of its name. "And I smelled that piece of deer meat cookin' a long ways before that," he added, grinning.

Jonah was prone to exaggerate on occasion. Jordan chuckled and waved him on in. The old trapper dismounted and led his mule over to the stream near Jordan's horse. He dropped the reins on the ground, knowing the mule wouldn't wander. Solomon nudged up beside Sweet Pea and stuck its muzzle in the water. It amazed Jordan that Sweet Pea tolerated the mule. It was a different story for the packhorse, however. It made the mistake of pushing in beside Sweet Pea, and received a sharp nip on its withers for the effort.

"I shoulda known you'd show up just when the meat was done," Jordan joked.

"Why, of course," Jonah replied smugly. "But I figured you'd be glad to share when you found out I've got a sack of coffee." He opened a pack and pulled out a sack of green coffee beans. "I traded some fox plews in Deadwood for this. A sack of coffee, and a few other little trinkets is about all I got for prime plews. A man can't hardly make a livin' no more."

"I reckon you're right," Jordan replied.

"But you look like you're makin' it all right since I last saw you."

Jonah shook his head and stroked his gray chin whiskers thoughtfully. "I don't know, Jordan. I swear I don't know how many more winters I can stand. The cold goes right to my bones anymore, and it aggravates my rheumatiz somethin' awful." He thought about that for a moment before continuing. "But damned if I wanna spend the rest of my days in a settlement. I couldn't wait to trade my plews and git outta Deadwood."

Jordan smiled. "I was there myself a few days ago. I musta just missed you. How long were you in Deadwood?"

"Just long enough to trade my plews," Jonah replied. "And long enough to hear about your little tussle with the vigilantes," he added. "I don't stay around places like that very long. There's too much trouble in that town. Why, some low-down varmint come into town and killed a woman in that eatin' place while I was there."

This captured Jordan's attention immediately. "The Trough?" he blurted. "One of the women at The Trough?"

"Yeah, I reckon. I don't know the name of the place. It were that place run by them women. Some feller just rode into town and shot one of 'em, pretty as you please, and rode on out. Hell, they said he knifed another feller before he kilt the woman. No, sir, I don't need to hang around a town like that."

Jordan was stunned for a moment before asking, "Do you know which woman it was that was killed?"

"No," Jonah answered as he went about smashing the coffee beans between two rocks. "They mighta said, but I don't know any of 'em, anyway — just one of the women is all I know." He looked up to discover the deep concern in Jordan's face then. "Why? Do you know them women?"

"I do" was Jordan's terse reply, the only response he could utter for a few moments as the shock of Jonah's news left him speechless. *Maggie? Hattie? Or was it the young girl he had just recently guided there — Polly?* "You don't remember hearin' a name?" Jordan insisted. "Maggie? Hattie? Polly?"

"I don't rightly recall," Jonah replied. It was obvious now that it was of more than casual interest to Jordan. "The feller that told me just said one of the women."

"Did he say who the killer was?"

"All I know is that it was some stranger, just come into town," Jonah answered. "I wish I could tell you more, but that's all I know."

Jordan leaned back against a tree trunk and closed his eyes while he tried to decide what to do. Maggie and Hattie were like family to him. They had stood by him when the whole town of Deadwood was out to lynch him. He had to go back to find out for himself which of the women had been killed. And then he had to find the man who murdered her. There was really no decision to be made. He owed it to Hattie and Maggie. The more the picture formed in his mind of one of them brutally cut down, the more tense he became until he finally stated, "I'm headin' for Deadwood at sunup."

"I figured as much," Jonah said. He had been reading the deep concern in Jordan's face.

It was a deep, moonless night that cloaked the sleeping town under a shroud of darkness, serving to soften the raw edges of the lawless mining settlement. In the lateness of the hour, even Sweeney's Silver Dollar Saloon was dark, the last drunken miner having gotten no farther than the corner of the building before slumping unconscious against the wall. A stray dog, searching for scraps, paused to sniff the sleeping man's trousers. Seeing the lone rider walking his horse slowly down the center of the dusty street, the cur dropped its head and slunk around the corner of the building, expecting some form of abuse. Deadwood, the town that never slept, finally lay in peaceful slumber.

With a cautious eye, Jordan rode past the darkened saloon, making his way unhurriedly toward the end of the street, past the jail and the blacksmith's forge, until he came to the alley that ran between The Trough and the hotel. There he paused for a few moments to look around before entering the dark passage.

"What tha . . . What is it?" Maggie Hogg stammered, having just been dragged reluctantly from a sound sleep.

"Somebody's knockin' on the door," Hattie responded, sitting up on the edge of her bed.

"What time is it?"

"I don't know," Hattie replied, her voice heavy with sleep. "I can't see the clock, but it's damn sure too early to get up." They heard the light tapping on the door again.

"Some damn drunk that can't find his way home, probably," Maggie growled. "Might as well see who it is, 'cause it don't sound like he's gonna go away." She reached under the bed and drew her pistol from the holster.

Hattie, standing by the door, paused to make sure Maggie was ready before demanding, "Who is it?"

"Jordan Gray," came the muffled reply.

Hattie quickly threw the bolt and opened the door. "Jordan — my God!" she exclaimed. "Come on in here!"

Upon hearing who their late-night visitor was, Maggie immediately got up from her bed. Jordan slipped inside the door as Maggie was lighting a lamp. Seeing the two partners, standing unabashed in their nightgowns, he realized the murder victim had been Polly Hatcher. While there was an immediate feeling of relief to find his two old friends safe, he could not rejoice. He did not know Polly well. The time spent with her was brief, but he was with her long enough to know that she was a decent girl, and undeserving of the end she had met.

"I apologize for wakin' you up," Jordan said. "But if I waited till sunup, somebody mighta took a shot at me."

"Boy, that's the God's honest truth," Hattie remarked. "What in the world are you doin' here?"

"Well, I ran into Jonah Parsons back in

the hills. He said a woman had been killed, and I came to see if you two were all right."

"It was Polly," Hattie replied softly, the mere mentioning of the name bringing a look of sad regret to her face. "My sister's baby, and I sent her back here alone like a lamb to the slaughter."

Maggie interrupted. "It weren't your fault, Hattie. None of us figured the bastard would do something like that." She then proceeded to relate the entire incident to Jordan. When she finished, he was left with a deep feeling of anger. He could think of nothing appropriate to say that might ease Hattie's feeling of guilt, except to echo Maggie's words.

"Maggie's right, Hattie. It wasn't your fault he killed her. A man like that would have eventually found a way to get to her. It was just a matter of when." No one said anything for a few moments, each forming an image of Polly's face in recall. Jordan found that the brutal murder of the young girl ignited a spark of fury inside him. According to what he had just been told, Polly had suffered a great deal in her brief journey on God's earth — more than he could reasonably explain. She had been forced to run away from her abusive husband, only to suffer the tragic encounter with Jim Eagle

— then to end her life at the hands of a vengeful killer. If there truly was a God who looked after good folks, why did He let things happen that way? He shook his head to rid his mind of questions that had no answers. Every time he delved too deeply into matters relating to God and the why of things, it only served to complicate his sense of reason. He found he was more comfortable when he just accepted what his eyes told him. For whatever reason, God made coyotes. The four-legged variety served a useful purpose. The two-legged kind served no purpose, and were best eliminated. Jordan decided at that moment that he would undertake the responsibility to rid the world of Bill Pike.

"This Pike," Jordan finally asked, "did a posse go after him?" When both women replied no at the same time, he shook his head in disgust. "They damn sure never missed an opportunity to get one up to come after me."

Maggie couldn't resist raising an eyebrow when she reminded him, "There ain't no sheriff here since you shot the one we had. And there ain't been nobody willin' to take the job."

"I didn't have much choice on that one," Jordan quickly replied in defense of Ben

Thompson's death. "I let him go, but he tried to put a bullet in my back."

"We never thought it was anything but that," Hattie immediately assured him. Maggie nodded her agreement.

"Anybody have an idea which way Pike headed after he killed Polly?"

"Nobody seemed to care but Toby Blessings," Maggie answered regretfully. "He said he saw a stranger headin' up the old east trail toward Wolf Valley."

"Who's Toby Blessings?"

She explained that Toby was a boy who had been totally infatuated with Polly. She paused, watching him closely. "You goin' after him?"

Jordan nodded thoughtfully, then replied, "I reckon." He missed the look of gratitude on Hattie Moon's face. "Now I expect I'd best get outta here and let you ladies go back to bed."

"Hell," Maggie snorted. "It ain't no use to go back to bed now. It's almost sunup — time to get the fire started in the kitchen stove."

Jordan walked over to the small window and pulled the heavy curtain aside. Maggie was right. The first rays of the morning sun were already probing the shadows between the buildings. They had talked longer than he intended. He had planned to be gone from Deadwood before daylight. "I'd best be goin'," he said.

Moments before Jordan looked out the window, Rufus Sparks took a shortcut behind The Trough on his way from the hotel to the stables. He stopped dead in his tracks when he saw Sweet Pea behind the building, standing, reins on the ground, patiently waiting. There was no doubt in his mind. No one else rode an ugly horse like the one he was gaping at — no one but Jordan Gray. His heart pounding, he turned on his heel and ran back up the alley to give the alarm.

At that early hour, there were only a few souls stirring, but Rufus' cry of alarm was sufficient to flush out several of the town's citizens. Whitey Hickson stuck his head out the door of the sheriff's office, where he had spent the night after staying at the Silver Dollar too late to return to his claim. Seeing Rufus running up the center of the street, he called out to the excited man, "Rufus! What the hell are you hollerin' about?"

Without taking time to catch his breath, Rufus stammered, "Jordan Gray, that's what!"

"What . . . where?" Whitey demanded.

"At The Trough," Rufus answered, still gasping for breath. "I seen his horse back in the alley."

Struck by an immediate fear that Jordan had returned to extract vengeance from the town that had caused him such pain, Whitey's first instincts were to lock the door and lay low until Jordan rode out of town. Only Rufus' excited insistence kept him from doing so. Whitey was forced to take some action. "Go get J.D.," he said. "He stayed in the hotel last night." He hurriedly turned to look for his boots. "And get anybody else you see," he called after Rufus, who was already on his way to the hotel.

In spite of the commotion already taking place in the street, Jordan was unaware that his presence was known as he stepped up in the saddle. The noise in the street was effectively muffled by the long alley that made a turn behind the kitchen before it opened by Maggie and Hattie's sleeping quarters. He was already seated aboard Sweet Pea, the two women standing by his stirrup, when the faint sound of some activity reached his ear.

"Uh-oh," Maggie said softly. "Somethin's goin' on. You'd better be careful, Jordan."

Thinking that to be sound advice, Jordan

decided it best to avoid the alley, and go around the other side toward the stables. He turned Sweet Pea's head and gave her a gentle nudge. "You two take care of yourselves," he said as he walked his horse toward the back corner of their little shack.

A rifle ball whistled past his ear just as he cleared the corner. By the time the sound of the shot was heard, he had dropped the reins, and pulled his Winchester. Overly apprehensive, Whitey had fired prematurely, jerking his rifle up and firing as soon as he saw Sweet Pea's head clear the corner of the building. Now he found himself in a bad situation because Jordan was quick to spot him behind the watering trough, and promptly sent a shower of lead his way. Unwilling to shoot it out with the likes of Jordan Gray, Whitey crawled away from the trough, and sought protection in the stable.

With no way of knowing where or how many were lying in ambush, Jordan was forced to make a decision. There was no option to stay where he was. He was going to have to make a run for it. Because the voices he had heard before seemed to have come from the head of the alley on the other side of The Trough, he guessed that his best chance of escape was out the north end of town past the stables. The only problem was the fact that Whitey was hiding in the stable now, and would be in position to get a clear shot at him as he rode past. He had decided he was just going to have to risk it when he was startled to hear Maggie's shrill voice beside him.

"Whitey! Hold your fire," she yelled. "I don't want you shootin' me!" Then to Jordan, she said, "Take your foot outta the stirrup and give me a hand." She reached up to get a boost.

Puzzled at first, he then realized what she proposed to do. "No. That's too dangerous, Maggie. You'll get yourself shot."

"Move your foot," she insisted. "He'd better not shoot me. Hattie'll cut off his rations — if she don't kill him." She rapped on his boot impatiently. "Move your foot, dammit, and give me a hand."

He still refused, unwilling to place her in harm's way. Sweet Pea had already started to walk toward the stable when Maggie suddenly grabbed his boot and jerked it out of the stirrup. Surprisingly spry for a woman of her years, she stuck her foot in the stirrup and grabbed onto Jordan's leg. He had no choice but to reach down and pull the determined lady up behind him, or else they both might have wound up in the dirt. "Maggie, you crazy . . ."

"Ride," she commanded, interrupting his protest. With both arms wrapped around his waist, she locked onto his back, and Sweet Pea was off with a bound. "Whitey Hickson may be a lot of things," she said, "but he ain't ever shot a woman that I know of."

"You might be the first," Jordan replied.

When Sweet Pea passed the stable at a gallop, Whitey ran out and raised his rifle to fire. Maggie was right. He couldn't take a chance on hitting her. He held his aim for a long time before he cursed in disgust, and lowered his weapon. He was standing in the middle of the street, watching the fleeing pair when he heard J.D. and Rufus running up behind him.

"Why the hell didn't you shoot?" J.D. demanded.

"He had Maggie up there behind him. I couldn't take a chance."

"Hell," J.D. snorted, "you coulda shot the horse."

"If he hadda, he'da got his ass full of buckshot." Startled, they turned to find Hattie standing at the corner of the building, holding her shotgun.

"You damn women," J.D. grumbled. Then he changed his mind about berating her, knowing he could never win that battle.

Turning to the other two, he said, "Reckon we oughta round up some more of the boys and go after him?"

"Hell, no," Rufus replied emphatically. "I ain't goin' after him."

"Me, neither," Whitey announced. "I'm gettin' damn tired of riskin' my neck goin' after that man. I say he's gone, well, good riddance. Who the hell ever said it was our job to go after every wild gunman that rides into town, anyway?"

J.D. stood thinking for a moment, then shrugged his shoulders indifferently. "Well, to hell with him, then. I need a drink." The three turned and walked toward the saloon.

"That's the smartest thing you ever did," Hattie clucked as they passed her. A scowl from J.D. was all she received in response. Already speculating upon the possibility of persuading Sweeney to open the saloon at this early hour, Whitey and Rufus ignored the remark.

Just past the edge of town, Jordan reined his horse up to a stop. "This oughta be far enough," he said. He held her arm while she dismounted. "It's a pretty good walk back to town," he commented apologetically.

"I reckon I can make it," she replied, laughing. Once she was on her feet, she straightened her nightgown. “I wonder how the town will like the new fashion?” she joked, pulling the gown up closer around her.

“You can take my coat,” he offered, reaching back for his pack.

She stopped him. “No. Hell, no. I ain’t worried about it. They all think I’m crazy, anyway.” She reached up and placed a hand on his arm. “You just watch yourself, Jordan, if you do run into that son of a bitch that shot Polly. He’s a mean one.”

He nodded. “I will, Maggie.” He nudged Sweet Pea, but reined her back after a few yards, and looked back at Maggie once again. “I’m much obliged, Maggie, to you and Hattie.”

“Don’t mention it,” Maggie replied, smiling.

Chapter 10

There was no point in wasting time looking for a fresh trail that might or might not be that of Bill Pike. Pike could have taken any direction away from Deadwood. Jordan knew if he ever met the man, it would have to be strictly as a result of pure luck. Where would a man like that likely head for? He could have decided to ride on to Bismarck and Fort Lincoln, or he might have returned to Fort Laramie. Hattie had said that the boy, Toby Blessings, had seen a stranger riding out toward Wolf Valley. That was a roundabout trail that crossed the main trail at the lower end of the valley. If a man continued on, crossing the main trail and heading west, he would eventually come out on the Belle Fourche — hardly the way to Fort Laramie. But Fort Laramie was where Pike had found out that Polly had gone to Deadwood. Jordan decided that because it was from Fort Laramie that Pike had come, he would most likely be heading back that way. But who could say for sure? Maybe he had reason to head for the Big Horns, or beyond.

Jordan had no idea what the man looked like — except for the fact he had a scar on his left cheek — or what kind of horse he rode, but Toby Blessings had seemed certain that the man he had seen on the Wolf Valley trail was Bill Pike. It was the only thing approaching a solid guess. There was nothing else to go on, so Jordan decided to follow the same trail.

As Sweet Pea carried him through the hills and valleys before the river, Jordan rode easy in the saddle, his mind occupied not only with thoughts of the manner of man he hunted, but also of obligations he had left behind in Laramie. When he had learned of Polly's decision to hire Jim Eagle as a guide, he had left a puzzled Lieutenant DiMarco wondering if his scout was going to return. *I expect I may have lost my job as a scout,* he thought. The possibility didn't overly trouble him. Scouting for the army was not his greatest ambition in life. He had witnessed Crook's arrival at Fort Laramie back in February, where the general had picked up three more companies of cavalry to join his campaign against the Sioux. At that time, Jordan was offered the opportunity to join a company of approximately thirty scouts under the command of Colonel Thaddeus Stanton. He had declined the offer. He judged the assembly of scouts to be no more than a collection of riffraff, cutthroats, and ne'er-do-wells — not the caliber of men he felt he could rely upon. The mere fact that, with that collection of scouts, Crook's column had attacked a Cheyenne village on the Powder River, thinking they had destroyed Crazy Horse's Sioux camp, was testimony enough that his assessment had been accurate. Until that point, the Cheyenne had considered themselves at peace with the army. Jordan had been at Fort Laramie when the news came back that Crazy Horse's village, his supplies and food stores, had been destroyed. He had been skeptical at once. His own feeling was that Crazy Horse was most likely camped on the east fork of the Little Powder. From what he had been told by Iron Pony, the village Crook's troops attacked was not as large as that of Crazy Horse. *Some scouts,* he had thought. *They can't even tell the difference between a Cheyenne and a Sioux camp.*

Now, as Jordan approached the Belle Fourche, General Crook's column was about to set out from Fort Fetterman, once again in search of Crazy Horse's Oglala Sioux. *He damn sure better be ready for a fight if he finds him,* Jordan thought. Then he put it out of his mind. He had other things to think about — primarily a man with a four-inch horizontal scar across his left cheek.

Jonah Parsons paused a moment to listen. Solomon, his mule, curled his upper lip and let out a low bray to alert Jonah that it had caught the scent of a strange horse. The mule was very seldom wrong about things like that, so Jonah got to his feet and moved away from the fire. *Might be a horse, might be a wolf or coyote,* he thought. There was no sense sitting by the fire where he would make an easy target. Unlike most white men, Jonah had no fear of trouble from Sioux or Cheyenne war parties. He was well known by local bands of both tribes, and generally accepted as one of them. Still, it was always best to be cautious anytime when traveling alone in this part of the world.

As usual, Solomon was right. Jonah knelt just below the rim of a gully, his rifle ready, his aging eyes searching the darkness for sign of any movement when he heard his visitor call out. "Hello, the camp!" It was a white man by the sound of his voice, but Jonah could not make him out as yet.

"Hallo, yourself," Jonah returned, still straining to see who was approaching his camp.

"I'm comin' in. All right?"

"Come on then," Jonah replied.

After a few moments, the form of a single rider appeared, moving up from the willows by the creek. Still cautious, Jonah remained where he was in the dark shadow of the gully, watching the stranger carefully. When it was obvious the man was traveling alone, Jonah stepped back into the firelight to greet his visitor. "Howdy," he offered guardedly, still wondering what possessed a man to be riding around the prairie in the middle of the night.

"Howdy," Bill Pike returned, and stepped down from the saddle. Noticing that Jonah was still careful to keep his rifle ready, he sought to put the old man at ease. "You got no call to worry about me. I just caught sight of your fire and thought you might have a cup of coffee to spare."

"You pick a strange time of night to travel," Jonah remarked.

"Well, to tell you the truth, I'm in a hurry to get to Fort Laramie. I'm plumb out of supplies, and I ain't had much luck huntin', so I've been ridin' at night to make up time."

Jonah studied the man's face for a moment. It was not a kind face, he decided. It might be a good idea to keep a careful eye on him. "Come from the Black Hills, I bet," Jonah finally said. "Lookin' for gold till your supplies run out."

A sly grin formed on Bill's face. "Well, now, that's a fact, all right."

Jonah relaxed his grip on the rifle. "There's coffee in the pot. Help yourself." He paused, watching for a moment as Bill filled a cup. "You say you're headin' for Fort Laramie?" When Bill nodded, Jonah continued, "Well, if you just come from the Black Hills, you ain't hardly headed to Fort Laramie. You're headin' west, toward the Powder River country." He pointed toward the south. "Laramie's that a'way." *And you ain't the first dumb-ass pilgrim to go wandering around lost,* he thought. "Git yourself some of that deer meat on the fire. I got plenty."

"Much obliged," Pike said, somewhat irritated to find out he had been traveling in the wrong direction. He tried not to show it as he eagerly helped himself to Jonah's supper. "I reckon a man gets a little confused travelin' at night."

"I reckon," Jonah replied while thinking that it never happened to him.

"Where are you headed?" Bill asked as he devoured a chunk of meat the size of his fist. Now that his hunger pangs were subdued, he glanced around the little camp, taking inventory of Jonah's possessions. Returning his gaze to the old man, he told himself that it might have been good fortune that he had stumbled upon Jonah's camp.

"Powder River Valley," Jonah answered in reply to Bill's question.

"What's at Powder River?" Bill asked.

Jonah shrugged. "Nothin' much but a whole heap of soldiers and maybe just as many Injuns." He could see at once that his answer puzzled his visitor. "The soldiers set out to find Sittin' Bull and his folks," Jonah explained. "They're supposed to have set up a stagin' point at old Fort Reno."

"What the hell would you wanna go there for?"

Jonah smiled patiently. It was like trying to explain the lure of the high mountains to a child. "There's bound to be a helluva fight when them soldiers catch up to Sittin' Bull and Crazy Horse."

Jonah's answer left Bill still puzzled. "You mean you're goin' there to see the fight?"

Jonah tried to explain that there were other reasons for his interest in the outcome of General Crook's campaign to force the Sioux back to the reservation. Jonah had many friends among the Lakota and Oglala bands. His concern was for their welfare, for he knew they would not go peacefully. He had never met General Crook or any of his officers, but they had evidently heard of him, for they had left word at Fort Laramie inviting him to join the company of scouts with the expedition. They had probably been told of his long years living with the Lakota, and figured he would be valuable to the campaign. Jonah was more interested in the fate of his adopted tribe. He was acting upon the general's invitation simply because he hoped to help prevent undue abuse of the free-roaming Indians.

"And you ain't never met any of the officers with the general?" Pike asked.

"Nope."

"They're willin' to hire you on, sight unseen? Pay you five dollars a day?" Bill asked. "For doin' what?"

"Like I said, scoutin'. Only I ain't sure I'll take a job to scout agin my own people."

"Hell, they's Injuns, ain't they?" Bill's mind was already working on a possible deal for himself. Five dollars a day for shooting

Indians sounded like something he'd be interested in. "How 'bout I ride along with you? I'd like to do a little scoutin' myself."

Jonah was hesitant, not at all enthusiastic about Pike's proposal. "I don't know, mister. I generally ride alone."

"Hell," Bill prodded, "you said yourself it ain't much more than two days from here. And then we can part company." He paused, waiting for Jonah's response. When Jonah continued to stall, he pressed. "Come on, old man. You know the way, and I don't. Just let me ride along with you till we get to the Powder, and then we'll part company."

Jonah shook his head impatiently. "How you gonna scout if you don't even know how to find Fort Reno?"

"You just get me there. I'll take care of the rest."

"All right," Jonah finally conceded. "I'll take you to Fort Reno, but you're on your own from there." He didn't care for the prospect of traveling with Bill Pike, but he figured that if he didn't take him along, the man would simply follow him. And it might be wise to have him closer just to keep an eye on him.

They struck camp early the next morning, and headed off in a northwesterly direction. The morning sun lit the tall peaks of the

Big Horn Mountains in the distance, causing them to sparkle like polished silver. The tallest in the chain of mountains, Cloud Peak, gleamed white and icy in the clear morning air. It was cold during the early hours, with a light frost on the higher ridges, but by midday, the sun had warmed the prairie to a more springlike comfort.

The two men rode along in silence. Few words passed between them the entire day until they made camp by the banks of a small trickle Jonah called Crow Creek. As a rule, Jonah talked very little at any time, usually no more than a word here and there to his mule. But his tongue could loosen up on the rare occasion when he had company, like a few days back when he had encountered his friend, Jordan Gray. This dark, bulky man with the scar on his face was of a different breed in Jonah's judgment, however. And Jonah found little to say to him. Watching the careless way Bill tended his horse, Jonah shook his head in disgust. He was overcome with a sudden nostalgic longing for the old days, when he felt like the only white man between the Belle Fourche and the Wind River Mountains. *It's getting so a man can't travel a week without running into some fool greenhorn from back east,* he thought.

In contrast to his silent traveling companion, Bill Pike became quite talkative once they made camp. Helping himself to Jonah's coffee and venison, he bombarded the old man with a flood of questions about the country they were riding into and the Indians who roamed the land there. Jonah reluctantly answered his questions, with no more than a grunt whenever possible.

"How much farther to Fort Reno?" Bill asked.

"Half a day," Jonah grunted.

"That way?" Bill questioned, pointing west.

"More or less," Jonah replied. "Just follow the crick — even you could find it." He couldn't resist adding that last barb.

"Is that so?" Bill responded. A thin smile creased his face. It was the news he wanted to hear. He stood up and gazed down the course of the creek for several long moments as if imprinting the direction on his mind. "Half a day," he muttered as he continued to gaze. Then he turned back to face the old man. "Like you say, even I could find Fort Reno from here." He favored Jonah with a wide smile. "I reckon this is where you and me part company, old man." He pulled his pistol and leveled it at Jonah.

Jonah acted instantaneously. Diving across the fire, he lunged at his adversary, drawing his knife as he rolled on the ground.

Startled by the old man's sudden reaction, Bill was nevertheless nimble enough to quickly step out of the way. At point blank range, he squeezed the trigger and took another step back as the bullet smacked hard into Jonah's chest. The old trapper continued to charge, a look of savage fury gripping his face. While constantly back-pedaling, Bill pumped three more slugs into him before he finally crumpled to the ground.

After a few moments to make sure Jonah was finished, Bill stepped closer to gaze down into his face. Although faint, there was a spark of life still burning in the old man's eyes. "You caused me to waste a helluva lot of lead, you old fart." He stood over him for a few moments more before leaving him to die while he returned to the fire to finish his supper.

He checked on the old man once more before bedding down for the night. "You're a damn stubborn ol' cuss," he complained when he discovered movement in Jonah's eyes. Not willing to risk a miracle recovery during the night, he clamped his hands tightly over Jonah's nose and mouth, and held them there until the old man finally cashed in. Jonah was so far down death's dark avenue that he made no effort to resist. Sitting on his heels, his hands clamped over the old man's face, Bill could not help but think about his father's death. "Maybe you'll meet up with my old man in hell," he said.

Satisfied that he would not be disturbed by a resurrection of Jonah Parsons during the night, he settled down by the fire to sleep. In the morning, he would sort through Jonah's possessions, taking what might prove useful, discarding the rest. He decided he would cut the mule loose, and take Jonah's packhorse. Pleased with the way things had worked out, he rolled over on his side and pulled his blanket over his shoulders. *It's been a good day,* he thought as he drifted off to sleep.

Colonel Thaddeus Stanton, commander of the company of scouts, studied the face of the man before him. He had to admit that the man standing in a confident slouch at the entrance of his tent presented nothing akin to the picture he had formed in his mind. When Colonel Bradley had suggested sending for Jonah Parsons, it seemed to Stanton that Bradley had referred to Parsons as an *old* scout. This man, with a gaze that could only be described as insolent, looked to be too young to have had all the experience he was said to possess. The colonel shook his head, dismissing his doubts. He had been wrong in his judgment of half the company of cutthroats who passed as scouts for General Crook — this one should fit right in. Stanton had come to rely upon the few good scouts he had already: Frank Grouard, Ben Clarke, Louis Richaud, "Big Bat" Pourier, and "Little Bat" Gaunier. These men had proven to be good dependable scouts, but they should benefit from Jonah Parson's many years living with the Sioux.

"All right, then, Mr. Parsons," Stanton said, signaling the interview's end. "I'll have the clerk add your name to the roster." He got up from the campstool he had been seated upon. "We'll be moving out in the morning, heading up the Powder. Reports we've been getting tell us that there are plenty of Indians camped along the Rosebud. The general thinks it may be the main camp."

Bill grinned and nodded. Then he turned and walked away, pleased with his successful charade. He hadn't the slightest notion where the Rosebud was, but he felt sure he could tag along with someone who did.

CHAPTER 11

It had been an erratic trail since leaving the old path at the south end of Wolf Valley. The tracks almost seemed to be leading in a great circle, and Toby wondered if the man he followed might be traveling a lot at night. There appeared to have been no effort to cover his trail. At first, Toby was convinced that Pike was heading for Fort Laramie, but then the tracks crossed the trail that led south and continued toward the west. Wherever they led, however, Toby was bound to follow.

Before noon on the second day, he came upon a campsite on the banks of the Belle Fourche. The tracks told him that Pike had joined up with someone there. The tracks combined, and three horses left the campsite together, heading northwest. Toby gave no more than a moment's thought to the dangers of riding deeper into Sioux country. He had to speculate upon the meaning of the other two horses, however. Was it a chance meeting? Or had Pike planned to meet someone all along? Toby could only know for sure that he now tracked three horses — either three men, or two men and a packhorse — he didn't know which. A new thought came to trouble him. Now that Pike was riding with someone, could he be sure which one was Pike? Thinking back, Toby realized that it had been dark when he had seen Polly's killer. Unknown to him, for no one had thought to mention it, Pike could have been identified by a scar on the left side of his face. He shook his head to free his concerns. There were too many questions to think about. He told himself that he would know which one was Pike when he caught up with them.

He saw the buzzards circling when still a mile away. The sight served to remind him that he was riding deeper and deeper into Sioux country. Although he had never been there, he knew that he could not be more than a day, maybe less, from Fort Reno, the abandoned army post on the Powder River. The trail he had followed from the Belle Fourche now seemed to be leading straight for the spot where the buzzards were circling. He stood up in the stirrups and looked all around him, suddenly feeling uneasy. The stark and silent Big Horn Mountains stood forbiddingly to the west, seeming to remind him that he was trespassing upon Sioux lands. He looked back across the broken prairie from whence he had come. Blank and empty, it stared back at him, and thoughts of being one man — alone in a hostile country — began to steal into his mind. He promptly scolded himself for wavering in his commitment, and tried to recreate the image of Polly in his mind. But the picture was vague and uncertain. That served to worry him, for he had thought the vivid image of Polly Hatcher would burn in his brain for all eternity. No more than a few days had passed and already he was straining his imagination to recapture the lines of her face. But then he brought to mind the dark shadowy figure of Bill Pike, riding hard on the Wolf Valley trail, and his resolve was strengthened once again.

As Toby approached the circle of buzzards, he became even more cautious, searching the prairie around him constantly. The object that attracted the great birds appeared to be in a ravine that led down to a small stream. He urged his horse forward and dismounted at the head of the ravine. Drawing his Henry rifle from the saddle sling, he moved cautiously down the defile, leading his horse.

The object that had attracted the attention of the grisly scavengers turned out to be a man's corpse. It was not the body of Bill Pike. Of that Toby was certain. This was quite obviously a much older man. He had been shot four times in the chest, and his face was frozen in his final display of rage. It was not a pretty sight, for the body was already bloated, swollen, and swarming with flies. Toby glanced up at the buzzards above him. They were getting closer and closer to the ground. "Man oughta have a decent burial," he mumbled. It was already in the shank of the afternoon, but he decided he would still take the time to bury the unfortunate man. He didn't doubt for a minute that this was more of Bill Pike's work, and was no doubt the unlucky man he had met at the Belle Fourche.

Using a short spade he carried tied to his saddle pack, he started scratching out a shallow grave. He tried to make a start in the hard rocky ground several times before he found a spot that accepted his shovel. Then he set to the task with a will, working hard to fashion a grave.

"I expect you'd be Toby Blessings."

The sudden utterance, though soft and

nonthreatening, was enough to startle the boy so that he stumbled over the edge of the grave in his panic. Already off balance, he lunged backward in an effort to reach his rifle, only to trip over his shovel and land on the seat of his pants in the pile of freshly shoveled dirt. Still trying to gain a defensive posture, he rolled off the pile, and settled in a sitting position. Completely flustered, he looked up at the lone rider sitting his horse casually above him on the rim of the ravine. He knew without asking that it was Jordan Gray.

"I didn't mean to spook you," Jordan said when Toby got to his feet and dusted off his trousers.

Somewhat shamefaced and feeling foolish after having shown such panic, Toby said, "Well, you scared the hell outta me." He reached down and picked up his spade. Looking hard at the stranger, he asked, "You're Jordan Gray, ain't you?"

"I am. How'd you know that?"

"I just figured," Toby replied. Then he added, "And that ugly-ass horse." Maggie, Hattie, and even Polly had talked enough about the broad-shouldered army scout and his ungainly horse to give Toby a fair idea of Jordan's appearance. He had to admit that, at times, Polly's talk about Jordan had caused him to feel a slight bit of jealousy.

Unaware of her uncomplimentary reputation, Sweet Pea pranced regally as she descended the slope of the ravine and halted obediently when Jordan dropped the reins and dismounted. With no more than a cursory nod to the boy, he walked over to take a look at the corpse. Although the bloated condition of the body made identification difficult, he recognized it at first glance. *Poor devil,* he thought, shaking his head sadly. *Sorry luck to cross paths with that murdering dog.*

Watching Jordan's reaction to the body, Toby asked, "You knew him?"

Jordan continued to stare at the corpse for a moment longer before turning away to face Toby. "Jonah Parsons was his name, and it was a sorry day when he met up with the likes of Bill Pike." He looked up at the ring of buzzards swooping just above the tops of the willows that lined the stream. "Let's finish that grave, and get him into the ground."

Together they finished burying Jonah amid a stream of raucous complaints from the disappointed buzzards rotating above them. When it was done, Toby looked expectantly toward Jordan. "Reckon we should say some words over him?"

Already walking toward his horse, Jordan replied, "Like what?"

"I don't know," Toby said, "Words of comfort, somethin' from the Bible maybe."

Jordan stepped up in the saddle. "Suit yourself. Words ain't gonna do Jonah much good now. Judging by the way that body was bloated, I'd say he has already met up with his Maker. And the longer I wait around here, the farther Bill Pike gets ahead of me." He wheeled Sweet Pea toward the stream, preparing to depart.

"Wait!" Toby exclaimed, running to his horse. "I'm goin' with you."

Jordan checked Sweet Pea for a few seconds while he thought it over. Maggie had said Toby was a decent kid, hard working and honest. But Jordan preferred working alone. Still, the boy had seen Pike, if only in a poor light. That was more than he could say for himself. Maybe it would be helpful to have him along. "All right, then," he said, "but let's get movin'. There ain't much daylight left."

They followed the trail left by Pike's horse and Jonah's packhorse for a distance of about two miles before Jordan decided Pike was headed for Fort Reno on the Powder River. After that, he was less concerned about tracking, and more interested in making better time. Sweet Pea set a steady pace that Toby's roan was hard pressed to match. At the end of the day, both rider and horse were more than ready to rest.

"Couple of hours in the morning and we oughta make Fort Reno," Jordan said as he pulled the saddle off Sweet Pea. It was only the second thing Toby had heard from Jordan since they left Jonah Parsons' grave. The first was "He's headin' for Fort Reno."

Toby had had plenty of time to speculate on the silent figure riding before him. He had heard people talk about Jordan Gray and, depending upon who was doing the talking, the scout was either a treacherous murderer or an honest avenger. Toby tended to put more stock in Maggie Hogg's and Hattie Moon's version of Jordan Gray. According to the two partners of The Trough, Jordan was a man to entrust with your life. Still, it didn't pay to put blind trust in anyone you just met in the middle of the prairie. Toby was careful to keep a cautious eye on his traveling companion. He rolled into his blanket that night with his pistol handy.

Although it was past the first of June, there was a light frost covering the ground when Toby opened his eyes a little after sunup the next morning. Looking at once toward the other side of the campfire, he was puzzled to find Jordan gone. Fearing something was wrong, he threw his blanket aside and sat up. His pistol in hand, he looked left and right expecting to find the worst.

"Don't get excited and shoot that damn pistol."

The voice came from the trees beside the stream, several yards behind him. *Dammit,* Toby thought, *why is that man always popping up behind me?* "What is it?" he blurted, still sensing that something was not right. Then he saw them — a dozen or more Indians, and they were heading toward them. Toby scrambled to his feet, and reached for his rifle.

"Take it easy," Jordan said. "They're Crow." He had watched them approach right at first light, and had positioned himself with his rifle in the trees by the stream. Relieved when he could see them well enough to identify them as Crow, he then was curious as to why they were riding away from the soldiers. He recognized two of the party right away, and knew that they were part of a company of scouts for the army.

As he watched, the party of Crows pulled up some seventy-five yards away, cautious now in their approach. Seeing them hesitate,

Jordan stepped out in the open and waved his rifle over his head. "Come on in, Iron Pony," he called out.

"Is that you, Jordan?" Iron Pony's reply came back, and he immediately prodded his pony forward.

"You're just in time for coffee," Jordan said when the Indians pulled up and dismounted. He was always happy to see his friends, Iron Pony and Otter, but he couldn't help but begrudge the time it would cost him to offer food and coffee to a party of Crow warriors. He nodded toward a grinning Otter, and offered a word of welcome in the Crow language to the rest of the party. Turning back to Iron Pony, he asked, "Why is it that you're headin' south? I thought you were scoutin' for the army."

"We go home now," Iron Pony explained. "Come back later." He went on to tell Jordan about the outcome of General Crook's expedition to find Crazy Horse's camp. According to Iron Pony, there were too many Lakota and Cheyenne. The column went into camp on the Tongue, and waited there until the Crow and Shoshone scouts showed up. By the time Iron Pony and his warriors arrived, the soldiers had moved down to Goose Creek, which puzzled the Crows. They were moving away from the enemy.

But after all the scouts arrived, they pushed north again up the Tongue, then crossed over to the Rosebud where they camped.

"The Sioux knew where we were all the time," Iron Pony said. "We saw Sioux scouts around us all the time. Still, Crook thought he was going to surprise them." He shook his head as if unable to believe his own words. "They attacked us one morning while the soldiers were still sitting around drinking coffee. We kept them from raiding the pony herds and chased them along the Rosebud. There were too many Sioux."

Iron Pony continued, saying that Crook had allowed his soldiers to be drawn out and stretched thin when they tried to pursue the Indians. Sioux and Cheyenne riflemen sniped at the soldiers from the gullies in the bluffs. Crook was forced to pull back in order to prevent major losses of life. Feeling they had won the battle, the Sioux withdrew and returned to their camp.

Jordan stroked his head thoughtfully. It sounded to him like the army had suffered a black eye in the initial round of fighting. "Where are the soldiers now?" he asked.

"Goose Creek," Iron Pony replied. "They say more soldiers coming, then they go after Sioux again. We're going home now, but we'll be back in two, maybe three weeks."

Finished with that subject, he inquired, "Where are you heading? To join the soldiers?"

"We're lookin' for someone, a murderer. Maybe you've seen him? A white man with a long scar across his face."

Iron Pony shook his head at first, then remembered. "The new scout has a scar on his face." He looked at Otter for help. "Parsons?" Otter nodded in agreement.

"Parsons?" Jordan echoed. "Jonah Parsons?" Iron Pony and Otter exchanged glances then nodded. He realized in a flash that Pike had not only taken Jonah's life, he had also stolen his name. "The army hired this man on as a scout?" When it was confirmed by both Indians, Jordan asked, "Is he still at Goose Creek?"

"He was there when we left," Otter said.

"Let's get goin', then," Toby interrupted impatiently, and started to get up.

Jordan stopped him with a firm hand on the boy's arm. "Just hold your horses. We'll let our guests finish their coffee first." He knew the importance of proper etiquette when dealing with Indians, and he didn't want to seem impolite by a hasty departure before giving the Crow scouts a chance to express their thanks for his hospitality. Toby frowned, unable to understand Jordan's lack of urgency, but he settled back down by the fire. Jordan turned his attention back to Iron Pony.

"Colonel Stanton — is he still commanding the scouts?" Jordan asked.

Iron Pony smiled and nodded. "Lead Bottom is still chief of all scouts," he said, referring to Colonel Thaddeus Stanton by the name the Crows had given him. It was inspired by the colonel's ability to remain in the saddle for long hours on end without dismounting to stretch his legs. Jordan knew Colonel Stanton well. He had scouted for him on occasion.

The coffee finished, the Crow scouts said their farewells and departed. Jordan and Toby saddled up and were soon on their way to Goose Creek. In less than an hour's time, they struck a large trail left by Crook's column on his march from Fort Fetterman. Jordan turned and followed the trail for another hour before reaching the staging point at Fort Reno. There, they saw supply wagons and tents for a hundred or more soldiers left to guard them. Jordan pushed on, hoping to reach Goose Creek by nightfall.

Midday found them at Crazy Woman Creek, after riding in the shadow of the Bighorn Mountains for half a day. At the rate they were traveling, Jordan realized that his plan to make Goose Creek by nightfall was not feasible. He elected to make camp near the ruins of Fort Phil Kearny, the site of the massacre of Captain William Fetterman's troop some years before. There was nothing much left of the old fort, but judging by the abundance of sign, Crook's column had apparently camped there on his march to the Rosebud. After the horses were unsaddled and left to graze, Jordan went about making a fire while Toby poked around some obscure articles left behind by the soldiers, hoping to find something of value. His search yielded a broken case of hardtack that had evidently fallen from a pack mule and rolled into some berry bushes. The contents were spoiled after a few days of frequent rain.

Jordan glanced up at his traveling companion when Toby came up to the fire, carrying an armload of dry branches. "Not much luck, huh?" Jordan said.

"Nope," Toby replied, surprised to hear Jordan initiate conversation. "Nothin' but some spoiled hardtack, and I don't like that stuff when it *ain't* spoiled." He had learned over the past two days that his somber partner wasted little energy on talk. He often thought about some of the things he had heard about Jordan Gray — some good, some bad. As far as he could decide, after having ridden with him a short time, the mystery of Jordan Gray lay somewhere in-between. He did decide, however, that his initial caution about the man was unnecessary. It was apparent that, like himself, Jordan Gray was after one man only.

"Maybe the next day or so we'll find some game, and we'll have somethin' to cook besides bacon," Jordan said. "The soldiers have run off all the game around here."

The next day before noon, they encountered pickets in the bluffs around Goose Creek. They were posted a good mile or so outside the camp proper. It was a big camp with the army supply wagons assembled in a huge circle between the two forks of Goose Creek. Jordan asked one of the pickets where he might find the scout company under Colonel Stanton's command. The picket didn't know exactly where Stanton was bivouacked, but directed Jordan and Toby to an area above the wagon corral where the main troops were encamped. "Much obliged," Jordan said, and prodded Sweet Pea. Toby followed, looking around from side to side, his hand resting on the stock of his rifle.

Riding along the left bank of the creek, they soon came to the main camp. As he looked around him, Jordan saw soldiers everywhere, but coming toward him, riding a chestnut stallion, was a familiar face. The name didn't come to him at once, but he remembered when the officer pulled up and recognized him.

"Well, Jordan Gray," the lieutenant declared. "I was wondering if you were going to participate in this action."

"Lieutenant Castle," Jordan acknowledged. "I thought you were assigned duty back at Fort Laramie, working for your father-in-law. What are you doin' out here?"

"I volunteered to join one of the reinforcement companies of cavalry after the first encounter with the Sioux on the Rosebud."

Jordan nodded, but refrained from passing on Iron Pony's view of that battle as a victory for Crazy Horse and the Sioux. "This here's Toby Blessings," he said, nodding toward the boy. "We're lookin' for the scout company."

Castle briefly recognized Toby with a nod before turning in the saddle to point toward the upper end of a long grassy tableland. "Colonel Stanton's tent is at the end of that plain, just before the bluffs."

"Much obliged," Jordan said, and nudged

Sweet Pea.

As Jordan and Toby rode off, Castle called after them, "I'd be glad to have you assigned to my company as a scout."

Jordan called back, "I ain't sure I'm gonna be scoutin' this time. Toby and me's got somethin' we've gotta do first."

They found Colonel Stanton in his tent, playing a game of whist with several other officers. The colonel excused himself for a few minutes while he came outside to talk to Jordan and Toby. "By God," Stanton exclaimed. "Jordan Gray — I thought you might show up." He extended his hand. "I can damn sure use you. Who's this you brought with you?"

Jordan smiled and shook the colonel's hand. "This here is Toby Blessings. I'm afraid I didn't come to join up with the column." The colonel's face immediately showed his disappointment as Jordan continued. "We ran into Iron Pony and a party of Crow Scouts yesterday," he said. "Accordin' to Iron Pony, you just hired Jonah Parsons on as a scout."

"That's a fact," Stanton replied. "I sent him off yesterday to see if he could locate the main Sioux camp." He paused, curious as to the nature of Jordan's inquiring. "Why? Do you have some business with

Jonah Parsons?"

"You might say that," Jordan said. "Not so much with Jonah as I have with his killer." Seeing his reply had confused the colonel, he explained, "We found Jonah Parsons' body two days ago. The man you hired murdered him."

Stanton was flabbergasted. "My God!" he exclaimed, at the same time feeling somewhat foolish at having been duped. "I had no reason to doubt the man's word." As he said it, he remembered thinking at the time that the man claiming to be Jonah Parsons was a much younger man than he would have expected. "Who is this impostor?" he asked.

"His name's Bill Pike," Toby volunteered, anxious to get on Pike's trail. "We need to get after him."

Jordan shot his impatient partner a quick glance before continuing. "Maybe you can tell us where Pike is lookin' for the Lakota camp," he said to Stanton. "Did he go out by himself?"

"No, I sent him out with two other scouts. They are to scout along the Tongue, and cross over to the Rosebud north of where the battle took place."

"Much obliged," Jordan said, and turned to leave.

A thought struck the colonel. "I expect if what you allege is true, this is a matter for the army to handle when Mr. Parsons . . . that is, Mr. Pike . . . returns from the scout."

"Yessir, I reckon so," Jordan replied as he and Toby prepared to climb into their saddles. *If he gets back,* he thought.

CHAPTER 12

Pepper O'Brien had been hunting and trapping the country from the Platte all the way north to the Judith River for more than fifteen years. During that time, he had never bumped into Jonah Parsons, although he had heard plenty about him. He guessed that they had never crossed paths because Jonah had lived with Crazy Horse's band of free-roving Sioux. And Pepper had made it his business to avoid the Sioux whenever possible — especially Crazy Horse's bunch.

He had to admit being somewhat surprised by how young Jonah was, now that he had finally met him. He and Royce Johnson had been detailed to accompany Parsons on a scout to find out where Crazy Horse may have moved his camp after the Rosebud fight. He had assumed that because he had lived with the Sioux for so many years, Jonah would have a fair notion as to where Crazy Horse liked to camp. As soon as they had left Goose Creek, however, Parsons had held back, allowing Pepper to lead the way up the Tongue. At first, Pepper guessed that Jonah was testing him and Royce to see how good they were. Now, after two days scouting the Rosebud above the valley where most of the fighting took place, Pepper began to question Jonah's skill as a scout. After riding with him for three days, Pepper decided he didn't like the man. There was something sinister and untrustworthy about him, and Pepper got the impression that Royce was of like mind. It was beginning to become painfully clear that this man claiming to be Jonah Parsons was in fact an impostor. Pepper decided to call his hand.

"How long did you say you lived with the Sioux, Jonah?" Pepper asked the casual question as they squatted around a fire, having their morning coffee.

Bill cocked a wary eyebrow and answered. "Longer than I care to think about," he said.

"How long was you married to that Sioux woman?"

"A spell," Bill countered, not anxious to give details he did not possess.

Catching a hint of what was going on, Royce chimed in. "You musta been no more'n a pup when you married her. You don't look all that old now." He shot Pepper a knowing grin.

"Yeah, I reckon" was Pike's curt answer. Not wishing the conversation to go any further, he got up and tossed the dregs of his coffee on the fire. "We'd best be movin'."

"I expect so," Pepper said. "Which way you think we oughta go? West to the Powder or east to the Bighorn? Where would Crazy Horse most likely go?" He winked at Royce.

Bill was beginning to get damned uncomfortable with the box he was being forced into, but he decided it important to try to bluster his way through. "I expect we'd better head west to the Powder. That's one of his favorite spots."

Neither of his two companions spoke right away, as they exchanged glances of total disbelief. Pike had walked right into it. After a long silent moment, Pepper closed the lid on the box. "I expect we'll be up to our asses in the Pacific Ocean before we strike the Powder if we head west. The Powder's to the east of us."

Realizing he'd been found out, Bill nevertheless attempted to talk his way out of it. "Hell, I know that. I meant to say east." He searched their faces, hoping to see they had bought the story. It was plain they had not.

"Suppose you lead us, you lying son of a

bitch." Pepper challenged. "Who the hell are you, anyway? You shore as hell ain't Jonah Parsons."

There was no use trying to prolong the charade. Bill scowled and turned to face Pepper. His pistol was in his hand. "This is who the hell I am," he growled. Pepper was taken by surprise by this sudden turn of events, and he realized too late that he had misjudged the evil in the man. He tried to scramble backward, but Bill fired at point-blank range. The first bullet caught Pepper in the face, the second in the chest. Pepper didn't even have time to cry out before collapsing flat on his back — dead.

Horrified, and as equally stunned as his partner, Royce found himself without a gun. His pistol had been hung over his saddle horn before he settled down by the fire. Now, as Pepper's face was split open by Bill's bullet, Royce scrambled to his feet and started to run for the horses. Bill gave chase immediately. Both men ran for all they were worth, Bill shooting at the terrified Royce. His aim was not that good at a dead run up a creek bank, so he missed the first two shots. Royce tried to zigzag, shrieking fearfully all the while. With only two bullets left in the .44, Bill stopped running and set himself to take careful aim. Royce dropped with two shots in his back.

Panting like a dog after chasing his victim, Bill walked slowly up to examine him. Though mortally wounded, Royce was still alive. "You done kilt me, you bastard," he forced the words out of his mouth, which was already filling with blood from his lungs.

Bill stood over the dying man, casually reloading his pistol. "The boys back at camp is gonna be real sad when I have to tell 'em you two was shot by Injuns." He curled his lip in a cynical grin. "I reckon you found me out. Was it worth it?"

Royce groaned with the pain that was now burning through his chest. "Oh, God," he gasped. "It hurts like hell." He turned pitiful eyes up to his executioner. "For God's sake, end it," he pleaded.

"Hell, you'll die before long," Bill growled. "What's the sense in wastin' another bullet?" He turned his back, leaving the man to suffer until death or the buzzards took him — whichever arrived first.

Concerned now that the pistol shots may have been heard by a roving party of Sioux, he deemed it prudent to vacate the ravine and start back to camp. Before leaving, however, he went back to take a look at Pepper's corpse, just to make sure he was dead. Satisfied that Pepper was done for, he then paused to consider which way they had come into this valley. "I may not know where the damn Powder is," he informed the corpse, "But I can damn shore go back the way we came."

Before mounting, he stopped to consider the dead men's horses. He was tempted to string them along behind him, but he knew he wouldn't be able to claim them if he took them back to Goose Creek. He decided they'd be too much trouble. *I'll just say the Injuns got them,* he thought. Neither victim had much of value. Bill took what he could use from the saddlebags and pockets, then hurried out of the valley. The creek and valley, named for the abundance of wild roses that grew in profusion along the banks, returned once again to silence, satisfied to be rid of him.

Backtracking by following the trail he and the other two scouts had taken into the valley, Bill had no trouble making his way back to the Tongue. Upon reaching the river, he turned south and followed it toward Goose Creek. As he rode, he rehearsed the report he intended to make when he got back to camp. *He was scouting ahead of the other two and, when he returned, he found that they had been ambushed by a party of Sioux war-*

riors. He, himself, was set upon by these same warriors, but he fought his way free, killing several of the savages in the process. Then, thinking it best to report the loss of two men to the colonel, he hightailed it back to camp. He liked the sound of it. It was downright heroic. So enthralled by his anticipated hero's welcome, he almost missed spotting the two riders on the opposite bank.

Seeing them just in time, Bill backed his horse into a gully lined with berry bushes, and hurriedly scrambled up to the rim to take a longer look. His first thought had been that they were Indians. A second look told him they were white men. Although from a distance, one of them could have been mistaken for an Indian. Bill studied the two as they followed the broken trail along the far bank. If they were army scouts, he had not seen them before. But in the short time he had been employed as a scout, he had not had the opportunity to meet all of them. He started to call out, but decided against it, reasoning that after they heard his story they might want him to lead them back to the bodies he had left behind. He preferred to give the buzzards and the coyotes a chance before anyone found Pepper and Royce. So he continued to lay low in the serviceberry bushes until the riders disappeared around a bend in the river.

Sweet Pea snorted and tossed her head as she usually did when catching the scent of a strange horse. Having learned to pay attention to the ornery mare's fits and moods, Jordan scanned the banks along both sides of the river, but could spot nothing out of the ordinary. He glanced back over his shoulder at Toby. The boy was plodding steadily along behind him, and showed no sign of concern. Jordan decided that Sweet Pea had probably sensed a coyote slinking along in the underbrush near the water's edge.

It was nearing dusk when they reached the Rosebud Valley, and although they had seen plenty of sign, they had spotted no hostiles. "There ain't much daylight left," Jordan commented. "I expect we'd better find a good place to camp. We can start lookin' for Mr. Pike in the mornin'. Accordin' to Stanton, he had two other men with him. If they scouted this part of the valley, we oughta be able to find fresh tracks of three horses easy enough."

A campsite was selected near the water where the Rosebud took a gentle turn toward the west before winding back on a more northerly course. There was good grass for the horses and a thick grove of willows to conceal their campfire. Jordan and Toby were not the first to select the spot. There were remains of an old fire tucked into a shallow gully that parted the willows. Jordan raked through the ashes. "Hard to say how long ago," he answered Toby's unspoken question. "At least a week, maybe more." He got to his feet again. "Let's see to the horses, and then we'll make us a fire."

They pulled the saddles off and hobbled the horses before leaving them to graze the new grass near the water's edge. Sweet Pea stamped menacingly when Jordan tied her feet. She was not accustomed to being hobbled. It was not her habit to wander far from Jordan, and she felt the need to show her resentment to what she deemed an insult. Knowing her feelings had been hurt, Jordan spent an extra minute stroking her neck and scratching behind her ears. He knew she wasn't likely to wander, but he wasn't willing to take the chance when there was such an abundance of Indian sign about.

The horses taken care of, they set about making coffee to drink with the little bit of bacon that was left. "We're gonna have to take some time to hunt before long," Jordan commented as he cut strips from the salted meat. "I can go just so long before I have to have some fresh meat."

Toby grunted his agreement, then said, "Jordan, when we catch up with Pike, I wanna be the one that shoots him."

Jordan took a moment to study the boy's face before responding. "Well, it doesn't make any difference to me whose bullet stops him. I reckon it'll just depend on what happens when we find him. Why, hell, if he just stands still and says, 'Go ahead, boys. Who wants the first shot?' then you're welcome to take it." Jordan watched Toby cock an eyebrow in response to his flip reply. Up to now, the boy had said very little about killing Bill Pike. In fact, he had little to say about anything — a trait that had pleased Jordan because it fit well with his own tendencies. He had evidently been smitten with Polly Hatcher. That fact was certainly evident.

Toby realized that his request may have sounded a bit naive, and he fumbled a bit when he said, "Well, I mean it's just that it's important to me to settle a score."

Jordan smiled and nodded his understanding. "If he's in this part of the valley, we'll find him. We'll do the whole world some good if we can kill that son of a bitch." He stopped to think about the statement that just passed his lips, and the casual irony behind it. He was struck by a brief moment of conscience, and he wondered at what point in his life he had come to talk about taking a human life in the same tone as killing a snake or a rodent. The spark of conscience lasted for no more than a brief moment, however, before flickering and dying when he recalled an image of Polly's face. Then he thought of Jonah Parsons, a man who had no enemies, white or red. Pike deserved a killing.

In the saddle again at daylight, Jordan and Toby started working their way south along the Rosebud, searching for fresh tracks or the site of a recent camp. There were many tracks, all from unshod Indian ponies, and a mass trail left by a large party of Indians. It was Jordan's guess that this trail was left when the Sioux retreated to their village after their victorious encounter with General Crook's troops. But the tracks Jordan and Toby searched for were not found until they had made their way some eight or ten miles toward the headwaters of the creek, and reversed their search to cover the same ground again.

They almost passed over them again before noticing two clear prints from a shod hoof beside a grassy bank that jutted out into the creek. "Whoa," Jordan called out. "I think we found somethin' here." He dismounted to examine the tracks more closely. "They seem to be pointing toward that ravine." He stood up and squinted against the afternoon sun as he studied the stand of cottonwoods that framed the entrance to a shallow defile. He was about to caution Toby to watch himself before riding into what could be trouble, but the boy didn't give him a chance. He kicked his horse hard, and charged into the mouth of the ravine, his rifle out of the sling. Jordan shook his head in wonder. Sometimes Toby could be exasperating.

Relieved to hear no gunshots, Jordan followed his impetuous young partner. He found Toby standing, staring at two bodies — dead for a couple of days by the look of them. "If I had to guess," Jordan said with no show of emotion, "I'd say these are the two scouts that went out with Pike." After a moment, he dismounted and stepped closer. "If I took another guess, I'd say this was the work of our man, Pike, 'cause it don't look like the work of Indians." There were no signs of mutilation, no missing scalps. He walked up the side of the ravine to take a look around. About a quarter of a mile down the valley, he spotted two horses grazing in the tall grass. They were still saddled.

Toby climbed up beside him, and immediately spotted the horses. "I expect we'd best round up them horses," he said. "I reckon we'll be totin' those fellers back to Goose Creek." It seemed the Christian thing to do.

Jordan didn't comment for a minute or more as he continued to stare out across the valley. When he finally spoke, it was in a soft, unemotional voice. "I expect we'd best forget about the horses, and leave the bodies where they lie." He pointed toward the high grass between the water and the horses. Toby stared at the spot indicated for several moments. Seeing nothing unusual, he looked at Jordan, puzzled. Jordan pointed again. This time he saw a gentle movement of the grass. He continued to stare and finally he saw what Jordan was pointing out. Forming a half circle, at least a dozen Sioux warriors were gradually closing in on the unsuspecting horses, their movement through the grass like that of a fox.

"Goddam!" Toby gasped, and started to raise his rifle.

Jordan immediately knocked it down. "Be

still, dammit! You wanna get us killed?" When Toby settled back, Jordan said, "There's a dozen warriors out there that we can see. There's no tellin' how many more there are that we can't see." He motioned toward the horses behind them. "Let's just back down off this rim nice and easy, and walk the horses out of this ravine. If we can cross over to the other side of the water before those Sioux find out we're here, we can probably ride on out of here with our scalps."

Toby acknowledged Jordan's instructions with a brief nod, and immediately backed down the side of the ravine. After another look to make sure they had not as yet been discovered, Jordan followed. There was no indication that the Sioux suspected their presence, but Jordan knew it would only be a matter of time. Finding two horses with white man's saddles and other gear, they would soon comb the ravines and gullies in search of the men who rode the horses. They would find the bodies of the two white scouts quick enough, and that might be the end of it. *On the other hand,* he thought, *they might want to find out who did the shooting.* At any rate, it was best to put a little distance between them and the Indians.

Using the ravine for cover, they led the

horses down into the water before climbing into the saddle. Once mounted, they pushed on across in water that came up to the horses' withers in spots before they scrambled up the opposite bank. Everything was going well until Toby's horse stumbled going up the bank, causing it to slide back a few feet. Unfortunately, it slid close enough so that its rump was in range of Sweet Pea's muzzle. As she was apt to do any time she was presented with the opportunity, Sweet Pea took a sizable nip out of the roan's hide, causing the surprised horse to squeal with pain and begin to buck.

"Oh, shit," Jordan muttered, and drove his heels into Sweet Pea's flanks. The mare responded, driving up the bank past Toby who was doing his best to remain in the saddle. "Don't you fall off that damn horse," Jordan commanded as he rode past, grabbing Toby's loose reins as he did. Wasting no time to look behind them, he galloped away from the creek bank, leading Toby's horse by the reins. In his mind, he pictured the warriors stalking the two stray horses, and figured they would probably pause when they heard Toby's horse squeal. With no way of knowing what had caused the sound, they would have no reason to immediately give chase. But when they discovered the two bodies, they would no doubt figure that the horse they heard cry out was ridden by a white man. And when they figured that out, Jordan intended to be a couple of miles away.

It was a reasonable plan, and may have worked had not another file of Sioux warriors appeared on the bluffs directly before the fleeing white men. Jordan pulled up sharply, causing Toby's horse to slide to a stop behind him. While he considered his options, Jordan tossed Toby's reins back to him. For the moment, white men and red exchanged stares, both surprised by the encounter. Suddenly, the silence was broken by a high-pitched call from one of the warriors on the bluff. Jordan didn't have to know Lakota to figure the warriors stalking the horses were being called to close in behind them. He turned to Toby. "I hope that horse of yours can run," he said.

"He'll hold his own," Toby replied.

Jordan was relieved to notice that the boy, though worried, showed no sign of panic. "Well, I reckon it's gonna be a horse race," he said. "Ready?" Toby nodded, and Jordan smacked the roan sharply on the rump, causing the startled stallion to bolt. Sweet Pea took off in pursuit without Jordan's urging.

The chase was on. Overtaking Toby's horse almost immediately, Sweet Pea surged ahead, and Jordan led as they raced along the narrow, grassy valley. The Sioux hunting party gave chase at once, descending from the bluffs and angling across the tablelands that sloped to the river. Avoiding the clumps of wild rose bushes that grew in profusion in the valley, Sweet Pea pounded the earth beneath her hooves, seemingly aware that she was being tested — and the ornery mare was determined not to lose the contest. Jordan bent low over her neck. His one objective at this point was to gain the end of the valley where the bluffs closed in to form a narrow passage. His major concern was Toby's horse, for he didn't know the strength of the stallion. One misstep as they galloped across the uneven ground and the race would be over. Glancing back over his shoulder, he was gratified to see that Toby's statement was accurate. The horse was holding its own, although falling back a little from Sweet Pea's torrid pace.

Several shots rang out as the Indians tried for lucky hits, but the distance was too far for accuracy. The bullets fell harmlessly in the grass behind them. Glancing over his other shoulder, Jordan caught sight of the Sioux he had first seen stalking the scouts' horses. They were racing along the other side of the river, and would have to cross over before warranting his concern. He returned his attention to the party driving to cut him off before he reached the end of the valley. Their swift ponies were equally up to the task, but the race was gradually going to the two white men — thanks to their initial lead.

After what seemed an eternity, Jordan reached the end of the meadow where the bluffs closed in. Reining Sweet Pea back hard, he was out of the saddle before she slid to a stop, rifle in hand. Moments later, Toby galloped in. "Get the horses back in that gully," he directed, handing his reins to the boy. "I'll slow our friends down a little." He ran back to a gully at the opening of the passage and settled himself to wait for the pursuing hunting party to get in range. It didn't take long, for they were already within two hundred yards when Jordan and Toby reached the temporary safety of the passage. He waited, taking an occasional glance back to see that Toby had the horses out of the line of fire. Jordan was as good a shot with a Winchester as any man, but he knew the effective range of the repeating rifle was one hundred and fifty yards at best. And he was not one to hope for lucky shots, so he waited. Toby scrambled up beside him, his Henry in his hand.

"Wait till they get to that little ridge," Jordan said, pointing to a swell in the open meadow about one hundred yards distant. "Take careful aim. You take that buck on the paint. I'll take the one next to him on the gray." The two warriors he singled out were racing ahead of the others. Jordan was confident that if they knocked those two down, it would effectively put a stop to the charge. The warriors would not continue to rush foolishly into an ambush.

Steadying their rifles on the rim of the gully, they waited patiently until the two leading warriors reached the designated spot. Almost in unison, two shots rang out, and the two warriors tumbled from their ponies. The other warriors scattered, immediately seeking cover. Jordan cranked another round into the chamber and sent another of their attackers to the ground before they could gain the protection of the rise.

"By damn, we stopped 'em," Toby exclaimed, his eyes wide with excitement.

Jordan reloaded his rifle, replacing the two spent rounds before answering. "We made 'em blink, but we sure as hell ain't stopped 'em." He slid back from the edge of the gully, and got to his feet. "Come on, we'd better not be sittin' here when they get up in those bluffs above us."

Realizing then that the encounter was far from over, Toby scrambled back after him. "You think they'll come back for some more after we already killed three of 'em?"

"They'll come back for more *because* we killed three of 'em," Jordan replied matter-of-factly. "And we ain't got more'n about ten or fifteen minutes before those bluffs on both sides of us will be swarmin' with 'em." Taking no further time for explanations, he ran for his horse. Toby paused only for a moment before following right on his heels. Thoughts of Bill Pike were far from their minds at that moment.

Riding as fast as possible over the narrow trail that followed close by the river, they hurried to reach a sharp bend about fifty yards ahead. Once they reached it, Jordan figured they would be shielded momentarily from Sioux rifle fire from the bluffs. The horses, only briefly rested after their sprint across the valley, responded once more to their masters' urging. But the angry Sioux warriors were quicker to reach positions among the crevices along the bluff than Jordan had expected. With still more than a dozen yards to safety, the cracking of their rifles suddenly split the air, sending lead snapping and ricocheting off the rocks around the fleeing pair. Jordan and Toby barely reached cover before a blanket of rifle fire covered the ground behind them. Safe for the moment, there was no choice but to keep moving. The Sioux warriors held the high ground and would soon trap them in a cross fire from the bluffs above them on both sides of the river.

"Come on!" Jordan called back to Toby when the boy reined back on his horse. "Our bacon is cooked if we stop here." He nodded toward the steep bluff above Toby's head. "If we're still sittin' here when they get to that spot, they can shoot right down our shirts." He nudged Sweet Pea, and the mare sprang forward along the bank. Although tiring quickly, Toby's roan gamely followed.

Knowing Sweet Pea's strength, Jordan's plan initially was to simply outrun their attackers. That plan had to be abandoned, however, because Toby's horse began to fall back before they had galloped another two hundred yards. Jordan pulled up to let Toby catch up. "Brownie's give out," Toby exclaimed when he reached Jordan.

Jordan nodded. He could see that for himself. He scoured the bluffs above them, looking for a place to make a stand. Another hundred yards or so and they would have cleared the narrow canyon, and come out on another meadow. One thing was clear — they could not stay where they were, for they were down at the water's edge while the Indians would soon be swarming the bluffs above them on both sides. Now that Toby's horse was too tired to make the all-out dash up the open valley, it might be suicide to continue following the river. Searching the gullies and ravines that cut the bluffs down to the water, he made his choice. "Up there," he said, pointing. "Let's lead the horses up that gully to the top of the bluff. It looks like it might be deep enough to hide the horses. We oughta be able to hold 'em off for a considerable time up there."

At this point, Toby had no opinion one way or the other. Whatever Jordan said was what he was ready to do. He hurried into the mouth of the gully, leading his horse after him, picking his steps carefully as he followed Jordan up the steep defile. Once they reached the top, they quickly looked the situation over. The gully they had just ascended from flattened out near the top of the bluffs. Now they were no longer below the warriors, but Jordan decided the position was too open after all. He looked around for an alternative, cognizant that the Sioux warriors could appear at any moment. "Up there!" Toby blurted out, pointing toward a large outcropping of rocks halfway up the hill behind them.

"That's as good as any," Jordan immediately agreed, and started running up the grassy meadow that sloped up from the bluffs. As soon as he reached the safety of the massive rock formation, he led Sweet Pea to a spot behind the rocks where she would be shielded from rifle fire. Toby followed suit. They had no sooner gotten their horses to safety when the first of the warriors appeared, winding their way quickly and carefully along the many slashes and gullies near the top of the bluffs. It was obvious that the Sioux thought the two white men were still following along the water's edge below, for they took no notice of the slopes above them, or the occasional rock formations on the grassy hillside. Jordan looked at Toby and nodded his approval on the boy's selection for ambush. Toby responded with a nervous grin.

"Let's wait and let 'em get directly below us. Then shoot fast, but aim careful," Jordan said. His hope was that if he and Toby could take out a few more of their party, the Sioux might decide their medicine was not strong, and break off the assault. He took an extra moment to study the boy's face as Toby concentrated on the bluffs now below them. There was nervous anticipation there, but no fear. Jordan decided the boy was all right.

It wasn't much of a battle. The unsuspecting Sioux had no reason to believe the two white men were not still hurrying along the river as it cut through the narrow pass. As a consequence, they were completely unprotected from the two repeating rifles above them on the hill. Jordan and Toby held their fire until the warriors reached a point directly below them. Jordan counted eight, five of whom carried rifles. When the lead warrior stopped, evidently discovering tracks where the white men had followed the gully up from the water, he turned at once to scan the hillside above them. His gaze darted across the grassy slope, and finally lit upon a large rock outcropping. Too late he realized that he was looking at two rifle barrels staring back at him. The next moment the Indians found themselves in a blistering barrage of rifle fire as Jordan and Toby cut down on them. Four of the warriors fell before the remaining four could scramble to safety in the gully. Effectively held in check, they had no choice but to descend the gully that Jordan and Toby had climbed up, for that was the closest cover available. A few random shots were fired back, but they glanced harmlessly off the rocks before the warriors retreated.

"Well," Toby sighed. "I reckon we stopped 'em again."

"I reckon," Jordan replied. He had a feeling that the loss of four more lives might be enough to discourage further pursuit. The Sioux hunting party had paid a terrible price in their efforts to capture the two white men, and it should be painfully clear that further pursuit would cost more lives. Few things were certain, however, so he deemed it best to take leave of the Rosebud for now.

Thoughts of Bill Pike and their reason to be in hostile territory resurfaced with the recent Sioux threat over. The image of the two white corpses returned to Jordan's mind as he led his horse over the top of the ridge. Had it not been for the sudden arrival of the Sioux hunting party, he might have been able to pick up Pike's trail away from the scene of the murder. *It didn't matter,* he thought. *Where would Pike likely go?* He would hardly ride deeper into hostile country, if he had any sense at all. He would most likely head back to Goose Creek, and the protection of the army because he was unaware that his masquerade as a scout had been uncovered. Jordan shared his thoughts with Toby, and the boy agreed with his reasoning.

"I'm sorry Brownie wasn't up to out-runnin' them Indian ponies," Toby felt compelled to say as he followed Jordan down the western side of the ridge. He was more than a little embarrassed that the sleek roan stallion had proved to be no match for the mangy-looking mare.

"Turns out it didn't matter, did it?" Jordan replied. "I think we put too steep a price on our scalps for 'em."

Toby couldn't help remarking, "I always thought Brownie was a pretty stout horse, but that blame mare of your'n —" He didn't finish.

Jordan smiled when he replied. "Sweet Pea was tired, too. She's just too damn stubborn to admit it."

CHAPTER 13

Sergeant Cary Cox rapped lightly on the tent pole before entering Colonel Stanton's tent. "Colonel, sir, Parsons is back," he said, a spark of urgency in his tone. "Pepper O'Brien and Royce Johnson are both dead, killed by Sioux hostiles. Jonah was just lucky he got out with his scalp."

Stanton put down the journal he had been writing in, and paused a moment to consider what his sergeant had just said. "Is that a fact?" he finally answered. He had issued orders to be notified immediately when the man claiming to be Jonah Parsons returned to camp. Pike was the man's real name, according to Jordan Gray, but Stanton had decided to keep this information to himself for fear that Pike might accidentally be tipped off. He intended to have him put under arrest as soon as he was back. Stopped momentarily by the sobering news that two of his best scouts had been killed, he had to consider the circumstances of their deaths. If they had truly been killed by hostiles, maybe they had found Crazy Horse's camp. If so, Pike could possibly be of some use even if under arrest for murder. "Sergeant Cox, take a couple of men, and bring Parsons to me."

"Yessir," Cox responded, puzzled by the order. "You want me to detail two men to go with me to tell him?"

"I believe that was what I ordered," Stanton replied curtly. "And I didn't say tell him to report to me — I said *bring* him to me."

"Yessir," Cox again responded, and turned at once to leave the tent — too long a soldier to further question orders.

When informed that Colonel Stanton wanted to see him, Bill Pike naturally assumed that the colonel wanted information about the fight with the Sioux. "Sure," he responded. "I'll be along directly, soon as I get myself somethin' to eat." He preferred to have as little contact with the army officers as possible.

"My orders are to bring you to the colonel *now,*" Cox insisted.

Pike was somewhat surprised by the sergeant's abrupt response. He glanced at the two privates accompanying Cox, neither of whom seemed the slightest bit interested, and a worm of worry began to tunnel away in his brain. Why did it take three soldiers to tell him the colonel wanted to see him? *Well,* he thought, *I ain't got much choice.* "Well, hell then," he said. "Let's go see the damn colonel."

Sergeant Cox dutifully escorted Pike to the colonel's tent. Stanton was standing outside awaiting them. "Here he is, sir," Cox said. "Will that be all?" He and the other two soldiers turned to leave.

"Not quite all," Stanton replied. "You men just stand where you are."

"Yessir," Cox said. He had better things to do, but his expression never revealed his impatience. He took one step backward to stand beside the two privates, his eyes straight ahead to avoid the curious glances of the two.

Stanton turned his full attention to Pike. "Now, then, *Mr. Parsons,* tell me what happened."

Pike repeated the story he had already told several times since riding back into camp. He modestly related how he had done his best to lead the other two scouts out of danger, but they had been killed by the hostiles. Stanton kept pressing him about where they had been attacked, and what sign, if any, had they seen of the Sioux village. Pike's answers were vague and hesitant. Stanton soon came to the conclusion that Pike wasn't even sure where he had been. He was not completely convinced that he and the other two scouts were even attacked by hostiles.

"Mr. Pike, I'm not sure you have any idea where to look for the hostile camp."

Pike was quick to protest. "Oh, I've got a'plenty ideas where them red devils is holed up. I've done a heap of scoutin' in this country." He looked anxiously at the colonel, confused by Stanton's intense stare. It then registered that the colonel had addressed him as *Mr. Pike.* In a moment of panic, he blurted, "Parsons. My name's Parsons."

Stanton had already seen the guilt in his face. "Mr. Pike," he repeated. "That is your name, isn't it? Bill Pike?"

"Why, hell no. Who told you that?"

"An old friend of Jonah Parsons found his body where you left it after you murdered him. I expect you'll hang for that." He shifted his gaze to Sergeant Cox. "Place Mr. Pike under arrest, Sergeant Cox."

Astounded after listening wide-eyed to the colonel's astonishing accusation moments before, Cox was quick to respond. The two soldiers standing by suddenly realized why they were there, and reacted as well. Pike found himself securely restrained before he could raise a hand. "Hey, wait a minute!" he protested. "I ain't kilt nobody. That old coot was already dead when I found him."

"Is that a fact?" Stanton replied sarcastically. "Well, I'm sure all that will be considered at your trial. There's also the matter of O'Brien and Johnson. I'll be sending out a scout detail to find their bodies." He shifted his gaze to Sergeant Cox. "Escort the prisoner to the adjutant's tent. I'll be along directly to file the charges." That said, he turned and went back into his tent.

Captain Herbert Livesey was not particularly pleased to be presented with the problem of Bill Pike. When the regiment was in the field, there was no stockade to incarcerate felons, so the question that confronted him was what to do with Pike. Livesey was not, in fact, the regimental adjutant. He was the acting adjutant while the troop was in the field. The most he had been called upon to deal with was drunken soldiers, fistfights, insubordination, and dereliction of duty — all offenses that could be dealt with handily with company punishment. Leaving the prisoner under heavy guard, he went to confer with General Crook on the situation. Crook's initial reaction was to simply shoot the man and be done with it. Upon further discussion with his staff, however, he changed his mind. Because Pike was a civilian, it was decided the best course of action was to escort him back to Fort Fetterman to be incarcerated in the guardhouse to await trial.

Instructed to assign one officer and four enlisted men to escort Pike, Livesey immediately thought of Winston Castle. The young lieutenant was newly transferred to the regiment and, as junior officer, he was the obvious selection. Most new officers were anxious to prove themselves in any assignment. As he suspected, Castle eagerly accepted the thankless task, and the escort party prepared to get underway early the next morning.

After the standard breakfast of coffee, hardtack, bacon, and a little sugar, the guard detail set out for Fort Fetterman. Lieutenant Castle led, followed by two troopers. Behind them rode a silent and sullen Bill Pike. The other two troopers brought up the rear. It was a diverse collection of troopers. Lieutenant Castle, erect and proper, still new to the frontier, in command of four regimental derelicts. When called upon to detail one man for the escort duty, each of the four company commanders naturally took the opportunity to send their worst soldier. Consequently, the guard detail was made up of four misfits who could, by no stretch of the imagination, be mistaken for model soldiers. There was no need for a guide. Even if Castle wasn't sure of the way back to Fort Fetterman, there was a broad enough trail left by the massive column on the march out to Goose Creek some weeks back.

The prisoner escort made good time, reaching a campsite on the banks of the Crazy Woman Creek at the end of the first day. Lieutenant Castle ordered Wheeler and Reed to gather wood for a fire while Ives and Slidell were assigned to guard the prisoner. When their supper was finished, Castle retreated a few yards from the others to sip his coffee away from the banter of the enlisted men.

Bill Pike grimaced when Ives clamped the manacles back on his wrists. "How about you leave these damn things off so I can sleep?" he complained. "You got two men watchin' me all the time. I ain't goin' nowhere."

Slidell grinned, enjoying the prisoner's discomfort. "We don't want you gettin' too comfortable. Do we, Ives?" Ives made no comment, but went on to lock Pike's chains, a grin on his face to match Slidell's. Slidell continued to amuse himself. "What if we was to forget to lock them cuffs? You could make a run for it. Then I'd have to put a bullet in your behind."

"Yeah," Ives said, joining in the fun, "and then we wouldn't have to ride all the way to Fetterman." He winked at Slidell. "Whaddaya say, Pike? We'd give you a head start, say a couple dozen yards or so. Wanna try it?"

"You can kiss my ass," Pike growled, causing both men to chuckle.

Leaving the prisoner to sulk by the fire, Slidell and Ives withdrew a few feet to make themselves comfortable against the trunk of a large cottonwood. Riding as the rear guard most of the day, the two had often fallen back far enough to talk without being overheard. Although assigned to different companies, they had found right away that many of their interests were shared — especially their dislike for army life on the frontier. Ives confided to Slidell that he had entertained thoughts of deserting ever since starting out on the first day of this campaign when the column had marched out of Fort Fetterman in a blinding snowstorm. Slidell admitted that he had similar notions when he had seen so many civilians at Fort Laramie passing through on their way to the gold strike in the Black Hills. The more they talked about it during the long day, the more they had become convinced that they had been handed a golden opportunity with this assignment. Now, as Slidell pointed out, they were already a day's ride away from the column. It would be a simple trick to take off during the night when they were pulling their shift at guarding Pike.

"What are you two jokers talkin' about?" Private Reed inquired as he sidled over to join the conversation.

"Oh, nothin' much," Slidell replied. "We was just sayin' how much we admired bein' in the army."

"Ha!" Reed snorted, and sat down. "I thought for a minute there you might tell me a lie."

"We was just wonderin' about the lieutenant over there," Ives said. "I don't know much about him."

Reed shrugged. "There ain't much to know, I reckon — West Point, I heard — married the post commander's daughter at Fort Laramie." He turned his head to glance at Lieutenant Castle, who was still quietly sipping his coffee. "Green as Carolina grass," Reed said. "He don't know an Injun from a railroad conductor."

Slidell grinned and winked at Ives. "Well, that just puts the frostin' on the cake, don't it?" Ives chuckled in response. Reed grinned as well, unaware of the significance of the remark.

Later, when it was time to turn in, Lieutenant Castle was about to give orders for the guard detail. He had planned to rotate the four men on one-hour shifts throughout the night when Slidell made a suggestion. "Beggin' your pardon, Lieutenant, but it might be better if we partner up, and stand two-hour shifts. That way one man can keep an eye on Mr. Pike over there, but make sure the other man don't go off to sleep. Me and Ives can take the second shift if that's all right with ever'body."

It seemed sensible to Castle, and he really didn't care as long as the prisoner was watched throughout the night. "All right," he said, "if that's the way you'd prefer it, we'll do it that way. Reed, you and Wheeler take the first shift, and wake Slidell and Ives up in two hours. Tomorrow night, Slidell and Ives can take the first shift." The guard rotation set, the detail settled in for the night. On the opposite side of the fire, a scowling Bill Pike attempted to make himself comfortable with his wrists locked together and a chain doubled back around a willow trunk.

It was a little past midnight when Reed awakened Slidell. Slidell sat up without protest, and reached over with his foot to nudge his partner. Ives awakened with a grunt, taking a few seconds to realize where he was. "All right, boys," Slidell said cheerfully, "you can go get your beauty rest now." He looked over at the prisoner, curled up around the willow, seeking warmth against the cool night air. Satisfied, he then looked at the lieutenant, fast asleep and snoring softly. *Like babes,* he thought. In a short time, Reed and Wheeler would join them.

Reed awakened in a fit of discomfort. He rolled over on his side and pulled his blanket up over his shoulders. After a few moments, he turned back on his other side, still chilly. It was then he realized that the fire had almost died out. *Damn,* he thought, and rose up on his elbow. Looking around him, he couldn't see Slidell or Ives. Looking quickly toward the willow, he was relieved to see Pike still wrapped around the tree. He still had a feeling something wasn't exactly right, however. Where in hell were Ives and Slidell? And why in hell had they let the fire die out?

He craned his neck to look behind him. Wheeler was sleeping peacefully, a low raspy snore issuing from his lips. About to convince himself that everything was all right, he decided to see what time it was, but he found it difficult to see his pocket watch in the deep darkness. So he picked up a splinter of wood and held it in the coals until it suddenly burst into flame. Using it as a light, he peered at his watch. What he saw immediately alarmed him. It was a quarter past four.

He rolled out of his blanket and scrambled to his feet, looking about in the darkness for Slidell or Ives. They were nowhere to be seen. *Those two no-good . . .* He didn't finish the thought when he suddenly realized that two of the horses were missing. Slidell and Ives were not sleeping on duty. They were gone — deserted! "Well, ain't this a pickle?" he said aloud, both amazed and disgusted.

Lieutenant Castle was properly alarmed when awakened by Reed a few minutes later. His first thought was concern for how the desertion of two of his detail would look to his superiors. He knew he should do something about it, but at the moment he wasn't sure what that might be. Maybe he should order the others to mount up and go after them — he wasn't sure. That idea was quickly squelched when Reed told him there was no sense trying to trail them in the dark. Because it would soon be dawn, Castle decided to eat breakfast, and wait for light enough to look for a trail.

When the sun finally made its appearance, it revealed two sets of tracks leading down into the creek — and that was as far as the trail led. "They coulda gone up or down stream," Wheeler said. "It could take us all day, lookin' up and down this creek, trying to find where they come out."

"Hell, they're gone," Reed stated flatly. "With the start they got on us, we'd never catch 'em, anyway."

The lieutenant was thoroughly perplexed, feeling helpless to act. Unsure of what he should do, he accepted the troopers' opinion, and announced that they would continue on to Fort Fetterman as they had been ordered to do. Reed and Wheeler were already grumbling about the extra responsibility they had been dealt by the desertions.

The only person amused by the situation was Bill Pike. "Hey," he yelled, "how 'bout unlocking my hands before I have to piss in my pants."

"Go ahead and piss in 'em," Wheeler

replied, but Castle ordered him to free Pike's hands.

Following the old government road, the reduced guard detail reached the ruins of Fort Reno at midday, and Castle permitted a brief rest for the noonday meal. It was still about eighty miles from there to Fort Fetterman. And although he wanted to make the trip in as short a time as possible, he was persuaded to allow a little extra time for Reed and Wheeler to search about the camp for any food supplies that might have been left behind when the column moved through some weeks back. The prisoner was secured to a tree trunk while the two troopers foraged for whatever might be found.

Pike had become more and more insolent after the desertion of Slidell and Ives — to the point of unspoken defiance. Despite the fact that he was always kept in chains, his demeanor was that of a man who gave no serious thought toward remaining in custody. When Reed and Wheeler disappeared beyond the still-standing chimneys of the old officers' quarters, Pike's surly scowl suddenly turned into a wry smile. Shifting his body around to face the lieutenant, he spoke, "It's been three solid days since I last took a shit, Lieutenant. And I feel a powerful urge right now."

Castle, his face screwed up in undisguised irritation, responded, "The guards will be back in a few minutes. They'll take you to relieve yourself then."

"I'm hurtin' pretty bad, Lieutenant. It's boilin' up in my guts somethin' awful. I don't know if I can hold it till then."

"I guess you'll just have to," Castle replied.

Pike made a show of agonized discomfort as he shifted his body back and forth. "I don't think I can," he groaned, and gazed at the lieutenant plaintively. "If you would just unchain my hands, I could get it done real quick." When Castle showed reluctance to do so, Pike pleaded, "Hell, if you could just free up one of my hands, I might be able to shit right here — if I can just get my britches down."

The man's plight was desperate. Castle could appreciate that, but he was still reluctant to free Pike, even for the short time it would take for a man to evacuate his bowels. He stood and looked impatiently toward the ruins of the old post, but Reed and Wheeler were out of sight. Turning his gaze back to light on Pike, he was met with an expression of deep misery. Winston Castle was not a hard-hearted man by nature, but he was not inclined to release a man as dangerous as Bill Pike. He looked again toward the ruins, hoping to see Reed and Wheeler returning. They had evidently gone on down to the creek, for there was no one in sight. Pike began a low mournful moan.

"All right," Castle conceded. "I'll free one hand so you can get your trousers down, but that's all. You can relieve yourself right where you are." He wished that Wheeler had not already started a fire to boil some coffee. It would have been more desirable to be a little more distant from the spot where Pike defecated.

With his pistol in one hand, and the key to the manacles in the other, Castle carefully unwound several links of the chain that Reed had wrapped around the tree trunk. His eyes locked on Castle's, Pike gazed at the lieutenant with the look of a grateful hound. He eagerly held his hands out to be released. "One hand," Castle reminded him.

"My right hand," Pike pleaded. "I can't do nothin' left-handed."

"All right," Castle said, and unlocked the manacle on Pike's right hand.

"I reckon we'd best get on back before the lieutenant thinks we took off after Slidell and Ives." Reed tossed the empty container aside. Their search for discarded hardtack had been unsuccessful. Scavengers had long since picked the campsite clean of anything edible. "Reckon Castle might let us take a little time to hunt somethin' to eat?"

Wheeler shook his head. "I doubt it. I think he's wantin' to shed himself of the prisoner as soon as he can."

"Ives and Slidell mighta had the right idea," Reed mused aloud. "Wonder where they headed?"

"Knowin' Slidell," Wheeler responded, "I know they didn't head up to Montana. He ain't likely to expose his sorry ass to them Cheyenne and Sioux. They either headed south or took off to the Black Hills."

"I expect so," Reed agreed. He gave the empty container a kick. "Yessir, them boys mighta had the right idea, all right."

"Damn! Look at that!" Reed grabbed Wheeler's arm just as he was about to step up onto a large flat rock near the water's edge.

"Damn!" Wheeler echoed, seeing the cause of Reed's alarm at that instant. There, coiled on the rock, was a large rattlesnake, its head raised, ready to strike. Wheeler would have stepped right in front of it if Reed had not grabbed his arm. The buzzing of the reptile's rattles had been muffled by the sound of the water gurgling around the rocks. Both men took a step backward.

"He's six foot if he's an inch," Reed speculated.

"He's meat," Wheeler pronounced, and drew his revolver from the holster. Steadying his gun hand with his other, he took careful aim at the angry snake. "Just hold still, darlin'," he cooed, trying to get a bead on the swaying head.

After a long moment passed and Wheeler had still not fired, Reed chided him. "Hell, if I had my pistol, I'da done blowed his head off."

"He won't hold still," Wheeler complained.

"Lemme have the pistol. I'll fix him quick enough."

Rather than yield to his companion, Wheeler fired. The rattlesnake dropped immediately, shot through the head. "Goddam," he exclaimed, impressed with his own marksmanship. "He's meat now."

Both men stepped closer to gawk at the dead reptile. After a moment to make sure the snake was truly no longer a threat, Wheeler reached down and picked it up. "Damn! That sucker's heavy. Look at that, Reed. His body's as big around as my leg." Then a mischievous thought crossed his mind. "We could have us a little fun with this jasper." He nodded his head toward the old fort ruins above them.

Reed caught on immediately. "I expect he heard that shot. He's probably already nervous about that." It was common knowledge among the men that Lieutenant Castle was a greenhorn as far as duty west of the Missouri was concerned. "He'd probably shit his pants if we dropped this beauty at his feet." They both giggled at the picture the thought invoked. "Come on, let's go see if them new lieutenants shit yellow like a baby."

Still about fifty yards away, they could see the prisoner chained to the tree and the lieutenant sitting close by. "Now what the hell is he doin'?" Reed commented.

"He's probably tellin' ol' Pike about the price of sin," Wheeler said, causing both men to chuckle. It was an unusual sight, for Castle had never said more than a mouthful of words to the prisoner before, wanting as little to do with Pike as possible.

The lieutenant appeared to pay them no mind as they approached. His back to them, he continued to sit near the tree where Pike was chained. Dragging his trophy behind him, Wheeler had a grin spread wide across his face in anticipation of Castle's reaction when the rattlesnake was plopped down before him.

"Well, we didn't have no luck," Reed said as they walked up.

"You still ain't got no luck."

Both men were startled when Pike spoke. Before they could react, Pike placed a foot in Castle's back and shoved the corpse over on its side. Too late, they discovered the lieutenant's revolver in Pike's hand. Reed reacted, anyway. He made a run for the rifle in his saddle boot. Pike put two bullets in his back before he had taken three strides. He then calmly brought the pistol around to aim directly at a stunned Wheeler, who was still holding onto the huge rattlesnake. "Now if you don't want the same, you'd best fetch that key laying on the ground yonder."

Wheeler started to do as he was told, then hesitated as he thought the situation over. "What's gonna keep you from shootin' me after I give you the key?"

Pike frowned, obviously irritated. "Well, I'm sure as hell gonna shoot you if you don't," he replied.

"That may be so," Wheeler said, still pondering his chances, "but you'd still have one hand chained to a tree."

A flash of anger sparked in Pike's eye, but was quickly extinguished to take on a gentler gaze when he realized that Wheeler was right. "Hell, man, you've got it all wrong. I didn't wanna kill your partner there," he said nodding toward Reed's body. "But he was tryin' to get to his rifle to shoot me. He didn't give me no choice. All I want is to get myself the hell and gone. I got no reason to wanna kill you — honest to God, man. But I will if you don't fetch me that key."

Wheeler studied Pike's face, trying to read truth there. In the final analysis, it came down to one simple fact — if he didn't do as Pike wished, he was going to die. That much was certain. He decided to take the one option that offered a chance for survival, slim as it might be. "All right," he said, finally releasing the snake. As he did, he thought of the pistol in his holster. His right hand was free now.

Reading his thoughts, Pike warned, "I'd cut you down before you even got it outta the holster."

Knowing that to be the truth of the matter, Wheeler shrugged and picked up the key. "Just take it easy, man. I ain't gonna try nothin'." He moved closer to Pike, but stopped short of handing over the key.

"There ain't no need for anymore killin' here. I ain't the one that wanted you arrested. I was just doin' what they ordered me to do. I don't care one way or the other."

"I know that," Pike said. "You ain't got nothin' to worry about. Just stick that key in here and unlock me from this damn tree, and me and you'll be square."

"That suits me," Wheeler replied, and fit the key in the lock. That done, he stepped back a couple of steps while Pike pulled the remaining coils of chain from the tree.

Once free of his chains, Pike favored Wheeler with a wide grin. Wheeler returned it with one of his own. An instant later, it turned to a look of horror as Pike raised the pistol and pointed it directly into Wheeler's face. The impact of the bullet at such close range knocked the stunned victim down — an ugly black hole centered in his forehead.

Pike watched dispassionately as Wheeler's lifeblood formed a crimson pool under his head. Satisfied that the man was dead, he then turned his attention to the snake. Talking to the dead man, he said, "I wonder if you was thinkin' 'bout eatin' that thing." He considered that possibility for a few moments before discarding it. "I ain't eatin' no damn snake," he stated. "I ain't no damn savage."

Chapter 14

When Jordan and Toby rode into camp at Goose Creek again, it was to find an army preparing to march. The Big Horn and Yellowstone Expedition was once again on the move. General Crook, still smarting somewhat from eastern newspaper accounts of his initial attempt to destroy Crazy Horse's band, was anxious to launch the second attack. Additional companies of infantry had arrived, and the supply wagons had been left behind. Supplies were to be carried by mules, their main burden being grain for the animals. The entire area around the forks of Goose Creek was alive with activity as infantry and cavalry companies prepared to take to the field again.

The scene was somewhat discouraging to Jordan. It struck him as organized confusion at best. He had gambled on the premise that Bill Pike had returned to the encampment, but judging by the amount of activity among the departing troops, it might be difficult to find his man. Motioning Toby to follow, he guided Sweet Pea across the lower fork of the creek to the spot where he had found Colonel Stanton's tent before — only to find it no longer there. Instead, he encountered a group of soldiers from the Third Cavalry sitting around a small fire. Their horses were standing nearby, saddled and saddle packs loaded. The men glanced up with no more than casual interest when the two civilians rode up.

"Can you fellows tell us where Colonel Stanton is?" Jordan asked.

One of the men, a corporal by the stripes on his sleeve, answered, "I wouldn't know, friend. I don't know who Colonel Stanton is. We just got here from Fort Fetterman day before yesterday." He looked around at the others only to see equally blank expressions, then turned back to Jordan. "What unit is he in?"

"He's head of the scout company," Jordan replied. "Where are the Crows camped?"

"There's a bunch of Injuns camped about a mile up the creek." He pointed toward the northwest. "I don't know if they're Crow or Shoshone."

"Much obliged," Jordan said. He turned Sweet Pea away, and glanced at Toby. "If we find Iron Pony, he can probably tell us if Pike came back to the scout company."

They had started back toward the union of the two forks of the creek when Toby suddenly pulled back hard on the reins. A rider on the opposite bank had caught his eye, and in that moment he thought it was Pike. Without waiting for an explanation to Jordan, he drove his horse into the creek, and charged up the other side to intercept the rider. Toby had only seen Pike from a distance on that late evening near his claim. But the heavyset man with the full dark beard, leaning forward in the saddle, seemed to be a dead ringer for the man fleeing Deadwood on that night.

Puzzled by Toby's sudden decision to gallop into the creek, Jordan pulled Sweet Pea up sharply, and peered after his young partner. When he saw the rider on the opposite bank, he immediately followed after Toby, pulling up behind him a few seconds after Toby confronted the man. "Who the hell are you, mister?" he heard the boy blurt out, uncertain now that he was face to face with the rider.

"Who the hell wants to know?" the man replied, not the least bit intimidated by the brash young boy.

Jordan answered Toby's demand. "He's

Frank Grouard, if I recollect correctly." Jordan had met the white scout briefly when Colonel Stanton had solicited Jordan's help on the campaign against the Sioux. He remembered Iron Pony saying that Grouard and a few others were the only competent scouts among the thirty or so white men the colonel had employed.

"Jordan Gray, right?" Grouard greeted the buckskin-clad scout.

"Frank," Jordan returned.

"You come back to join the expedition?"

"No," Jordan replied. "I'm lookin' for a man." He nodded toward a subdued Toby. "*We're* lookin' for a man. That's the reason my brash young friend here was fixin' to shoot you." Grouard cocked an amused eye in Toby's direction. Jordan went on. "Fellow's name is Pike, and he was ridin' with your company of scouts. We trailed him as far as the Rosebud, but we got jumped by a Lakota war party before we could catch up to him."

"You're talkin' about that feller that called hisself Parsons. Is that right?"

"That's the man," Jordan replied.

Grouard nodded knowingly. "Well, I can save you some trouble there. Colonel Stanton had that feller put under arrest. They've already took him back to Fetterman to stand trial for the murder of Jonah Parsons. I knew that feller was full of bullshit after I talked to him for five minutes. I told Stanton I didn't want him ridin' with me. Stanton sent him out a few days ago with two pretty good scouts, Pepper O'Brien and Royce Johnson. Pepper and Royce didn't come back with Parsons — or Pike, if that's his real name — and now I've got to go out to see if I can find them."

"I reckon I can save you trouble there," Jordan said. "We found your two scouts near the Rosebud. They were both dead, and it didn't look like the work of Indians."

"I figured as much," Grouard said. "That bastard. The colonel shoulda just strung him up as soon as he came back." He gave Toby a quick glance, then shifted back to Jordan. "What are you fellers huntin' him for?"

Jordan briefly related the reasons he and Toby had taken on the mission of tracking down the blatant murderer. They both had scores to settle with Pike. Grouard expressed his understanding for their mission, but assured them that they were too late to administer their personal punishment. The army had taken over the situation, but they could take solace in the certainty that Pike would hang.

The news was met with mixed feelings on the part of Jordan and Toby. As far as the boy was concerned, he had been cheated out of the vengeance that he so desperately wanted. Jordan, although almost as passionate for revenge at first, could be more philosophical about the issue at this point. The matter was simple to Jordan. The murderer needed to be stopped, and he didn't feel anyone else was going to undertake the responsibility. That is, aside from Toby Blessings, and Jordan was not confident Toby would have come out on top in a match with Bill Pike. Maybe it was just as well that the matter would be handled by a military court. He was not especially fond of the role of executioner, anyway.

"Well, I'd best be gettin' along," Frank Grouard said. "Look me up if you decide you wanna come along with us to fight Sittin' Bull and Crazy Horse." He saluted with a single finger to his hat brim, and rode away.

Jordan nodded in reply, and he and Toby watched the stoutly built man as he guided his horse along the creek. Their search apparently ended, Jordan shrugged and said, "Well, I reckon the army has finished our job for us."

Toby's need for vengeance was not satisfied, however. His passion for Pike's blood was fueled by his love for a woman. That the love affair had been one-sided made little difference to him. He had pledged his devotion to Polly Hatcher with all the passion in his young heart. And that passion needed desperately to be involved in the final reckoning of one, Bill Pike. "I'm goin' to Fort Fetterman," he announced. "If I can't put the bullet in him that kills him, then I've got to see him hung. I want to see that son of a bitch dead."

Jordan studied the young man's face for a few moments. There was no mistaking the fact that Toby meant what he said. Jordan felt it would be better for Toby if he put Bill Pike behind him, and went on with the rest of his life. But he refrained from trying to advise the boy. Toby was man enough to make his own decisions. After a long moment, Jordan said, "I'll ride with you. I might as well head back to Fort Laramie." He glanced at the figure of Frank Grouard, almost out of sight by then. "I reckon I've killed all the Sioux I care to." He had really given thought to joining General Crook's troops no more than a fleeting moment.

"Suit yourself," Toby said. Although making an attempt to sound independent, he was more than grateful to Jordan for accompanying him. Early the next morning, they were once again on the trail — this time the government road back to Fort Fetterman.

"Looks like they camped here," Jordan commented upon finding recent ashes of a campfire by Crazy Woman Creek. "Good a place as any — we might as well camp here, too."

There was good grass and ample water available, so they pulled their saddles off and let the horses graze. Toby looked around while Jordan built a fire. Watching as Toby poked around the tree where there were signs that someone had been chained, Jordan wondered if he had ever been that much in love with a woman. It seemed many years since his wife and child were killed. It was something he didn't think about if he could help it, for when he did, it always stirred a bitter bile in his gut. He supposed he had been just as smitten with Sarah as Toby seemed to be with Polly. It was just so long ago, and so much had happened between then and now, that it was hard to remember ever being as young as Toby. Since Sarah's death, he had only given thought to one other woman, Kathleen Beard, the post surgeon's daughter. She had served as his nurse while he recovered from gunshot wounds in the hospital at Fort Gibson. At the time, he was puzzled by the amount of attention he received from the comely young woman. He had supposed it was her fascination with a *wild creature* — as she had laughingly referred to him then. It went a little deeper than that, but he was too stupid to realize it until it was too late. It was too soon after Sarah's death to permit thoughts of another to take hold, but after leaving Fort Gibson, he had found that he could not rid his mind of Kathleen.

After months of trying to convince himself otherwise, he finally admitted that he was in love with the girl. By the time he made up his mind to do something about it, she had decided he was a lost cause. Being a practical woman, and realizing she was not getting any younger, she made a practical decision, and accepted a marriage proposal from Lieutenant Thomas Jefferson Wallace. That, in itself, was reason enough to detest Lieutenant Wallace, but Jordan had already developed a strong dislike for the arrogant officer. News of Kathleen's engagement had struck him with a profound sense of loss.

Realizing that he was allowing his mind to wander back into places that brought only pain, he quickly brought it back to the present. He elected then to think of things that brought him pleasure — like the cool night air and the peaceful quiet of the prairie away from the noisy army camps. "Who the hell can blame the Sioux for not wantin' to go to the reservations?" he blurted aloud. "Damned if I'd give up my way of life."

"How's that?" Toby asked.

Realizing then that he had spoken his thoughts, Jordan replied, "Nothin', I was just mumblin' to myself — I need to get some coffee made."

The next morning, with the horses grazed, watered, and rested, they were back in the saddle. It was Toby who was impatient to ride. Jordan was in no particular hurry, but he was attuned to Toby's urgency. They made good time, and noontime found them about a mile northwest of the ruins of Fort Reno. It was here that they were first alerted that something was wrong.

Jordan spotted it first — a ring of buzzards circling in the sky ahead. Half a mile farther, off to their left on a gentle rise, a lone horse grazed leisurely in the high grass. It was saddled and, at that distance, they could see that it was an army saddle. It raised its head and whinnied when they approached. Sweet Pea snorted in reply. There was no need for either man to waste words of warning. Both Jordan and Toby tensed as they proceeded cautiously toward the riderless horse. It stood obediently waiting while they approached. Jordan reached over and picked up the loose reins.

"Injuns?" Toby wondered aloud.

"I don't know," Jordan replied. "I don't hardly expect an Indian would have let the horse go."

They rode on, guiding on the circle of buzzards. After covering another half mile, they arrived at the ruins of Fort Reno. The ring of scavenger birds was hovering directly overhead. Jordan took a careful look around them before riding in. The closeness of the buzzards would indicate that the birds sensed no threat of danger, but Jordan was still alert to the possibility of ambush. Impatient, Toby pushed on ahead. When Jordan followed him, it was to find the boy staring at three corpses sprawled near the ashes of a campfire.

"Well, I don't reckon I have to ask if one of those bodies is our man, Pike," Jordan commented as he rode up and dismounted. It didn't take a great deal of investigating to see what had happened. "Lieutenant Castle," Jordan said, recognizing the young officer from Fort Laramie. He at once thought of the officer's young family, and his wife now a widow. A series of deep bruises and broken skin tattooed the lieutenant's neck, obviously the cause of his death. There were no bullet holes or other wounds. Apparently, his windpipe had been crushed, and probably with a length of the chain lying at his feet. The other two bodies had been shot — one with a bullet hole in his forehead, the other a few yards away, shot in the back. Since all three bodies were wearing uniforms, there was no need for close examination to know that Pike was not one of the dead.

"I thought that feller, Grouard, said there were four soldiers in the guard detail with the lieutenant," Toby said, just remembering.

"He did," Jordan replied. "Maybe the other two helped him pull it off. Or maybe they deserted before they got this far."

Now there was the question of whether they were trailing one man or three, and there were too many tracks around the old ruins to determine which were new and which weren't. The road had been traveled a great deal lately by army troops going and coming, but Jordan searched anyway, hoping to find some cluc that might tell him which tracks were Pike's. He soon abandoned his search. This time, Toby didn't bother to suggest the Christian thing would be to bury the bodies, but Jordan couldn't bring himself to leave the young officer's body for the buzzards to feast upon. Picturing Mary Castle's face in his mind, he didn't like the prospect of someday having to relate the circumstances of her husband's death. He resolved that he would at least be able to comfort her with the knowledge that her husband had had a decent burial.

A few miles past Reno, they came upon another saddled horse wandering free. Toby went after it, and soon had it trailing along behind Brownie. "I reckon there's another horse out here somewhere," Jordan speculated. "He wasn't takin' a chance on being caught with horses wearin' a US brand."

The more Jordan thought about it, the more he was convinced they were still chasing one man. He just couldn't see a man like Pike teaming up with the two deserters. Pike was a lone wolf. The riddle to be solved was where would a lone wolf likely be headed? With no identifiable trail to follow, it was little more than a guessing game. He couldn't go back to Deadwood — he would most likely be strung up for killing Polly. And to go back into the Powder River country would be heading straight into a swarm of Sioux and Cheyenne. Because there was nothing but speculation to go on, Jordan decided their best chance was to continue on the government road to Fort Fetterman, and beyond to Fort Laramie. His reasoning was that Pike could assume that there were no witnesses to tell of his arrest or the murder of his guards. There was no telegraph between Goose Creek and Fort Fetterman, so he had to figure he could be long gone before the army was even alerted that the guard detail was missing.

It was late in the afternoon when the buildings of Fort Fetterman came into view. Located on a plateau above the valleys of the North Platte and LaPrele Creek, the post was not one of Jordan's favorite places. Generally known as a hardship post among the soldiers who were unfortunate enough to be stationed there, Fort Fetterman was the cause of many desertions. Fresh food and supplies were not available on the site. Everything had to be hauled in from Fort Laramie or Medicine Bow Station on the Union Pacific Railroad. It was a constant complaint from the soldiers that the soil was not capable of supporting even a small garden. Jonah Parsons had told of spending a winter there many years back. He said it was a toss-up as to whether he was going to starve to death or freeze solid. Blizzard after blizzard paid regular visits, and the wintry gales never ceased. Jonah claimed that he had a ringing in his ears on into the following summer as a result. Due to the inhospitality of the location, there were no more than a few homesteaders scattered nearby. So there were no social opportunities for the off duty soldier — the only diversion being an establishment known to the troops as the "Hog Ranch," staffed by a few *prairie belles* as rough as the rugged land.

Jordan and Toby went directly to the log building pointed out as the post headquarters, where they were met by a Sergeant Murray. Murray informed them that the post commander was off up the river somewhere fishing, but he assured them that he was the one who actually ran the post. When Jordan described the man they were trailing, Murray remembered Pike right away. "Yeah, solidly built man, had a scar on one side of his face. He rode in two days ago. Didn't stay long, not even overnight — I saw him in the sutler's store. He bought a few things and left right away."

"Did he say where he was headin'?" Jordan asked.

"Back east," Murray answered. "That's all he said. I didn't push him for more 'cause he didn't seem like he wanted to talk. I figured him for just another drifter, and let him be." The sergeant stepped outside with Jordan and Toby. "What did you say you was following him for?"

"He's killed some folks, seven that I know of, five of 'em soldiers. We found the bodies of the last three back at Fort Reno two days ago." He then went on to explain that Pike was being escorted to Fort Fetterman for trial, and the three bodies were part of the guard detail.

"Well, forevermore," Murray exclaimed. "And he was right here on the post. The colonel's most likely gonna send out a patrol to look for him."

"Maybe," Jordan said. He shot a quick glance in Toby's direction when the boy showed a slight look of alarm. "I don't reckon Toby and me'll wait for the army to get a patrol mounted." This last, he said for the boy's benefit, knowing that Toby wanted to beat the army to Pike. "We've got a couple of the army's mounts we'd just as soon get rid of. Can you take 'em off our hands?"

"Shore can," Murray replied, and walked to the hitching post with Jordan. Noticing

Sweet Pea then, he couldn't help but remark, "I'm surprised you didn't swap horses when you had the chance."

Weary of defending his horse, Jordan just smiled and said, "Didn't think of it."

Content to have Fort Fetterman behind them, they followed the North Platte toward Fort Laramie. It would be a two-day ride, less if they pushed the horses hard. Starting out with only a few hours of daylight left, they were determined to close the distance between them and the outlaw. Already trailing Pike by a couple of days, it was hard to say if they were gaining on him or not until they stumbled upon a recent campfire around noon the next day. They paused to rest the horses and look around the campsite for sign. It was here that lady luck decided to glance in their direction.

"What is it?" Toby asked, noticing that Jordan was kneeling over a patch of bare ground near the ashes of the fire.

"Might be a break," Jordan said without looking up. Toby came over to see. Jordan looked up at him then. "I believe Mr. Pike will be slowin' down pretty soon." He traced his finger along a hoof print in the soft dirt. "His horse is about to throw a shoe." Toby bent low to see for himself. There was no doubt about it. The shoe was loose, as evidenced by the double print in the dirt. "He probably didn't get very much farther before the horse lost it," Jordan said.

Still two days ahead, but unaware of his pursuers, Bill Pike cursed his horse for throwing a shoe. He pushed on, forcing the animal to keep up a steady pace until the horse began to limp slightly. Still with no compassion for his mount, Pike whipped the horse unmercifully. By his reckoning, he could be no farther than ten or fifteen miles from Fort Laramie at this point, and he was intent upon reaching the post before dark. With each mile, however, the horse's hoof became more and more tender until, finally, it began to limp in earnest.

"Damn you!" Bill lashed out at the helpless animal, and with great reluctance, dismounted. He would have shot the horse then and there, but even in his fit of anger, he realized he would then have to carry his saddle himself. Frustrated and hungry, for he had finished the last of his meager rations that noon, he started walking, leading the lame animal.

He had covered little more than a mile when he came to a small stream that emptied into the North Platte. He paused for a moment to let the horse drink. Then as he was about to cross over and be on his way, he detected a movement in the corner of his eye. His reflexes were swift. In a flash, he drew his pistol and turned, ready to fire. Expecting an Indian or a soldier, he was astonished to find he was facing a small boy armed with a fishing pole. The boy, even more startled, froze, his eyes wide and growing every second as he stared at the gun barrel.

Pike relaxed and returned the pistol to its holster. "Boy, that's a damn good way to get your head blowed off," he said. "Where the hell did you come from, anyway?"

"Down by the river," the youngster replied. He held his catch up for Bill to see.

It was only one catfish, and hardly of a size to make a meal, but the sight of it immediately reminded the outlaw of his empty stomach. "Here, lemme see that fish," Bill demanded abruptly. The boy dutifully complied. Pike held it up before his eyes to examine it more closely. Satisfied that it was edible, he looked around him for something to build a fire with.

The boy studied the strange man with a white scar parting the dark beard on one side of his face. He wasn't entirely comfortable with the man's brusque demeanor, and it was beginning to look as if he was not going to return the fish. He remained still for a few seconds while Pike, clutching the catfish possessively, looked around for wood. He had already dismissed the boy from his mind.

"You hungry, mister?" The boy finally broke his silence.

As if just then remembering the boy standing there, Pike cocked an eye in the lad's direction. "Damn right I'm hungry. You got anything else with you besides this slimy little fish?"

The boy shook his head. He didn't care for the stranger's unfriendly attitude, but his parents had taught him to be respectful of his elders. "No, sir," he replied. "But if you're hungry, Mama can fix you somethin' to eat."

This immediately garnered Pike's attention. He looked all around him now, searching for sign of a house. "You live near here?"

The boy nodded, then pointed toward a low ridge to the north. "On the other side of yonder hill," he said.

This was pleasing news for Bill. He needed food, and he needed a horse. His belligerent attitude swiftly changed, and he broke out a crooked smile for the boy's benefit. "Well, then," he said, "let's go see your mama." He handed the catfish back to the boy. "What's your name, son?"

"Jeremy," the lad replied.

"Well, Jeremy, I'm mighty glad I run into you. Lead away."

The boy crossed the tiny stream, and started up a path that led along the bank toward a narrow gap where the stream cut through the ridge. Pike followed along behind, leading his lame horse. On the other side of the ridge, they came to a modest cabin built of logs. Pike wasted no time in taking a quick assessment of the homestead. He was hungry. There was no doubt about that, but there were other things he needed — a horse for certain. So he was quick to look toward the corral. It was of crude construction, built of gnarled pine logs that were no doubt not straight enough for use on the cabin roof. But there was a horse and two mules inside. The discovery brought a smile to Pike's face. He shifted his gaze to the chickens pecking near the cabin door, and his smile grew wider. *Yessir, Jeremy. I'm mighty glad I run into you.*

He glanced again at the stock in the corral. "Where's your pa, boy?"

"I think he's in the house," Jeremy replied. "Pa ain't workin' the place today."

"Oh, he ain't, is he?" Bill responded. "Why ain't he workin' today?"

Jeremy looked back at the stranger in surprise. " 'Cause today's Sunday — Pa don't work on Sunday. It ain't right to work on the Lord's Day."

"So today's Sunday," Pike said. "I didn't have no idea." He was about to remark that the devil worked every day when a woman appeared in the cabin doorway. "Is that your mama?"

"Yessir," Jeremy replied. The woman turned her head to make a comment to someone inside, and a moment later Jeremy's father appeared in the open doorway. "Pa," Jeremy called out, "this feller's horse is gone lame." His father stepped around his wife, and walked out in the front yard to meet them. "And he's hungry," Jeremy added.

"John Dunstan," his father said. "This is my wife, Helen. We ain't got much to offer, but I'm sure we can fix you up with somethin' to eat." Hearing her husband's comment, Helen Dunstan nodded politely, then disappeared inside to see what she could come up with to feed the stranger.

"Well, now, that'ud be right Christian of you," Pike said, doing his best to affect a friendly face. Despite his efforts, his grizzled features, long accustomed to an evil scowl, presented a twisted facade more akin to pain.

Dunstan was not at ease with the dark stranger. There was a look of hard violence about him that triggered an instant warning. John Dunstan was a Christian man, and he would not deny hospitality to strangers in need, but he made a mental note to lecture Jeremy on the scarcity of food. Anxious to speed the stranger on his way, he said, "My wife'll fix you somethin' to eat. Why don't you set down beside the cabin in the shade, and Jeremy'll fetch you a cool dipper of water from the springbox." He motioned his son toward the stream with a nod of his head. "I ain't no horse doctor, but I'll take a look at that hoof."

Pike smiled. Although Dunstan was trying to disguise it, his sense of distrust was apparent to even one as insensitive as Bill Pike. No longer concerned with his horse's welfare, for he already had his eye on the injured animal's replacement, he nevertheless made a feeble attempt to continue the game. "Well, now, I appreciate it." Feeling it necessary to assuage the man's suspicions, he said, "I'm an army scout headin' for Fort Laramie with some important messages for the general."

"Well, we'll try not to delay you, Mr. —"

He paused.

"Pike." Bill filled in the blank.

"Mr. Pike," Dunstan echoed. He lifted the horse's leg and examined the injured hoof. "Looks like he's throwed a shoe."

"Yeah," Pike replied while taking the dipper of water from Jeremy. After a long drink of the cool water, he added, "He throwed it about a mile back. I had to get off and walk."

Dunstan stared at the badly injured hoof. It showed signs of tenderness that would hardly result from walking a mile. He had no sympathy for a man who would abuse any animal, especially his horse. Another precaution that stuck in his mind was Pike's comment that he was carrying dispatches for the *general* at Fort Laramie. Colonel Bradley was the post commander at Laramie. There was no general there. He would have thought that an army scout would know that. Just another drifter, he thought, or a deserter — there were certainly plenty of them hitting the high road. Maybe instead of heading for the fort, Mr. Pike was heading away from it. *Well,* he thought, *we'll give him something to eat, and send him on his way.*

"There ain't much you can do for this horse's hoof. It'll heal if you keep the weight off of it. But you can't ride the horse till it heals."

"That's what I figured," Pike said. "But I got to git them messages to the fort."

Dunston realized that he was in a box now. It would be extremely bad manners to suggest to the man that he had best start walking if he wanted to make the fort before morning. It was either that or hitch up the wagon and carry Pike to Fort Laramie in the morning. He didn't relish that idea, but he didn't know what else to do. Reluctantly, he offered the invitation. "I reckon me and Jeremy could take you in to the fort in the mornin'. It ain't hardly ten miles from here. There ain't no room in the cabin, but you're welcome to sleep in the barn tonight."

Pike had a different solution to his transportation problem, but he decided not to reveal it at the moment. *Might as well take advantage of the hospitality,* he thought. "Why that's mighty neighborly of you," he said. "I could use a good night's rest before I start out again."

Helen Dunston arrived with a plate of food just in time to hear Pike express his appreciation. She set the plate down beside Pike, then stepped back, giving her husband a questioning look, hoping she had heard wrong. He frowned and shook his head, knowing he was going to have some explaining to do later.

"Why in the world did you tell that man he could stay here tonight?" Helen Dunstan demanded when supper was finished and Pike had retired to the barn. "He's the evilest-looking man I've ever seen — nothing but a common drifter. We'll be lucky if he doesn't run off with the livestock while we're asleep in our beds."

"I didn't know what else to do," John replied in defense. "I couldn't just order him to start walkin'. I mean, his horse did go lame." He placed the bar across the door. "Besides, I aim to set up all night and watch the barn. He ain't goin' nowhere without I see him."

As he said, John Dunston sat awake for almost the entire night. Sitting beside the window, his rifle propped against the wall beside him, he kept a close watch on the barn until just before daybreak. He didn't realize he had drifted off to sleep until his wife shook his shoulder. He bolted from his slumber so violently that he knocked his chair over.

"John!" Helen exclaimed. "It's just me. Everything's all right." A moment later, she heard the rooster announcing the arrival of the new day.

Fully awake then, he picked up the chair and moved back to peer out of the corner of the window. There was no sign of activity from the barn. The horse and the mules were standing peacefully in the corral. Nothing was out of place. He looked at his wife and shook his head, thinking what a fool he had been to sit up all night while their guest slept soundly in the barn.

"I guess I'd better get coffee started," Helen said with a sigh. "Jeremy's friend will want some breakfast before he leaves." As she said it, she made a mental note to talk to her son about inviting strangers home with him.

There was still no sign of movement in the barn by the time John left the cabin to feed the livestock. He dragged the barn door open and stepped inside to find his overnight guest just stirring from his bed in the hay. "Damn! That's the best night's sleep I've had in I can't remember when," Pike said, greeting him. His tone was almost cheerful. "I never did sleep worth a damn on the ground." He got to his feet and took a few steps away from the hay to relieve himself. "Better than a feather bed," he commented as he patiently emptied his bladder.

"The missus will have breakfast ready in a few minutes," Dunston said. He glanced back toward the barn door, concerned that his wife might walk in to look for eggs while Pike was still performing his toilet. Much to his relief, the footfalls he heard on the hard-baked clay turned out to be Jeremy's. She had assigned the boy that duty on this morning.

"Mornin'," Jeremy said with a definite lack of enthusiasm, and went straight to the nests along the back wall of the barn. Shooing the hens away, he gathered the few eggs he found and returned to the cabin.

The mood at breakfast was considerably lighter than the somber tone of supper the night before — the prospect of saying goodbye to their guest being the primary reason. What discomfort remained was felt by Helen Dunston due to the crude gaze that Bill Pike fixed upon her as she moved about the table. She was reluctant to speculate on the thoughts behind those dull eyes — a fear that even the homeliest of women felt around a man of suspect morals.

"Well, I expect I'd better hitch up the mules," John Dunston said, and got up from the table. "We'd better get movin' if we're gonna drive into Fort Laramie and get back before dark."

Pike turned his coffee cup up, draining the last of it, wiped his mouth on his sleeve, and gave Helen a satisfied smile. "Yeah, reckon it's time to get movin'," he said, getting up from his chair. "But there ain't no need to hitch up your wagon. I've got a better idea. I'm gonna trade horses with you." Before Dunstan could reply, he said, "You'll be gettin' the best part of the deal, 'cause my horse is a heap stouter than your'n, and his hoof will be as good as new in a few days."

Dunstan didn't know what to say at first, but he didn't see a trade of the two horses being to his advantage. In his opinion, there was no comparison between them — his horse the better by far. Glancing at Helen's startled expression, and then at Jeremy's anxious look of concern, he turned back to Pike's smiling face. The stranger's confident grin told him that there was little room for negotiation. "Thanks just the same," Dunstan finally replied, "but I don't reckon I wanna trade horses."

The malicious grin remained frozen in place on Pike's grizzled face as his dark eyes narrowed slightly and locked on Dunstan's gaze. "I'm givin' you a helluva deal for that piece of crow bait. It's just your good fortune you caught me in a time of need."

"Nossir, I reckon not," Dunstan gave his final say on the matter. "Now I'll hitch up the wagon and take you to Fort Laramie. There's horses for sale there."

"I ain't goin' to Fort Laramie," Pike replied.

Dunstan paused with his hand on the door latch. "I thought you had dispatches for the army you had to deliver."

Pike shrugged impatiently. "Well, I ain't. I got no business at that fort." Then his patience, limited at best, dissipated completely. "Dammit, I need that damn horse, and that's all there is to it. I'm tired of pussyfootin' around with you." The grin that had remained in place before was now transformed into an angry glare.

"John, let him have the horse." Helen Dunstan read the depth of violence in the angry man's eyes. She feared for her husband's safety.

"No," Dunstan replied firmly, aware of his young son's eyes upon him. "Now I reckon it's time for Mr. Pike to leave." He pulled the door open.

"It's time for Mr. Pike to leave," Pike mocked sarcastically. "You damn fool, I gave you a chance." He pulled his pistol and fired two shots into the startled man's chest. Dunstan fell back against the doorpost, his knees buckling. Then he slid down the post to the floor.

Helen screamed in horror, and ran to her husband's side. Unmoved by her despair, Pike shifted his gaze to the boy. He had seen the double-barreled shotgun propped in the corner, and he watched Jeremy to see if the boy had any notions about making a move toward it. But Jeremy was paralyzed by the sight of his dying father, slumped in his mother's arms as she pleaded with her husband to live. Satisfied that there was no immediate threat from mother or son, he walked over and removed the shells from the shotgun. "All right," he ordered, "that's enough. Let's go outside."

He motioned toward the door with his pistol. When Jeremy did not move, Pike gave him a kick in the seat of his pants. It was enough to break the stunned youngster's paralysis. Jeremy stumbled toward the door, almost falling over his mother's feet. Pike grabbed the stricken woman by the collar and dragged her outside. "Come on. He's dead. Stop your blubberin'. It's his own damn fault."

Once they were all outside, Pike ordered Jeremy to saddle the horse. The boy, devastated a few moments earlier, now found his backbone. "I ain't saddlin' no horse for you," he spat in defiance. "You killed my pa, and I'll hunt you down till I kill you!"

Pike recoiled slightly in surprise. Then the grin returned to his face. "You little shit, I believe you would." The pistol spoke once more, the force of the bullet knocking the boy back against the cabin wall, where he fell dead.

The impact of her son's brutal murder coming upon that of her husband's was too great a shock for the woman's shattered mind to withstand. Her eyes fluttered briefly, and then she collapsed on the ground. Pike paused to stand over her for a few moments before turning to go into the barn to fetch his saddle. In the length of time it took for him to saddle John Dunston's horse, the man's new widow slowly regained consciousness. When she began to stir, Pike paused again to watch her, curious as to what her reaction might be. It was not long in coming, and the reverse of what he anticipated.

Opening her eyes from what she prayed had been a bad dream, she was devastated to find it had been all too real. Gripped by many emotions, from hopeless and terrifying despair to a sudden burning fury, the latter taking control of her mind, she struggled unsteadily to her feet. In uncontrolled rage, she suddenly charged headlong at her antagonist, hurling her fragile body at Pike. With one foot in the stirrup already, he barely had time to withdraw it and prepare to meet the crazed woman's charge. Bracing himself, he stepped aside, causing her to collide with the horse's belly. When she bounced back from the collision, he took a step toward her and unloaded a right hand, his fist catching her square on the chin. She dropped like a sack of grain on the ground. "Crazy bitch," he muttered.

He started to step up in the saddle again, but hesitated to take another look at the woman lying at his feet. With husband and son no longer a threat, he let his mind dwell on the woman's bare leg for a moment. It had been a long time since he had known a woman. He reached over and pushed her skirt up with the toe of his boot, revealing loose-fitting cotton drawers. It suddenly became an obsession with him to see what the drawers concealed. His lust fully awakened now, he tied the horse to the gatepost, and returned to draw his knife. Sticking the blade under the waistband, he ripped the garment from top to bottom. Then he sat back on his heels to gaze at the bony pelvis and pale thighs. She was not a pretty woman. Life on the open prairie had taken the bloom from her youth many years before. This would have ordinarily made little difference to a man of Pike's moral fiber. It was the fact that he had never seen gray pubic hair before. It looked unreal, eerie in fact, and the sight served to cool his passion. "Damn," he swore. She opened her eyes at that point to find him hovering over her. She immediately screamed and struck him in the face. His reaction was swift. In a fit of anger, he buried the knife in her abdomen.

Helen Dunston's final moments in this world were long and painful. Oblivious to the woman's suffering, Pike delayed his departure long enough to ransack the cabin in search of anything of value. There was little to find: a shotgun, a box of twelve-gauge shells, a small silver chain, a locket with a faded picture of a baby inside. The only item that caught his fancy was John Dunston's razor. The handle was pearl with a pattern of onyx inlaid to form the shape of a diamond. Pike opened the razor and admired the honed edge of the spotless blade. Dunston must have valued the razor highly, judging by the condition it was in. Pleased, Pike nodded smugly to himself as he ran a finger over the inlaid pattern. His thoughts were interrupted by the sound of moaning outside, and he stepped to the door to make sure the woman was no threat. He stood there and watched her for a moment in her desperate attempt to stem the flow of blood from the ragged gash in her abdomen. Satisfied that she had not moved from where she had fallen, he continued his search of the cabin.

Outside again, he stuffed the few trinkets he had found into his saddlebags, only glancing down at the dying woman as he walked past her. Her painful moaning was weaker now, but still constant to the point where it began to annoy him. He decided to end it. Opening the pearl handled razor, he started toward her, but had second thoughts. *The razor was too fine a thing to soil on a bony old woman's throat,* he thought. So he put it back in his pocket and, as he had done before, he knelt beside his helpless victim and smothered the life from her lungs. When she finally quit struggling, he got to his feet and, on a sudden impulse, decided to burn the cabin.

Chapter 15

"Injuns?"

"Maybe," Jordan replied as he continued to gaze at the lone column of smoke in the distance. "It's mighty damn close to the fort though. Could be some homesteader clearing some land." Even as he said it, he doubted it.

Toby got up from his knee where moments before he had been studying the hoofprint in the sand. Although neither voiced it, they were both thinking the same thing. Someone might be in trouble, but there was a strong reluctance to leave the trail they had been following. There was a long moment of hesitation while Toby climbed back in the saddle, and then conscience got the best of Jordan. "I expect we'd best have a look on the other side of that ridge."

Toby didn't answer at once. There was nothing in his young life more important than catching up with Bill Pike. There had been nothing uppermost in his mind than the fear that Pike might get away, and go unpunished for the evil he had done. When he realized that Jordan was going to investigate the smoke off to the northeast, however, he begrudgingly gave in to conscience as well. He stood up in the stirrups, peering at the trail far up ahead, searching for a landmark. "That looks like a stream or somethin' about a half mile up ahead. "We can pick up his trail there when we come back," he suggested, unaware that Pike's tracks took an abrupt turn to the north precisely at the stream, heading straight for the column of smoke.

Guiding on the smoke, they rode for almost a mile before reaching the ridge. Upon gaining the crest, they stopped to survey the land beyond. There was nothing but uneven prairie, broken by cuts and draws for perhaps another mile before giving way to the stream, which was bordered with cottonwoods and willows. The smoke was clearly coming from the trees on the far side of the stream, but the source of the fire was hidden from their view. Even though he couldn't see it, Jordan was fairly confident at this point that it was a cabin that was burning. The speculation was reason enough to approach with caution. It would be somewhat surprising, but not out of the question, that a Sioux war party would strike a homestead this close to the fort. Iron Pony had warned him that the Lakota and Cheyenne were emboldened by their success against General Crook's troopers on the Rosebud. "We'd best be careful how we approach that cabin," Jordan advised. "That party might not be over."

Leading off, he angled down the ridge and made straight for a stand of willows at a bend in the stream to the south of the fire. He figured that way they'd have less chance of meeting a war party that might just be leaving the scene. His reasoning was that a Sioux raiding party would most likely escape to the north, away from the direction of the fort.

Once the safety of the trees was reached without mishap, Jordan dismounted and signaled Toby to do the same. "We'd best leave the horses here till we see what's what," he said. "Check your rifle," he added, for he could hear the sound of horses snorting and an occasional squeal. With no further hesitation, he made his way along the bank of the stream, weaving through the thick clump of willows. Toby followed in his footsteps. When he reached a point near the edge, he dropped down on one knee. Parting the branches before him, he saw the burning cabin. There was no sign of anyone about. He shifted his gaze to the small corral. There were two mules and a horse in the corral, which seemed strange to Jordan — a Sioux raiding party would have taken the livestock. The squealing and snorting he had heard before was due to the fact that the wind had shifted and was blowing the smoke and cinders from the fire toward the penned-up stock.

Reasonably sure whoever was responsible for the fire was gone, Jordan pushed through the branches and stood out in the open. Toby came up beside him. They both discovered the bodies at the same time. One, a woman's, lay between the cabin and the corral. The other was that of a boy. It was slumped against the burning wall of the cabin, the flames barely a foot or two above his head. "Lord have mercy," Toby muttered. His words trailed off, leaving him nearly speechless before the grim scene.

"Here, hold my rifle," Jordan said, handing the Winchester to Toby. He then made a quick dash toward the fire, grabbed the boy's feet, and quickly dragged the body away from the burning building. The heat of the flames almost took his breath as he hurried out of range. "There's another one inside," he gasped as he laid the body beside that of the woman. "I just caught a glimpse of his boots just inside the door." He paused to look back at the cabin, which was now an inferno. "Nothin' we can do for him. Better let the stock outta that corral before they start trying to come over the rails." Toby nodded, and went immediately to remove the gate rails. The two mules bolted out ahead of the horse. Jordan and Toby exchanged surprised glances when the horse followed, limping noticeably. They knew without commenting that it was the horse they had been tracking.

Jordan caught the horse as it hobbled by him, and confirmed that the favored hoof was the only one without a shoe. He released the horse and watched for a moment as it followed the mules to water. Then he looked back at the bodies on the ground. "Ain't no need to look for tracks of this son of a bitch," he uttered. "Just follow the dead bodies." Their quest became even more urgent than the simple seeking of revenge. The man they hunted held no regard for the value of human life. Everyone he had dealings with was in mortal danger.

"He can't be gone long," Toby offered, judging by the intensity of the fire. Aware that they had succeeded in cutting the distance between them and the man they hunted, his comment was obviously a question as he awaited Jordan's reply.

"No more'n an hour, I'd say," Jordan responded, thinking of the short lead Pike now enjoyed. After a moment's hesitation, he gave in to conscience. "We ought to put these bodies in the ground first." He might have been tempted to leave them to the buzzards, but it was a woman and her son. It didn't seem right to leave them there for the scavengers to feed on. Toby nodded his head in agreement, knowing it was the right thing to do.

Though done in great haste, Helen Dunston and her son, Jeremy, were laid in a shallow grave near the stream. When it was done, Jordan began scouting along the path that followed the stream back toward the Platte, looking for confirmation that Pike had headed back toward Fort Laramie. He soon found what he was looking for — fairly fresh hoofprints following the trail back along the stream. "He can't be more than two or three hours ahead of us," he said.

There was no doubt about Pike's intended direction. His tracks led straight back along the stream to intercept the government road toward Fort Laramie. Concerned only with making up time now, Jordan and Toby didn't bother scouting the trail before them. It was obvious that Pike intended to follow the road to the fort. It was unlikely that the outlaw would venture near the military post itself, finding it less risky to stop at the little settlement nearby. Ordinarily, a traveler would find a need to visit the sutler's store on the post. But Jordan assumed that Pike had most likely supplied his needs with goods ransacked from the cabin they had just left. With that in mind, he decided the first place to look for Pike was Skelley's Saloon.

Jack Skelley, a swarthy Irishman with dark black hair, and features to match, operated a business he loosely referred to as a saloon. It was, in fact, an undisguised den of iniquity, preying upon the bored and lonesome soldiers of Fort Laramie. Skelley claimed to have served honorably with General Sherman's army when it swept through Georgia. Not one of his customers really cared whether he did or not, although most figured it more likely he deserted before he ever saw the Chattahoochee. The big Irishman greeted everyone with a wide, toothy smile, and a glass of poison that was best described as embalming fluid — and that was what counted to a lonely trooper — that, and maybe a tussle with one of the tarnished ladies who showed up from time to time to accommodate his need for companionship.

Skelley's original establishment had consisted of a large canvas tent. He situated it within a mile of the post. It soon caught the attention of the post commander, however, and Colonel Bradley closed the soldier trap down. Unfazed, Skelley moved his business two miles south of the fort near a fledgling settlement of houses. With no real competition, the business thrived, and soon Skelley was able to replace the canvas tent with a permanent building — complete with a bar and several tables. On this day in early spring, Skelley was in the process of mending a broken table leg when the stranger rode up to his saloon.

Skelley stood up from his work to look his visitor over through the open door, waiting until the rider pulled up before the building. One glance from Skelley's experienced eye told him that this stranger should best be watched closely. There was a mean look about him as his stare fixed upon the burly barkeep standing in the door.

"You open?" Pike asked.

"Always open, friend," Skelley responded.

"Looks like you need somethin' to cut the dust from your throat. Come on in."

Pike stepped down, and looped the reins over the hitching post. He paused at the door and took a good look around before stepping into the dim interior of the building. Inside, he paused again to let his eyes adjust to the darkness. His gaze settled on the table lying upside down in the light of the one window in the room.

"A couple of soldiers got a little rough in here last night," Skelley said. "I had to bean one of 'em. The damn fool fell across the table and broke the leg."

Not really interested, Pike fixed on the barkeep with a dull stare for several moments before replying. "You got anythin' fittin' to drink back there?"

"Why, hell yeah," Skelley responded, moving toward the bar. "You want beer or whiskey? I've got some good rye whiskey that's strong enough to wash away a man's sins."

A single grunt was as close to a laugh as Pike could get. "Gimme a shot of that, and I'll see how big a liar you are."

Skelley produced a bottle from beneath the counter, blew the dust out of a shot glass, and set it down on the counter before Pike. He raised the bottle to pour, but hesitated before filling the glass. "I don't believe I've seen you around here before. Wouldn't hurt to see the color of your money. Whiskey's four bits a shot."

Pike scowled. "That's a little steep, ain't it?"

"Good rye whiskey like this costs a little more than most of the rotgut you'll find anywhere else around here," Skelley said, still waiting before pouring. "Look at it this way, it'll make you drunk a helluva lot quicker, so you're savin' money in the long run." He flashed a wide, toothy grin at Pike. "Now, let's see your money."

His scowl still in place, Pike reached into his pocket and pulled out a small wad of money. Skelley, his smile genuine now, filled the glass to the brim, with prospects in mind for gaining the whole wad. "Hell, I'll have one with you," he said, and produced another glass. He picked up the bottle and carried it over to the table. With a hand from Pike, he turned the table up on its legs again and set the bottle in the center. "Set yourself down, friend. The first one's on the house."

"That's more like it," Pike said, his tone still gruff, but he sat down at the table with Skelley. As soon as Skelley poured, Pike picked up the glass and tossed the contents down. His teeth clenched in a painful grimace as the strong whiskey burned its way down his throat. "By God, you're right," he gasped when he could talk again. "It wouldn't take much of that stuff to lay a man out cold."

Skelley chuckled. "I told you it was the best." He picked up his glass and sipped a little of the fiery liquid. "Just take her a little slower, and you can enjoy it a helluva lot longer. Me and you'll be good friends by the time we finish this bottle."

Pike cast a suspicious eye at the swarthy barkeep. "Yeah, I expect we might, but I ain't plannin' to pay for a whole bottle of whiskey, especially when you're drinkin' half of it."

"There he is!" Toby blurted, sighting the horse tied up in front of the saloon. "We caught him!" He kicked his horse hard, charging down the ridge toward the wooden building with the word SKELLEY roughly painted on the front.

"Hold on!" Jordan shouted, but the boy was already halfway down the slope. The single trail they had followed from Dunston's cabin led straight to the saloon, and there was only one horse tied up at the rail. So it was reasonable to assume that Toby was right, but Jordan would have preferred to be a little more cautious. That choice was no longer available to him, thanks to Toby's impulsive action. Now there was no course left but to follow the headstrong boy, and hope he didn't walk in blazing away and killing some innocent settler having an early drink.

In his haste for vengeance, Toby was out of the saddle before his horse was fully stopped. Not taking time to tie the horse, he drew his pistol and stormed into the open doorway. Once inside, he hesitated, for there were only two men in the saloon, both seated at a table by the window, and no one behind the bar. Toby had never been this close to Bill Pike. At that moment, he wasn't sure which man was Pike. The two were close in appearance. Either one could have been the man who killed Polly Hatcher. Still hesitant, he called out, "Bill Pike!"

Although Skelley was taken by surprise, Pike did not hesitate. At first sight of the excited young boy with a gun in his hand, Pike had reached under the table and eased his own pistol out of the holster. He didn't wait for explanations. As soon as Toby yelled out his name, he fired. With the pistol under the table, his aim was unsure, so his first shot was wide, ripping into the doorframe.

But his second shot caught the boy near the collarbone, slamming him backward through the doorway, into the arms of Jordan, who arrived just in time to catch him before he fell. In the chaos of the moment, Skelley attempted to lunge out of the line of fire, turning over the table and his chair in the process. It was enough to spoil Pike's aim, and the shot he fired at Jordan splintered the edge of the wooden door. He didn't take time to try to get off another shot, but took the few moments when Jordan had his hands full holding the wounded boy to dive headlong out the window.

"Get him!" Toby yelled as Jordan eased him down on the floor. The blood was already soaking his shirt.

With no way of knowing the connection between Pike and Skelley, Jordan, his pistol drawn, had to first concern himself with the bartender, who was crawling across the floor toward the bar. "Don't shoot!" Skelley screamed. "I ain't got nothin' to do with him!" Jordan turned his attention back to Toby, intent upon stopping the boy's bleeding.

"Don't let him get away," Toby pleaded. "Go after him."

"I'll get him," Jordan promised. "You just take it easy till I get back." Feeling confident that Toby wouldn't bleed to death, he got to his feet and ran for the door, only to be forced back against the wall when Pike emptied the remaining three bullets from his six-gun through the open doorway. A moment later, Jordan heard the sound of a horse's hooves as Pike fled the scene. One more look back at Toby to be sure he was all right, and a glance at Skelley who signaled that he would take care of the boy, and Jordan was off.

Sweet Pea stamped her feet impatiently as Jordan untied her reins. The ornery mare knew instinctively that she had to run down the horse galloping away up the slope. Jordan had barely thrown a leg over when she bolted after Pike, gobbling up the incline and racing along the top of the ridge. The half-mile lead that Pike held would not last long as Jordan laid low on the determined mare's neck. There was no need to encourage her. Jordan knew that she would run until she caught the roan — or until she dropped over dead.

Only a quarter mile ahead now, Pike's horse stumbled slightly as he whipped it ruthlessly. The horse, though tiring rapidly, recovered and leaped a narrow gully as Pike desperately drove it toward a line of trees at the base of a hill. The lead had shrunk to less than a couple hundred yards when Sweet Pea glided over the gully, hardly breaking stride. Feeling his pursuer closing in on him, Pike drew his pistol, and in a desperate attempt to slow Jordan down, tried to shoot behind him, only to hear the firing pin click on an empty cylinder. In a panic to reload, he fumbled with the weapon and dropped it in the dust, leaving it behind. His efforts resulted in slowing his horse down as it groaned for breath. Pike whipped it furiously with the reins. The roan was not short of heart, but it had no more to give, and the relentless mare was no more than a dozen yards behind now.

Pike realized that the chase was over. He cursed the roan as it stumbled to a halt. With a dark scowl on his face, he turned to meet the onrushing mare, drawing his rifle from the saddle sling. There was no time to aim the weapon. Sweet Pea, her nostrils flaring, her broad chest glistening with lather, her legs pumped powerfully, drove forward like a small locomotive. Jordan could only hang on. At this point, he could not have stopped the belligerent mare if he had wanted to. There was a solid thump of horseflesh as she plowed into the hapless roan, her powerful chest impacting with the roan's belly. The resulting collision knocked the exhausted horse backward to land on its side, and threw both riders from the saddle.

Pike tried to hold onto his rifle, but lost it when he hit the ground. As soon as he could recover, he scrambled on all fours to retrieve it as Jordan rolled a few feet away to regain his feet. Unable to get to his own rifle, which was still on his saddle, Jordan charged toward Pike. His hand on the rifle now, Pike turned to find Jordan practically on top of him. He tried to bring the rifle up to shoot, but Jordan aimed a boot that caught the outlaw under the chin. The crack of his jawbone resounded like the snap of a pistol shot as he was knocked over backward and the rifle was sent flying. Jordan was quick to follow up with another kick to the dazed man's ribs. Pike gasped loudly as the breath was knocked from his lungs. Rolling over in desperate pain, he knew he must fight or die. Oblivious to the broken jaw that caused him to suck air furiously through his nose, his thoughts were now only of survival, and he tried to back away from the relentless attack. Caught up in the fury of the confrontation, Jordan stalked him step-by-step, images of Jonah Parsons, Polly Hatcher, and Toby Blessings flitting briefly before his eyes. There was no thought of mercy, for Bill Pike had never traded in mercy. His victims demanded death, nothing less.

Pike struggled to get to his feet. With one hand holding his broken ribs, he managed to draw the pearl-handled razor he had taken from John Dunston's cabin. Leaning forward in a painful crouch, he waved the razor back and forth, threatening. Jordan continued to advance, oblivious to the danger, closer and closer, until Pike suddenly lunged, aiming for Jordan's throat. Quick as a cat, Jordan stepped to the side, and with a massive right hand, smashed Pike's face, knocking him sprawling. He attempted to stagger to his feet, but he had been knocked senseless by the powerful blow. When he tried to steady himself, he fell back against Jordan's horse. Sweet Pea reacted violently, rearing up, and coming down hard on the ill-fated man, her hooves stamping the life from his bosom.

Jordan backed away, not sure if the wild-eyed mare was out of control as she trampled the now lifeless corpse. After a few minutes, she calmed down and backed away from the body to stand and stare at the bloodied remains. Then she turned her head and gazed beseechingly at Jordan. He whistled softly, and she came obediently to him, pressing her muzzle against his chest. He stroked her neck for a few moments while he gazed blindly at the remains of Bill Pike. Then he turned and led the mare away, leaving the corpse to the buzzards.

CHAPTER 16

"Well, it's a miracle you aren't dead, young fellow," Captain Beard commented stoically when he examined Toby's wound. "The bullet isn't near the heart or lung, but stuffed with that old rag, it's a wonder gangrene hasn't set in." He looked up accusingly at Jordan. "Whose idea was that?"

Jordan shrugged defensively. "We had to stop the bleedin'," he offered. It was actually Skelley who had stuffed the wound with a bar towel, but Jordan had not seen fit to remove it before carrying Toby to the post surgeon.

"Well, it did stop the bleeding, I guess," the doctor admitted reluctantly. "And the wound doesn't look like it's festering — probably because the towel's soaked in whiskey." Turning back to Toby, he said, "I'll bandage you up properly. I'm going to leave that bullet right where it is. You should heal right over it." Then he winked at Jordan before joking, "Might cause him to lean a little to the left when he walks." Toby grinned weakly, doing his best not to show his discomfort.

"I thought I recognized that horse. There couldn't be two like that." Surprised to hear a woman's voice, they all turned to see the surgeon's daughter enter the office. Kathleen Wallace covered the room with a casual smile that froze only slightly when it settled upon Jordan Gray.

"Mrs. Wallace," Jordan acknowledged politely with a nod of his head.

"Kathleen," the surgeon greeted his daughter. "Where are you off to?" Before she could answer, he continued, "This young man is Toby Blessings. Seems he's gotten himself shot." He looked back at the boy, and jokingly lectured, "That's likely to happen to folks that hang around Jordan."

Kathleen smiled again at Toby. "Father's right," she said. "A person can get into a great deal of trouble with Jordan Gray." Her smile stiffened when she met Jordan's gaze, losing her composure for a brief moment before recovering to go on. "I was on my way to visit Sergeant Grant's wife when I saw that awful-looking horse of Jordan's tied out front. And I couldn't pass without stopping in to see an old friend." Feeling Jordan's eyes upon her, she turned her attention to Toby, pretending to evaluate her father's job of bandaging. "Not bad," she said. "Not as neat as I would have done, but not bad." Directing her gaze at Jordan again, she said, "I suppose you'll be around for a few days while his wound heals."

"I don't have much choice," Jordan replied without explanation as they left the boy to rest and moved to the outer office.

Captain Beard explained for him. "The provost marshal wants Jordan to hang around for a few days while they investigate the death of a man over near that man Skelley's place." He cocked a suspicious eye in Jordan's direction. "Seems the man was stomped to death by a horse. I didn't see the body, but Lieutenant DiMarco said that was pretty much the look of it."

"Why do they want you to stay for the investigation?" Kathleen asked Jordan.

He shrugged indifferently. " 'Cause I was the only witness, I reckon." A faint smile touched his lips. "That, and the fact that I'm ridin' the chief suspect."

"Well, I've got my rounds to make," Captain Beard announced, signaling an end to the visit. "Let your friend rest here for the night. Then he should be all right to ride." Jordan nodded, and he and Kathleen walked outside to stand on the small porch.

"You can walk me over to Mrs. Grant's quarters if you like," Kathleen offered.

Jordan hesitated for a long moment before replying. "I thank you, but I reckon I'd better not. I've got to take care of the horses, and set up a place to camp." It had been hard enough to try not to think about her over the past year. Already, this casual encounter was beginning to stir up memories best left alone.

She was at once offended, but quickly realized that he was attempting to avoid disturbing thoughts that were bound to arise between the two of them. "Oh, well, some other time." She managed to say it casually before spinning abruptly on her heel and leaving him standing there holding Sweet Pea's reins.

He paused for a moment, watching her walk away. The unexpected encounter had left him a little sad as it brought back thoughts of what might have been. But he was wise enough to know that it would never have worked out. He was a son of the mountains, born to roam the slopes and valleys. Even if circumstances were different, it could have never worked for Kathleen and him. He knew he would have made an honest effort to change his life for her sake. But any wild animal that was caged would eventually break out — or die trying. She had made her choice, married her arrogant lieutenant, and set herself up for a secure life as an army wife. So be it.

He would never know the softness of her body, the touch of her hand, the secret thoughts that filled her mind. He could only imagine the passion she was capable of. Those thoughts were beginning to crowd into his mind again until he was distracted momentarily by a hawk wheeling high above the parade ground, its forlorn cry seeming to call out to him. He thought about that for a moment, then told himself, *I'll never soar above the ground like that hawk, either, but I can climb to the top of the highest mountain in the Rockies if I need to see the view.* He would get over Kathleen, he decided at that moment, maybe as soon as he returned to the mountains.

He turned to face Sweet Pea. The belligerent mare tossed her head impatiently. "You're as anxious to get outta this army camp as I am," he said and climbed in the saddle. "We'd best go make a camp. Tomorrow we'll fetch Toby. Maybe in a day or two we can take him back to the Black Hills. I expect Hattie and Maggie are gettin' pretty worried about that boy." He paused to think about the prospect of another trip to Deadwood. "Besides," he said, "I ain't been shot at lately."

The employees of Thorndike Press hope you have enjoyed this Large Print book. All our Thorndike, Wheeler, and Kennebec Large Print titles are designed for easy reading, and all our books are made to last. Other Thorndike Press Large Print books are available at your library, through selected bookstores, or directly from us.

For information about titles, please call:
(800) 223-1244

or visit our Web site at:
http://gale.cengage.com/thorndike

To share your comments, please write:
Publisher
Thorndike Press
10 Water St., Suite 310
Waterville, ME 04901